Killers

An Ellen Parker Novel

Steven M. Silver

Steven M. Silver

© Steven M. Silver

ISBN 978-1-7352051-1-3

Dedication

The Once and Future Duck – for being there.

Acknowledgments

Hunting serial killers makes for dramatic movies and hopefully interesting novels – in real life, it can be unending stress, frustration, and unrecognized hard work. For those who want to go more deeply into this very dark area, a good start is Morton, R. J. (Ed.) *Serial murder: Multi-disciplinary perspectives for investigators,* which can be found at http://www.fbi.gov/publications/serial_murder.htm.

I strongly recommend former FBI agents Douglas' *Mind Hunter* and Ressler's *Whoever Fights Monsters.*

I have played slightly with the geography of Chester and Cumberland Counties and more so with the operating procedures of the Chester County Sheriff's Office. Over the years, primarily because of my involvement in the local critical incident debriefing program, I met with several Deputy Sheriffs and was impressed with their professionalism, hard work, and community involvement. However, none were involved in the writing of this novel in any way; all errors, therefore, are mine, as are the liberties I've taken with their procedures.

Art Peterson, noted Chester County cabinet maker and wood artist, helped supply some of the details of Mr. Klemmer's day job. The histories of southern Pennsylvania in general and Chester County in particular are filled with artisans of all types and he is among the more cheerful of the breed. I greatly appreciate his providing me with education before embarking on his fabled New Mexico Expedition. Welcome home, Art!

Eric Strehl, as always, is thanked for his cover design, encouragement, and hunt for shrubberies.

Southern Pennsylvania
Spring, 2003

Chapter 1

The Pennsylvania April breeze pushed aside the scattered leaves left from the nearly forgotten fall as it muscled its way down off the mountain to settle into the valley. The dead woman formed a low windbreak and leaves settled beside her, helping to hide the dry pool of blood but not distracting the flies and small insects. The breeze hesitated, as if reacting to what it discovered, and then ceased its movement. There was silence then, pressing down around the body like a giant, invisible hand. If there had been anyone to listen, only the insects, as always indifferent, were heard. The breeze remained still as the morning sun climbed and then it was reborn with the rising thermal currents, drawn upward now, working its way through the trees, and away from the body as if gently fleeing.

Down the hill, halfway down to the valley road that bisected the state park, a dog and man moved carefully along the contour lines. They moved quietly, the dog because that was his nature when searching and the man because that was his nature wherever he was. They moved along the hillside and occasionally turned and went higher before returning to their original path.

The black and white dog was a Border Collie named Cracker and he was a search and rescue dog. Cracker worked with his mouth open, his natural expression almost a smile. When he paused to consider something, his mouth closed but his eyes never lost their alert sparkle.

Near him was his handler, a tall, lean man whose face had the reddish tint of someone who had spent much of his life in the sun. He wore his hair cropped so short as to be invisible until the very top of his head where it was little more than a brown and white dusting. His blue eyes had the same intelligent alertness as the dog's and, if someone had pointed that out to him, he would have taken it as a compliment.

The dog and man pair moved perpendicular to the movement of the air – Cracker hunting scent while the handler, a retired Marine named Dave Maddux, watched the dog. It is said that eighty percent of canine search and rescue training is training the handler to pay attention to the dog, who already knows how to track a scent.

1

Cracker wore an international orange reflective vest; within large white circles on the sides were a pair of red crosses. Maddux wore old jeans and a faded military jacket. What the two wore seemed to be a natural part of both dog and man.

Maddux enjoyed the work. It let him play with his dog, a secret joy last experienced when he was a boy forty years before. Besides, and this he had admitted at more than one 12-Step meeting, it got him out of the house, into the woods, and away from the bottle. Beyond that, and he never admitted this part to anyone, he was drawn to the work because it gave him back much of what he had left in the Marines, most especially a sense of doing something that mattered.

The other piece that he did not tell anyone else, and usually kept hidden even from himself, was that each successful find in some way balanced the scales inside him. In a time of fire and confusion, he had had to give orders and people that he knew died – the killing he had done personally seemed insignificant in comparison to the weights of the deaths of the young Marines who had followed the orders of their gunnery sergeant. Those weights never left his scales; there were no time machines, no way of changing the past. But the scales could be brought to some approximation of balance by putting something on the other, the positive, side. Each person found – child, wandering old person, lost camper – was one of those small weights. When he told himself that all the training and working with Cracker mattered, it meant more than finding something to keep him busy.

Today mattered. Somewhere in these woods, a little boy named Jeff Tulane had wandered off from his family campground. He had been missing for almost a full 24 hours before anyone had thought to call in a canine SAR unit. The first impulse, to gather a group of people together and go looking for him, calling his name fruitlessly again and again, had been indulged with the usual results.

The local town constable finally had called the nearest State Police barracks. The trooper taking the call had a book of protocols to follow, including one for search and rescue requests, and it incorporated the knowledge that groups of men stomping around the woods almost never found anyone. Children in particular, because of their size and fear, would be even harder to find. In fact, hearing his name called might have convinced young Jeff he was in serious trouble, leading him to burrow in under a fallen tree or get under a bush, invisible to anyone who walked by.

2

The Cumberland County Canine SAR unit, like many, was made up of volunteers and responded to the call with more than a dozen people. Maddux and Cracker, together for three years, were one of four teams searching segments of the area. Maddux carried a pack on his back containing first aid gear, food and water for Cracker and himself, clothing, and a survival blanket. A radio was clipped to his belt while a GPS locator was looped to his left wrist. Their segment was divided into blocks, though the terrain and air flow the pair encountered finally determined how they searched their segment.

Maddux glanced down at the locator every minute or so, checking their position, and continually studied the shape of the ground and the movement of the air. For his part, Cracker understood to cross the breeze at a right angle whenever possible but he would occasionally glance back at Maddux who would silently nod to confirm the dog was moving correctly.

Sometimes Maddux would want a particular area checked closely; gullies might be sheltered from the breeze and holding their scent like a cradled mystery. He would make a low whistle to attract Cracker's attention and then gesture left or right. Cracker would grin – he enjoyed obeying The Man's commands - and would take in the area indicated.

Their search grid was on the northern edge of the park, five miles north of Carlisle, the county seat. Cumberland County drew its northern edge along the curving up-thrust of the Appalachian Mountains, formed when what became New Jersey drifted into the side of the North American continent. To the south, a curve of mountains paralleled those to the north as they arced from the northeast to the southwest and crossed into Maryland. To the northeast, the county encountered the sprawl of Harrisburg and stopped at the Susquehanna River.

No states in the eastern United States have as much unpopulated land as Pennsylvania. The entire center of the state was remarkably deserted, dark forests covering the rolling hills of the Appalachian Mountains in a pattern the Iroquois of three centuries before would have found familiar. People lived in the hills in small communities, sometimes in isolation and the population numbers never seemed to grow much – the days of iron and coal were over for Pennsylvania. Maddux grinned; the hills of Pennsylvania were a great place to live if you liked the outdoors – tree-huggers and hunters were welcome – or if you liked to be left alone.

Maddux glanced upward. The slope of the park rapidly increased and he doubted a child would continue very far in that direction – kids tended to go downward but the area had to be excluded in the systematic search. The breeze was coming up from the valley and working their way perpendicularly across its flow meant Cracker was getting a good sample of what lay below them. As they finished their path, they would have to go uphill another hundred yards before reversing course in order to check the next broad block of the hillside.

For Cracker, everything was as it should be. The Man was with him and they were in the woods playing The Find Game. Cracker knew they played The Game because of how The Man looked and dressed and because The Man had put the reflective vest on him, wrapping it around his body and securing it to his collar.

The various odors Cracker came across were, for him, almost visual. He could feel the smell go past him and get the sense of its size and power, comparing it with the incredibly huge library of smells he knew. With an ability to smell which was perhaps 300 percent more acute than that of a human being, Cracker was using a sense which gave him a moving, three-dimensional picture of the world around him.

As he trotted across the stream of the breeze, he raised and lowered his head, sampling the air at different heights. He used the movement of the breeze and the relative location of the smell and its condition to locate the source as a three-dimensional target in his awareness.

Cracker smelled the squirrel nest in the tree a hundred yards away, the four crows sitting on a low branch beyond the nest, the lingering trace of two deer who crossed through the area three hours earlier, all that and more and, despite the urge to go, see and, perhaps, chase, Cracker just noticed them and kept searching. They were not part of The Game, they were not what he was trying to find.

Maddux watched the black and white dog cut the breeze, moving back and forth, occasionally pausing, its ears flicking forward as it considered a new scent, and then moving on. It was getting warm as the sun climbed overhead and he figured he would be stuffing his jacket into his pack before too much longer. His radio hissed and he pulled it to his face, his eyes still on Cracker.

Hey, Maddog, you there?

It slightly irritated the former Marine in him – once one, always one – that the other members of the unit had never learned proper radio procedure, but he had learned to go with the flow.

"I'm here, Jack," Maddux said. His voice was a little gravelly but it could be Drill Instructor sharp when he wanted it to be. "What's up? Over." Cracker glanced back at him and then went on with his searching.

Status check.

Damn. Maddux glanced at his watch. He was late calling in his quarterly hour check. The folks in the unit might not have been perfect in their radio procedures but they ran their searches by the book, especially when a dog team was out without a safety man. The safety's job was to watch the handler and make sure he didn't walk off a cliff while watching the dog; unfortunately, they were a little short of people just now.

"We're about three quarters through our second block," he said, unconsciously using the plural while his eyes followed Cracker. "Nothing at all so far. We'll be going uphill for the last pass. You want us to go over to area Charlie as planned, over?"

Roger that.

There was a long hiss of empty static and a slight sound of country and western music in the background. Jack was probably slow letting go of the mike button while he noted the check in his logbook.

Maddux slipped the radio back into its pouch. He'd give Cracker some water before they took on the third block and take off his jacket at the same time. He glanced at the GPS locator and matched it with his folded map of the park. He nodded and gave Cracker a soft whistle. The dog paused and looked at him, his head canted to one side. Maddux gestured up the slope and Cracker turned uphill, glancing behind him as he led Maddux. A few minutes later, Maddux peeled off his jacket and gave Cracker a little water from a plastic cup. Then they went back to work.

The trees weren't dense and Maddux could see glimpses of the park road below them in the distance; moving sparkles of chrome and glass picked out the road through the trees. Still, the occasional brush tended to come in fairly heavy patches. He made sure Cracker checked in them closely. Kind of place a kid would hide.

They were just coming to the end of the block and Maddux was thinking about the path they would take to the next search area when the wind hesitated and then shifted. Now it was coming down from the mountainside, almost exactly opposite of what it had been doing. Maddux frowned as Cracker turned and looked over his shoulder. With only a little of the block left to

5

search, the shift would force them to go lower on the hillside to make sure they were covering the last piece. He shook his head; there was always something.

Maddux started to whistle when Cracker gave him a full alert. The dog was frozen in place, ears cocked forward, his whole body pointing slightly uphill into the slight, hesitant breeze and toward a clearing just out of the search block. Cracker's smile was gone and he was studying the hillside seriously.

Damn, that's further than anyone thought a kid would go.

Maddux, looking in the same direction as the dog, reached for his radio as he strode towards Cracker. The clearing had the dog's attention but Maddux could see nothing.

"Show me, Cracker," he called, and the dog lunged up the hill and into the clearing. Maddux keyed the mike.

"Base, Maddux. We got an alert here on the northwest corner of my second block, over." You were supposed to wait for something definite but Maddux knew Cracker and he had found human scent. He struggled to control his breathing as he increased his speed, trying to keep the dog in sight as it moved quickly into the clearing.

Not our boy, Maddog. Was just gonna call you. Debbie and Terry found him just now. Kid's okay.

Maddux was into the small clearing. There were no trees but the spring weeds of various types were doing quite well. He could see Cracker, now stopped and not moving. Weird. The dog was trained to come back to him and then show him where the person was. He keyed the mike as he approached the dog, which was intent on something but showing no excitement, its head noticeably sagging.

"Well, hell, Jack, Cracker's got something here, hold on..." Maddux instinctively reached down and scratched the dog's ears as he came up on it and looked where the dog was looking. Some sort of cloth or something. Why was the dog acting so weird? Then he saw.

"Base, base, this is Maddux. We got a body up here." Maddux paused, swallowing hard. He had seen dead before, but he had never seen a murder victim.

"Base, you better tell the troopers to get up here. We'll back up and preserve the scene. Looks like a murder."

Man, you sure?

He started to lead Cracker back down to the edge of the clearing, both of them glancing back over their shoulders as they went. Even when the weeds and brush hid the body from view, the image kept filling his mind.

"Yeah, Jack, I'm sure. It's a woman. She's dead." He paused, making himself breathe. "She's had her throat cut."

Chapter 2

Maddux had seen death before, had seen what gunfire and shrapnel did to young flesh, and had learned to hold his reaction like a snake, a dangerous one that had to be held tight or it might hurt him. He had lived with a belly full of snakes, paying the price for their imprisonment with alcohol and a lost marriage, until he had no choice but to root them out, one at a time, and finally deal with them.

Part of him seemed to stand back and observe, noting the dead woman did not bring back any of the old snakes. There was a small sense of satisfaction in that, tinged with something that was almost guilt.

The rest of him was recoiled from the image. Maddux sat quietly on a tree trunk, mechanically scratching Cracker's ears, waiting for the police.

Cracker sat close to The Man, pressing against his calf. This was not how The Game was supposed to go. The person was not alive and the black and white dog felt as if things were wrong, very wrong, and that in some undefined way he had failed The Man. Cracker glanced up at The Man from time to time seeking reassurance but saw his grim expression.

Maddux saw Cracker looking up at him and made himself smile. Dogs read people better than people usually did. He stretched the smile into a grin.

"Good dog," he said, stroking Cracker's head. "Nice job."

It was a good try but Cracker partially saw through it. He kept his head low and the tongue-hanging smile was gone. Maddux nodded as he used two fingers to scratch the dog's chest; when they got back to the team site he would have one of the others hide and then he and Cracker would search for him. Cracker would get his success and be praised. In the meantime, it was important to let him know that he had done nothing wrong.

Maddux heard sirens in the far distance. He knew they would come up the park road and would probably take one of the firebreak roads cutting through the state forest he was, or had been, searching.

The sirens lasted only a few minutes – the police were deployed, along with his team, at the camping site where young Jeff and his family stayed. He and Cracker worked at the edge of the area their estimates said the boy would have

8

wandered in the length of time he was missing. The sirens of the police car and the ambulance made a discordant, sorrowful harmony that barely entered into their chorus before they trailed off as if embarrassed. They stopped somewhere below Maddux and Cracker, hidden by the trees. Maddux guessed they stopped where they saw his pick-up truck.

The police, two of them, trudged up through the trees with a pair of EMTs and Jack. Cracker alerted to them before they could be seen, probably picking up on their noise. Maddux stood and waved. Jack, obviously the guide with his GPS locator in his hand, waved back. The uniforms paused, had a quick conference and one cop, a woman, and an EMT went back the way they came, while their partners followed Jack.

"Hey, man," Jack said, holding out his hand, his thin, bearded face tight with concern. Maddux shook the hand almost automatically and nodded silently. Jack stood beside him and gestured towards the approaching officer and EMT.

"They're gonna get the vehicles and bring 'em up a firebreak a couple of hundred yards down from here and then come up as close to here as they can. Four wheel drive stuff. This here's Sheriff Robert Donner," he finished as the officer walked up to him. The officer held out his hand.

In many ways, he looked like Maddux. About average height, he wore his hair burr short. What there was of it showed gray. His dark blue uniform, American flag on one shoulder, Cumberland County Deputy Sheriff patch on the older, was razor sharp, as were the eyes that looked out dubiously on the world from behind steel-rimmed glasses tinted yellow. His face was square and deeply lined and beaten from a career spent in the sun and weather.

Maddux took the hand and shook it.

"I'm Deputy Sheriff Bob Donner," Donner said in a voice with the rasp of two blocks of granite turning against one another. "Cumberland County Sheriff's department. The State Police are going to be here soon. Our job is to secure the crime scene area. You found the body?"

"No," Maddux said. "Cracker did." The dog looked up at the mention of his name. "He alerted to the scent and led me to it." As he talked, Donner took out a notepad and a silver pen and took notes. "It's up there," he said, gesturing. "Other side of the clearing, maybe fifty yards away, if that."

"How close to the body did you get?"

"About fifteen feet away. Cracker stopped there, I walked up and saw, and we made the call."

"You didn't go any closer? Then how...?"

"How did I know she was dead?" Maddux paused, glancing towards the clearing. "Seen dead before," he said, his voice flat. "I could see part of the wound. That much blood, no way she could be alive." Donner's mouth tightened slightly in response and he made a note.

"She's lying with her head uphill. She's face down and her arms have been taped behind, looked like duct tape. I couldn't tell what her other injuries were, but she's had her throat cut. There's blood everywhere..." His voice trailed off.

"How long after you saw the woman did you make the call?"

"Immediately. I was already talking to base when I saw her." Jack nodded in agreement.

"Yeah, Maddog was calling in and I'd just told him about us finding the boy." He kept nodding his head. "I got his 'time-of-call' logged in if you need to check."

They could hear the sound of engines coming. A heavy, police four-wheel drive vehicle led a slightly larger vehicle decked out in white, red, and blue medical emblems, as the two carefully made their way up an ancient fire road less than a hundred meters away. They stopped and the woman officer, bringing with her a large roll of yellow tape, led the way over to Maddux and the others. Donner did not bother with introductions.

"Here's what we're going to do," Donner said, raising his voice slightly so the approaching people could hear him. "Mr. Maddux is going to walk us up to within sight of the body." He turned towards Maddux. "At that point, I'd like you to come back here. One EMT will be with me and confirm the woman as dead. The other waits here. Deputy Book, I'll want you to tape off the area around the body, at least 25 feet away." He paused and looked up into the clearing. "Questions?" There were none.

As Donner started forward, Maddux gave Cracker a flat handed signal. *Stay and wait for me.* He walked beside the deputy in silence, the EMT, a large first aid kit in his hand, and the other deputy following.

For a moment, Maddux had a feeling of panic when he didn't see the body, but then he saw the depression in the weeds ahead. He stopped.

"She's there," he said, gesturing. Donner held his hand up slightly and Maddux took that as his signal to leave. He started to turn away and then stopped.

"One thing, forgot to say," Maddux said and Donner paused and looked back at him. "At about the ten o'clock position from the body, no more than a yard away, you'll see a bunch of her hair. It looked like it was hacked off her head."

As he walked away, Donner glanced at the other deputy. "You can start circling the area from here. Use the saplings here in the clearing for now, but we may have to drive some stakes."

The woman nodded and moved off. Donner gestured to the EMT and they walked up to the body.

"All right," Donner said. "Just tell me for the record she's dead and then back off. I want to keep the scene as clean as possible."

The EMT, a young man a little overweight with a shaggy blond mustache that made him look younger, nodded silently, took a step forward and crouched beside the body. After a moment, he rose and stepped back. His breath came out in a long sigh and Donner wondered if he had held it the entire time.

"Deputy, she's dead. The Staties will bring a medical examiner with them, but it looks to me like she's been dead for a full day. She's got some cuts on her arms and legs and back but they're minor slashes."

"Okay, partner. Go on back to your vehicle. I think the troopers will release you but standby until they make it official."

The EMT nodded and turned away.

"Hey." Donner's voice stopped him and turned back. "Nice work." The young man's face lightened slightly and he continued on across the clearing.

Donner moved slowly around the body, carefully examining the scene and very carefully placing his feet.

The woman looked to be in her mid-30s, about average height and weight, with her blond hair cut, almost shredded, very short. Wide bands of grey duct tape wrapped around her elbows held her arms together. She still wore purple and white jogging shoes, no socks. He glanced across the body. There were several clumps of hair hanging in the weeds and on top of the torn pieces of her clothes. *Maddux didn't mention seeing the clothes.* There were, as the medic observed, shallow cuts and nicks on her back, arms, buttocks, and legs. Dry blood pooled beneath her throat and torso and dried stains spattered the brush around her. Blood had dried on her hair, matting it together, and on top of her clothes.

Clothes and hair to the left. Guy was right-handed? Cut with his right, throw what he didn't want to one side with his free hand.

He moved up towards the head. The woman was face down. He crouched down. Her eyes were half-open; Donner had little sense of the poetic and no thought came to him about what she saw now. More grey tape across her mouth. The slash in her throat almost reached her right ear. He backed away and circled around her head, carefully placing each foot. He stopped short of the hair and clothes.

Donner saw that most of her clothes were lying in the same place, though part of a blouse was further away. The hair was mostly on the remains of her jeans. He looked at the neck wound. From her left side he saw it began well under the jaw. He nodded.

Looks like he finally came out here, the bastard.

He stood slowly and looked uphill. Donner could see his deputy making her way through the trees, securing the yellow police scene tape as she went.

"Book," he said, and the woman stopped. "See anything?"

"No, nothing," Book replied. "I think there's another fire or logging road or something over there." She gestured uphill with the roll of tape. "Hard to see from here, but it looked a little clearer in that direction. I don't think it's on my map." She paused. "Maybe they came down from there; there's some crushed plants.

He nodded. "All right. Finish taping then run a line of tape up along the route of travel. Maybe there will be tracks or some damned thing on the road. We'll maintain the area until the Staties get here."

Donner turned and carefully made his way downhill, his eyes on the ground and any possible path used by the perpetrator. Maddux, sitting beside his dog, and Jack were there, waiting.

"I'd like to keep the crowd down around here," Donner said. "Would it be all right with you two to go back to the campsite and wait for the state police there? They'll have someone to talk to you, maybe double-check the log for times and so on."

"No problem," Jack said, seemingly relieved to be moving away from the crime scene. Maddux stood silently. He wiggled his fingers and Cracker moved beside him.

"Was it as bad as I thought?" he asked the deputy. Donner nodded. "Then find the bastard."

Donner's granite rasp was glacially cold.

12

"Count on it."

The Pennsylvania State Troopers were highly professional and whatever they might have thought of local cops, their behavior gave nothing away. They got their briefing from Donner and made an initial, cursory viewing of the scene. One of them walked further uphill with Deputy Book, noting the apparent trail, and found the firebreak. They walked its length, finding nothing, until it hooked into the valley road. As she thought, it wasn't on their maps either.

Maddux gave Jack a ride back to the base area – more police cars passed them, including several that were unmarked.

"You think this is another one of them?" Jack asked.

"Hell," Maddux said, "I don't know. I hope not. I don't want to think that son of a bitch is over here now."

"The deputies think it is," Jack said, his fingertips drumming lightly on his chin. "The woman said this was number seven, if it is." He leaned back and sighed. "Makes you wonder if the world is going insane."

"It might be," conceded Maddux and his slowed down and turned into the campground parking area. "I haven't seen a whole lot to the contrary in the past couple of decades."

"I hear that," Jack said.

More police arrived as Maddux parked, along with the first of what would be an avalanche of news vehicles. As Jack walked over to the trio of vehicles that had served as the unit's base, Maddux saw the Tulane family had not yet left.

Maddux took Cracker over to meet the boy's family. The parents were still in the mode of being grateful for the return of their child and compulsively thanked everyone who had anything to do with the return of young Jeff, even a canine team that hadn't actually found him. Cracker seemed to accept the pats and chest scratches as his due. Maddux had learned to always see the families of successful searches - it made the unsuccessful ones a little easier to endure.

He walked with Cracker over to the team's base. Everyone was a strange mix of elation at the successful find – they always used just the one word – and low-keyed shock at the discovery of a murder victim. No one asked Maddux directly about what he had seen, for which he was grateful, but he explained anyway how they had found the body. He did not describe the injuries.

13

"Nice work, Cracker," one of the other handlers said and the dog grinned, understanding the phrase. The man looked up at Maddux. "My boy will do a quick hide if you want Cracker to find."

He did not have to add, *a live one.* It was protocol when the find was not a rescue, just a recovery; the search dogs could be just a depressed as a human when encountering death. Running a search for a living target seemed to help the dogs.

For that matter, paying attention to the dog, helping it deal with what it had found, seemed to help handlers.

After going a little way into the forest, Cracker found the handler's boy quickly, looking like a black and white torpedo following the air scent. Like all good SAR dogs, he did not bark but turned and stepped towards Maddux, his jaw open and tongue hanging in a large dog grin.

A pair of State Police investigators and an FBI Special Agent interviewed Maddux. The Agent stood back, letting the Staties ask the questions. The questions resulted in him describing what he saw and how he saw it probably three times over but Maddux remained patient. The Special Agent, crouching to scratch Cracker after getting a silent nod of clearance from Maddux, only asked if the dog alerted to anything prior to catching the scent from up the hill. Maddux shook his head.

"Sorry, no," he said. "I imagine you folks are going to do some shoulder-to-shoulder sweeps up there," he paused as all three officers nodded, "but you might want to run a dog before you do that. Your idea is a good one; Cracker might have found something else if we'd done a walk around. If something got dropped up there, a good dog will pick up on it."

"Agreed," the FBI man said, grinning as Cracker licked at his face. "We'll do that. Just checking."

Later, as Maddux loaded his gear back into his old Ford Ranger pick-up, with Cracker already wearing his special dog harness and sitting on the passenger seat, he glanced toward the road as more official vehicles, their multicolored lights strobing, made their way to the crime scene. He shook his head.

Maddux sat behind the wheel for a few moments, the engine idling. The dead woman lay in his mind, as she did in the grass – quietly, heavily, and unmovable. Other pictures followed, scenes beneath a sky turned black, hiding the sun, roaring red-orange flame all around, and, as far as he could see, scattered dark bundles, collapsed like rags, the remains of an Iraqi infantry

14

battalion, their fighting vehicles thrown about like toys discarded by angry children. He sighed and reached over and scratched Cracker's ears, who cocked his head in acceptance and appreciation.

"I think maybe we take in a meeting tonight," Maddux said softly to the dog, his voice barely above a whisper. Cracker seemed to smile in agreement, or maybe just in enjoyment for the smooth rubbing of his master's thumb in his ear. "Thought I'd kind of gotten that out of me, but I'll tell you, right now I'm thinking that maybe I'd like to go back into the killing business just one more time."

Maddux slipped the shift into drive and pulled out, waving to Jack and the rest of the team. He could feel the tempting pull of alcohol on him, still small, but knew with the help of the AA meeting, he would get passed it. Might not be easy, he knew. Sometimes it wasn't. He grimaced as he drove down the road. Nothing said he deserved to have it easy.

Chapter 3

Ellen Parker sat against the wall of the *Philadelphia Inquirer* conference room and counted to ten slowly. A young white woman with a raw-boned look that spoke to her southern Ohio roots, she carefully folded her hands and placed them on the table in front of her. None of the other eight people sitting at the oval table noticed, none except, possibly, Jefferson Johnson; his sharp eyes flicked towards her as the editor spoke but his expression remained still.

Johnson was her Intern Supervisor, in the formal language of her university's Department of Journalism. What it meant was she had never worked so hard in her life for anyone who was so grudging with praise. For six months, she had been over every square inch of the newspaper building, dug up items from the paper's archives, checked facts, re-checked them, read and re-read copy that other people were reading and correcting and ignoring her notes, and doing all the other things that seemed to be a part of the experience of a journalism intern.

She had loved it all up to this point. An idea she shared with Johnson had just been presented by him and it sounded as if he was claiming it for his own – he had not even mentioned her.

Ellen had the journalist disease, perhaps contracted with the eyestrain that came from staring at electronic copy and trying again and again to get it to read *right*. Studying journalism at Philadelphia's Temple University Department of Journalism had been the usual graduate school grind. But her internship had re-lit a flame that academia almost ground to ash. Along with the flame came a hunger for recognition, especially by one's peers. Johnson's failure to acknowledge the idea was hers was a slight that stung. Anxiety quickly joined the anger.

If Johnson ran with her idea, sure, that meant the idea was a good one, but it also meant she missed an opportunity. Would there be another? Her fear was that there would not be – in the real world, there were few opportunities for interns to stand out.

"So," the editor said, flattening his thinning hair with a habitual gesture, "you want to do this as a sidebar to the main story? You're going to have time to do this?"

At least he didn't say no, Ellen thought to herself. *Even if no one knows it was my idea, at least it will get done.* It was not much comfort but twenty-three years of life had taught her to take satisfaction where it could be found and on its own terms. She pushed her short, light brown hair back from her forehead, the only sign she gave of her irritation, and her eyes, falcon brown and gold, gazed steadily but she smiled as Johnson answered.

"Things are happening," Johnson said, nodding. "We've got another one," he added as he glanced at the other reporters at the table who had not seen his latest story's columns yet.

"Saw it on the news last night," someone said. "They sure it's the same guy? What's that, seven now?"

Johnson nodded again but remained silent as the editor spoke.

"Time," the editor said. He was a white man carrying too much weight who habitually wore his tie loose and he tugged at it. When talked about, the others called him "Big Sam." "Time is the issue." His eyes shot over to Ellen and then back to Johnson. "I don't want you missing any steps on this."

"It's Ellen's idea," Johnson said. "It's a good one."

Ellen felt her heart beat and beat again at the acknowledgment. She smiled at Johnson, but he only looked at the editor. Both the anger and the anxiety vanished, replaced by hope.

"Perspective of a killer," Johnson continued, "would work well. We've got the sidebars from families and police, but this would be unique. You're right about time. With another body found, things are going into overdrive."

A handful of people at the table nodded. A serial killer story was rare, fortunately for the general population, unfortunately for selling newspapers.

Johnson was working the story with the characteristic energy that had marked his career with a handful of Pulitzer nominations. A man with light brown skin, his gaunt appearance, was made worse by wearing his red-tinged hair almost military short. The gauntness convinced some who knew him that he stopped eating when chasing a story. When he talked about "overdrive," people took him seriously.

"So?" the editor asked. "How do you plan to do it?"

"Well, it was Parker's idea," Johnson said. "We can have her..."

"No," the editor said, shaking his head for emphasis. "Interns can't serve as reporters." Ellen felt the hope evaporate. This was the reality; no bylines for students.

"Not what I was going to say," Johnson said, smiling slightly. "She does the backgrounds, lines them up. When time permits, I swoop in and do the actual interviews. Just background, pretty much what she's doing now."

"All right," the editor said, nodding, his expression serious. "To be clear. Parker will gather background information with documentation, even set up the appointments if any of those people will talk to you, but she is *not* to interview anyone for publication. I don't want to hear from our lawyers, damn their black hearts, that we've lost a child in the wilderness. Clear?" He glanced over at Ellen, who instinctively nodded, and then back at Johnson.

"Not a problem," Johnson said and leaned back in his chair.

"All right," the editor said. "We have anything else to cover?" He looked around the table and the silence meant the meeting was over.

Glass enclosed the conference room while all of the reporters and other staff worked in low, open cubicles on the same floor. Ellen was not surprised when Johnson curled a finger for her to follow. He would want to talk to her privately and several of the others were staying behind in the conference room.

The *Inquirer* had several small rooms along the walls for interviews and Johnson led the way, flipping the *In Use* sign as they entered. As the door closed behind her, he turned and faced Ellen, folding his arms.

"You've got to learn," Johnson said, "to control what you give away with your face. Don't let them know what you're thinking, especially when you're angry."

"I wasn't angry," Ellen said immediately, grateful Johnson had not seen her fear.

"Of course, you were," Johnson said. "You thought I was not going to mention the idea was yours. Good thing to be angry about, by the way. Getting credit for ideas is important, especially for an intern."

"All right," Ellen said, "I was." She paused and took a breath. "I shouldn't have been."

"Because I've always treated you fairly?" Johnson snorted. "Look, princess, a journalism intern's life is usually one of wading through tons of meaningless bullshit doing the kinds of tasks that a well-trained cocker spaniel could do without breaking a sweat. Well, much to my surprise, you've done all that and will continue to do that, but this idea of getting some insight from a killer's perspective is not bad. Stories like this, there will be slack periods, though our boy seems to be pretty regular. So, we'll get it into the can and have it ready." He shook his head. "We're in competition for column space with the president and this little thing in Iraq. The more we have ready to go, the better."

Ellen nodded. Johnson was regarded, depending on which piece of rumor you listened to, as a complete asshole to work with or someone who'd teach you a hell of a lot if you showed you had both talent and interest. Ellen had spent the past six months hoping she had done the latter.

"Here's the thing, though," Johnson said, leaning back against a small table. "Our boy is not just any killer. He's an organized, intelligent serial murderer specializing in women. Most murderers are folks who've fucked up. Too much to drink, too much anger, lashing out and, oops, pardon me, the other person is dead. The rest are business people, trying to get something done that happens to require killing someone. Maybe get a new spouse, a rival drug dealer off a street corner, eliminate a rival for a promotion…" Johnson rubbed his chin and looked sardonic for a moment. "Hmm, interesting idea." He looked up and smiled. Ellen got the joke and returned the smile – Johnson thought he had a great sense of humor.

"Where was I? Oh, yeah, so talking to just any killer isn't what we need but it may be all we can use." He pursed his lips.

"You don't think," Ellen said, "we could get to any convicted serial killers? There are a few in prison."

"We might," Johnson said. "The FBI had a project of interviewing a bunch of them; used it to build a database. Data is still being gathered but they've had problems with funding. A lot of them lie, big or small, but the Fee-bees are pretty good at sorting through all that. Nowadays, all kinds of academics are in line to talk to them. Despite my fame, I don't know how much of a chance I would have to get someone to say yes or how long it would take. This whole story could end tomorrow or go on for years." He pursed his lips again. Finally, he nodded.

"All right, here's what we do," Johnson said. "Two-pronged approach. I'll get together with the feds on the task force and see if they can nominate a tame one for us to talk to. You, in the meantime, draw up a list of local candidates. Not our first choice, but they'll be our fallback. Men who killed women, men who've shown some degree of articulateness. Maybe someone who's gotten born again – they get the repentance thing going, maybe they'll talk to us. You talk to the prison shrinks, Graterford, Camp Hill, those places. See if they can get us inside."

"Got it," Ellen said. Now that her idea was getting transformed into a reality, she felt a small wave of fear return but showed none of it.

"Put together a list," Johnson said. "Talk to the prison shrinks but not the prisoners." He straightened up. "After we finalize the list, you'll work on developing a pitch. If it doesn't make you sound like a complete idiot, I may let you set up the interview."

"Understood," Ellen said, nodding. The fear slipped through her like an incoming tide; though the idea was hers, the possibility of actually talking to someone who killed made her stomach cold. She focused on what Johnson was saying.

"You got why Big Sam didn't want you doing any interviews?"

"It would be unethical," Ellen said. No interviews also meant the fear was pushed back, gradually getting further away from her. She smiled slightly.

"Screw ethics," Johnson said with half a laugh. "The paper doesn't want the liability. What if you talk to someone and they kill themselves? What if you make something up and we get sued?" He shrugged. "We've got more lawyers working for us than we do reporters and we've got a hell of a lot of reporters. Where are you in your reading?"

Johnson was referring to a list of books he had given Ellen three weeks before. All were on serial killers with several written by professional profilers. Fortunately for her graduate school finances, most of them were in her school's library. They had disturbed her sleep less than she had anticipated.

"Done," she said. "I also picked up one by Berry-Dee."

"What did you think of it?"

"I expected transcripts," Ellen said. "It's mostly summaries of conversations he had. I got more from interviews. Not bad at all."

"He's been focused on understanding them," Johnson said, nodding. "I've got two of his."

"I preferred John E. Douglas," Ellen said. "His three books on your list got the information across and managed to be good reads."

"A profiler's perspective," Johnson said, "and, for a cop, a good writer." He smiled and then his face went serious. "So now you're an expert?"

"No," Ellen said. "There's a lot I don't understand." *Much more than I can say.*

"So, what do you not understand?" Johnson asked. "Why someone could do something as horrible as killing?"

Ellen paused long enough that Johnson raised an eyebrow.

"Sometimes," Ellen said, "people kill because it's the best option. It's still horrible but…"

"Whoa," Johnson said and smiled. "Our princess is a moral relativist. Where's that coming from?"

Ellen felt herself blush slightly and she hesitated again before answering.

"My cousin Eileen," she said slowly, "was killed. We were kids. Around ten years ago, back in Ohio. It was an accident. Two gangs fighting over drugs, a stray bullet crossed the interstate and hit her."

"Sorry to hear that," Johnson said. His eyes were steady on Ellen, seeking something beyond her statement. Johnson was a skilled reporter and, despite Ellen's defenses, he saw something in her deeper than the usual graduate school anxiety. He let the silence draw her out.

"The men who did it," she said slowly, looking at Johnson, away, and back at him, "they were killed. Someone hunted them down and killed them one at a time." She said nothing else.

"Dangerous work," Johnson said slowly, "being in a drug gang." He waited but Ellen's gaze was steady as she looked at him and he realized she was not going to say anything else. He nodded.

All right, we all have secrets.

Johnson never told anyone but one of his secrets was enjoying working with interns. To cover it up, he adopted a curmudgeon style copied from a character he had seen on television many years before. If the intern was any good, he generally maintained the style for a time and then let it fade; then he acted almost as if working with a colleague.

Ellen Parker was a good intern, one of the best, and she always was thinking rather than looking for the expected answer. The idea of a piece using a killer was typical of her thinking. She could write – Johnson was astounded at the number of college graduates he encountered who were poor writers – and she had all the energy needed to remind him that he was fifty and she was twenty-three.

There was something about her, something behind those eyes. She did not rattle and gave the impression she would have been calm finding herself hanging by one ankle over a cliff in a thunderstorm at midnight. Johnson knew FBI agents and a Navy SEAL who had that same internal calm and he knew it was more than genetics – people learned that steadiness and he wondered what had been Ellen's classroom.

There was also, as if in competition, something else, something that seemed to be a part of fear, something that she was very good at keeping out of sight. He did not believe it was the usual student anxiety. It connected, he suspected, with the work she was doing on the killer.

I wonder why. Her cousin?

"I'll see who my Fee-Bee friend can refer us to," he said. "You start checking with the prison shrinks and see what they'll do." He nodded to Ellen and led the way out of the small room.

The four journalism interns shared two desks and four computers on the back of the floor and Ellen crossed the cubicle islands, heading for the space that they sometimes called "Purgatory."

Sitting at his own desk – his mini-office was bordered on one side by the glass wall of the building and higher than average insulated walls on the other three sides, a mark of his status – and gazed out the window as he punched numbers from memory into the phone. It rang twice.

Agent Callahan. The voice had a Boston accent and Johnson smiled; he had known Paul Callahan for eight years.

"Not this year," Johnson said immediately. "Never again. The miracle is over."

I refuse to be harassed by an Eagles fan. The Patriots will be back – you heard it here first.

"Nonsense," Johnson said as he leaned precariously and pulled open a file drawer. His fingers danced across the tabs of folders and pulled one out as he spoke. "New England has had its moment of glory."

Are you drunk?

"Of course," Johnson said with mock astonishment. "I'm a reporter, remember?"

Remind me to tell your wife.

"She encourages it," Johnson said as he opened the folder. "Says it makes her life bearable when I'm stupefied."

Probably true. So, what's up, buddy?

"You guys still short-handed?"

Since 9-11, of course. Bargan's been fighting like hell for more people and Quantico is trying to send us another person but things are pretty damned

22

tight. Hell, the word is we may lose him. With the war going on, who the hell knows?

"You want me to say something about it? Generate a little heat?"

No. Everything we're doing nowadays is limited by a shortage of agents. No sense squeaking for grease when there isn't any.

"Understood. Listen, I got something here I want to run by you. We want to do a sidebar of some kind getting into the perspective of a killer, preferably a serial killer. I know you people have that interview program…"

That's on hold. Shortage of staff. Let me leap ahead. You want to talk to one?

"That's the idea," Johnson said nodding, his eyes on the papers in the folder. He raised an eyebrow.

A number of them will talk to anyone who walks in the door but they are mostly bullshit artists. Johnson heard the FBI profiler sigh. *Once you get passed the florid psychotics, they're never as bright as the movies make them out but almost all of them think they are. The number of women who correspond with these characters while they are in prison will leave you with your head shaking. But to get back to your point, remember that very few of them go to federal prison. We may catch'em, or help catch'em, but it's the states that generally have jurisdiction. You need to talk to your commonwealth people.*

"Well, yes," Jefferson said, "I get that. But I was wondering if there were any you would recommend, maybe based on the interview program." His fingers typed on his keyboard and he looked at what came up on the display. He glanced at the file again and typed some more.

Well, I can check on that for you. I wasn't an interviewer. But you know the official database has its limits.

"All white males," Jefferson said, nodding as he remembered the report. "And only thirty-six." He rubbed his chin as he clicked through several pages on his monitor and then paused, an eyebrow rising.

Right, but it gives us a pretty good starting place. You have to remember, there have been damned few nonwhite or female serial murderers. Hard to build a database around so few cases of them. We have additional data but it's been developed under a variety of formats. One limit I referred to is that some of them from the original group are dead. The database was completed back in '85, remember. And some were pretty disorganized in their thinking.

23

That hasn't gotten better with time. Let me talk to our people who might have some ideas.

"I'd appreciate it," Jefferson said. "I got one other thing I want to ask you about."

Damn, you're going to need to buy me a hell of a dinner when I get into town. What's up?

Johnson eyes quickly traveled down the newspaper columns displayed on his monitor.

"What can you tell me about the death of an FBI agent named 'Steve Johnson' in Ohio back in 1994? And the Parker family?"

Chapter 4

Chester County Deputy Sheriff Craig Morgan never described himself as a patient man and sitting in the conference room watching the Sheriff (Morgan always capitalized the word mentally as well as when he wrote) talking with the big wigs running the serial killer task force stretched his patience. Sheriff Kate Walsh, one of the few female sheriffs in the country, was a no-nonsense blond whose quick smile did nothing to hide her intelligence and organizational abilities.

Serial murder was a specialist's crime, well beyond the resources of a county-level law enforcement agency, particularly when the killings moved outside the county. Once Sheriff Walsh realized what was happening, along about victim number three, the call for help went out. The federal team coordinated everything but tread lightly on the sensibilities of the other police agencies involved.

Morgan frowned; he hated waiting, especially in an over-crowded conference room with its prints of old Wyeth paintings hanging from the walls – in Chester County, it seemed to be the law that it was a Wyeth painting or nothing at all. Morgan grimaced; there wasn't enough room to stretch his legs out without hitting the fold-out chair in front of him. If sitting position in the room reflected hierarchy, then the fact that Morgan and his partner sat in the second row, just behind the state and federal representatives, suggested Chester County was at the center of things.

It was. The killer the task force pursued had left three bodies in Chester County. Only after the task force was formed did he leave his kills outside the county. The FBI and state profilers agreed he now tried to scatter his victims in what he thought was a random pattern. However, the location of the first three strongly suggested he was from Chester County and had started on familiar, comfortable ground.

Like most people, the killer's deliberate effort to appear random resulted in a pattern that was not. True randomness would result occasionally in clusters. The killer spread his bodies out, including leaving one across the

Mason-Dixon Line in Maryland. The others were in other Pennsylvania counties with the most recent the furthest west in Cumberland County.

To Morgan's left sat the representatives of the county's detective office. They worked for the district attorney, not the Sheriff, and most of their detectives were mobilized to work with the task force. Their Major Case Section had given up four of its seven detectives plus a sergeant.

The Sheriff's Office, as it was known, handled all the police security and community outreach functions for the county – firearms licenses, the D.A.R.E. program, courtroom security, and backed up the police departments of the county's communities. The detectives, well, *detected*, in Morgan's sardonic reference. They asked questions and gathered evidence but they didn't spend hours watching for speeders or responding to alarms or emergency calls. Morgan thought of them more as junior lawyers than real cops.

He was well aware that some of the county detectives thought equally disparagingly of the deputy sheriffs, referring to them as "county mounties" who wrote tickets to a quota and consumed far more doughnuts than was good for them.

Part of his feeling toward the county detectives came from *the incident* and he steered his thoughts from that subject. Not the time or place…

Besides, it was an indication of the seriousness of the situation as well as the general short-handedness of the county law enforcement services that the detectives and deputies were working closely together. Even people like Morgan and his detective counterparts kept their feelings out of sight while working the case.

Seven dead women made a lot of things snap into proper perspective.

Morgan's partner, Bobby Hamme, touched his arm. Hamme looked like a police officer. Wherever there was metal, diamond sparkles touched his brown and yellow uniform. Even the clips of his pens shone. Hamme wore his hair short, though not as short as Morgan who tried to hide his creeping baldness by keeping his hair to a faint brown rumor. Hamme had piercing blue eyes that he usually hid when outdoors behind incredibly dark sunglasses.

Hamme had worked on the Sheriff's D.A.R.E. program – this was a major activity by the department and generally had around five deputies working full or part-time in it – and then had been assigned to criminal investigation when another deputy moved into his slot. There was talk the department was going to get a K-9 unit but such rumors had been buzzing around the courthouse with rising and falling volume for years. Still, if it came through, part of the rumor was that another Corporal's position would open. Morgan would be in line for it. But Morgan thought Hamme would be better at it. There wasn't much that got past his partner and he was always cool under pressure.

"Morg," Hamme said, his voice low and almost hard to hear in the buzz of conversations around them, "the feds brought in another agent." He gestured to one side with a slight movement of his head. Morgan turned and looked at a woman wearing a sport coat talking to the county's chief of detectives.

She was a white woman, not tall, with an all-right face, and very light brown hair cut short enough to stay out of the way. She was athlete-slim, as far as Morgan could tell, and her eyes seemed to take in the whole room, including the fact that Morgan was looking at her.

She was attractive but Morgan paid little attention to that; divorced for a decade, he seldom considered a woman beyond his initial visual reaction. After that, if they were not a cop, witness, or suspect, they tended to fade from his awareness. That hadn't changed with several years of sobriety, the lack of which was one reason he was divorced.

That she was a federal agent was obvious. First, she dressed meticulously. Her coat, blouse, and slacks were certainly off the rack but she wore them like they were a uniform. Second, she had the "cop look" and she wasn't a local, all of whom Morgan knew. Third, as she shook someone's hand, Morgan glimpsed the dark metal of a handgun at her waist. Without seeing much of it he recognized it as a Glock 22, a .40-caliber standard issue FBI weapon.

Then they took her up front and introduced her to Sheriff Walsh and the other people sitting at the table at the front of the crowded room. The assistant district attorney smiled broadly and shook her hand a little longer than the others but the FBI agent seemed not to notice.

After a moment, the meeting began. The assistant DA quietly left the room; this was police stuff. The lead FBI agent and head of the task force, a tall black man named Bargan, took over.

"We've been reinforced," Bargan said, smiling slightly. He had a surprisingly deep voice that had to come all the way up from his shoes, Morgan figured, for someone with such an average frame. "This is Special Agent Karen Deevers," he motioned to the woman in the sport coat. She nodded towards the group. "Special Agent Deevers comes to us from the Behavioral Analysis Unit. She'll join Agent Callahan working up profiles and otherwise lending a hand. We're glad to have her."

There were murmurs and heads nodding. Bargan pointed to someone in the back of the room and the lights dimmed. He touched an open laptop computer on the table and from the back wall, a projector flashed into life.

"Here's what we have," he said. "The body was found by a canine SAR team. The victim, yet to be identified, is currently undergoing autopsy but the cause of death appears to be a knife wound to the throat."

The pictures advanced as he spoke, his fingertip lightly touching the keyboard and revealing horrific scenes that somehow seemed less real for being processed by electrons and a central processing unit.

"Like the others, the hair is blond, in this case with streaks of white. Clothes were cut away prior to death and thrown to one side first." Another picture and another flashed into existence. "No blood on any of the clothing other than a couple of small stains apparently from accidental nicks when her clothes were cut free."

"As you can see," Bargan said dispassionately, "the victim is white, in her mid-thirties. She's still wearing an inexpensive watch." Another picture. "Ankle bracelet." Picture. "But no rings or earrings." Another close-up picture caught a corner of an eye that stared at something out of the frame.

"She was bound, probably by rope that the perp took away with him. So, unlike some of the others, he didn't use duct tape." Bargan looked back at the audience. "We think he takes the rope and destroys it, just cleaning his trail. He leaves tape if he uses it because it's just too much of a hassle to unwind and gather up. All we've gotten from tape analysis, as most of you know, is that he uses latex gloves. Nothing yet for the DNA people."

"No obvious evidence of rape," Bargan added. He motioned and the lights came on. He touched the computer and the last picture vanished. "If the pattern holds, there won't be. This isn't about sex." He looked at Karen and then back at the group.

"Our people up here have been bouncing ideas off of the people down at Quantico," he said. "Special Agent Deevers, you've got the floor." Bargan sat down and Deevers moved in front of the table.

"I'm going to be a little repetitious," she said with a voice that carried easily to the back of the room. "I just want to make sure we're all on the same page. First off, the Behavioral Analysis Unit totally agrees with the work all of you up here have done. No one thinks you've missed anything." She paused, letting her words sink in.

"So we're all agreed that we're looking for a white male in his mid-thirties, right-handed, and a resident of Chester County. This is his comfort zone but he has pushed out into the surrounding area, perhaps to throw us off. He is intelligent, in part because he has left nothing behind, nothing our forensics people have picked up." Morgan noticed the use of the word *we* and nodded; good move, emphasizing that she was part of the team.

"Wound analysis indicates he is at least into his third weapon. Weapon one was used for victims one through four. Weapon two was used on number five. Weapon three was used on six. We don't know about seven." She looked around. "Changing knives is not a good sign. He's undoubtedly getting rid of them. We're not likely to find them in his trunk on a traffic stop. One profiler suggested that the use of a new knife is becoming part of the ritual."

Morgan heard Hamme quietly snort and nodded in agreement. Too many shrinks had too many theories to be useful.

"He keeps the earrings and rings as souvenirs, obviously. The previous victims did not all have both earrings and rings but all were believed to have one or the other at their deaths. So he's a collector. He undoubtedly has a hiding place for them but they will not be far from him, possibly in his house or near it." She smiled. "All of the obvious stuff, straight out of the book."

"Now here is what else may be going on," Deevers said. "The specificity of the hair, always light blond and/or white, suggests he has a special target in mind. Someone in particular who hurt him, and hurt him a lot, is the real target but he can't reach her. Maybe she moved away or she's already dead. Dear mom, maybe."

"We did the data search and we think these seven are not all he has done." She reached into her bag and pulled out a CD case. As she opened it, Bargan touched his laptop and a tray whined open. He nodded to the rear of the room and the lights dimmed again. He inserted the CD and for a moment worked with the computer. Deevers leaned over and pointed at something on the screen and Bargan nodded again.

A map appeared, one that encompassed eastern Pennsylvania, New Jersey, Delaware, and a large portion of Maryland. Red dots were scattered across it and were thick around Philadelphia, Wilmington and other cities.

"These are unsolved deaths of women," Deevers said. "Going back twenty years. The software was CrimeStat and a new package we're evaluating. They concurred." She nodded to Bargan and the picture changed. No longer was there red covering the cities. "Same time frame but killings in rural settings."

She looked at the group. "Our killer may be abducting within towns but he kills them in the countryside." The picture changed again.

"Killings by blade," Deevers said. "Of white women with light colored hair." Now there were only a small number of red dots. "This includes the Cumberland County victim. If we take away the latest seven…" She nodded and Bargan touched the keyboard.

Five red dots remained, all close to the outline of Chester County.

"Shit," someone said.

"Indeed," Deevers said. "Shit. These five are in two time groups. The first two occurred eleven years ago, both in Lancaster County, right next door. Both identified as prostitutes, one from York, one from Lancaster. Separated in time by three months in terms of when they were found but probably longer when the deaths occurred. The most recent three were five years ago, using the last one. One down in Maryland – that one the locals thought they had the perp, actually had him in jail, but the case fell apart when the man's alibi was confirmed. Second might be the first in this series as the body was found well after the crime was committed. Southern Chester County outside of Oxford. Third, that's this dot here, is in Berks County, just north of Chester County. Forensics tells us that one was killed very violently with lots of knife wounds after the victim had to have been dead."

She didn't bother to consult notes.

"Like the most recent seven, earrings and rings were gone. Where victims were identified, they appear to have been prostitutes, full or part-time." She motioned to someone in the back.

"I mentioned," Deevers said as the lights came on, "the one that was killed violently compared to the others. In the first pair, the York prostitute is believed to have died before the one from Lancaster. The remains of the Lancaster woman suggest the use of extreme violence. We are seeing, we think, someone whose pent-up rage escalates. That seems to be some sort of catharsis. That may lead to him shutting down activities for a while but, as you know, serial murders can take time off for any of a number of reasons." She looked around the room and paused.

"We think this one stopped killing because he is not a fool. We think he stopped because he did not want to attract a lot of attention from law enforcement. Both of these earlier sets ceased at precisely the point where someone floated the idea that they were connected." As a hand came up, Deevers quickly continued.

"No," she said, anticipating the question. "We don't think he learned what the police were hypothesizing. There was no follow-up on the idea and nothing showed in the press. It was just a coincidence in that sense. The point is, he closed up shop about the time he thought attention was being drawn to him."

"Do you remember any of that?" Hamme whispered to Morgan.

"Just vaguely," Morgan said. It was a while back and, besides, eleven years ago he had other problems...

"I wonder what the deal was with the guy in Maryland," Hamme said. Morgan nodded and held up his hand. Deevers pointed at him.

"That suspect in Maryland," Morgan said. "Are we sure he was cleared?"

"Yes," Deevers said. "He found the body and claimed he was not near the woman at the time of her death. Maryland thought he might be a perp coming back to the scene."

"I remember that," someone from the back said. Morgan looked over his shoulder at a gray-haired man in a brown state trooper's uniform standing up. He identified himself first. "Captain Terrence Brown, Investigation Command, Maryland State Police. He claimed he was with fishing buddies and it turned out he was. We just had a hell of a time finding any of them."

"Thank you, captain," Deevers said, being carefully polite. "His alibi turned out to be solid. He's excluded now because he died three years ago."

"That would rule him out," Morgan whispered to Hamme who smiled and nodded.

"But that takes us," Deevers said as Brown sat down, "to another point. A question has been raised. Are we dealing with more than one killer? While we know serial murderers are not always continuous in their behavior, we have not ruled out a copycat. Some of you may recall this point was raised in our teleconference of three weeks ago."

There were a few nods in the group, mostly from the front of the room.

"One suggestion, and one that we don't give a lot of hope, to be truthful, is getting a verification of any known violent types in Chester County. We've recommended building a database of men who have assaulted women on more than one occasion and cross-matching those names with anyone we run across in the current investigation. The hypothesis is that someone who hates women has modeled the behavior of our killer for at least some of the killings on our map. Unfortunately, as you know, some of the initial news reports in the past had a great deal of information about the specifics of the murders. While we've kept the lid on specifics in this latest string, if there's a 'number two' in operation, he would have picked up enough from the reports of the earlier killings to be difficult to tell from our current perp."

"Good point," Hamme whispered. Morgan could not tell if his partner was being sarcastic.

"One other thing," Deevers said. "This one is a very cool customer. Though he has centered his activities here in Chester County, his willingness to move outside the county means he can move outside of his comfort zone. It is clear that some of his victims were moved a considerable distance before being killed. That shows good control. And that dispersal was one of the things that kept him off a number of radars." She paused and looked around and smiled.

"That's all I have except to say I'm glad to be here," she said and stepped to one side.

"Wait a month on that," Bargan said as he stood, "and then get back to me." There was scattered quiet laughter from the group.

"All right," Bargan said, "check in with your team leaders for assignment updates. We'll get the forensic information online as soon as it comes in along with the report of the team personnel who were on site. Any questions at this point?"

There were none and people scattered into small groups. Morgan and Hamme worked their way to Sheriff Walsh who had taken position in a corner with a pair of county detectives.

"I think we need to be a little proactive on this database idea," Walsh said.

"In what way, sheriff?" one of the detectives said. Frank Lloyd by name, he was a bald-headed black man with a large mustache flecked with gray. He had a good reputation and Morgan thought he was pretty solid.

"We can pull names easily," she replied. "I'll get on the clerks to have that done immediately. But let's take it another step. Something Agent Deevers said got my attention. Maybe our target is not as cool as we've been thinking. Maybe these are the killings we know about but maybe he engages in less than lethal violence in between rounds of murder."

"Gotcha," Lloyd said. "The point she made about assaulting women."

"So, let's see if we can't scratch any names off the list," Walsh said. "Certainly, we can eliminate on the basis of not being available for some of the crimes where we can verify that. But what I'm thinking is taking a look at some who seem to be good prospects."

"Generate our own leads," Lloyd said, nodding. "I like that. And we haven't had a lot to do." The last comment was a reference to the dispersal of the bodies meant no single county was carrying the total load and the state and federal people had taken charge. Politely, of course.

"It will expand the field," Hamme said slowly. "Rather than just be a passive resource of names to cross-reference, we may generate a number of active suspects."

"Exactly," Walsh said. Hamme smiled, though whether at Walsh's agreement or something else Morgan didn't know – Hamme was sharp, though, and if he thought this was a good idea, it probably was.

"Where do we begin?" the other detective asked.

"Let's start," Walsh said, "with the most violent, those who have actually killed someone. Forget profiles for a moment. We don't have that many convicted murderers walking around in our county. Let's see how many of them we can eliminate."

Morgan nodded. Lloyd was right; being on the task force meant a lot of down time. This was definitely cop work. Sure, it was routine – go out, talk to people, check them out, move on to the next name on the list, but that was the bread and butter of police work. It might go nowhere, probably, but it was *working the case*. That was real police work and Morgan loved it.

"We'll filter the list," Walsh said. "Knock off people in jail during the killings, out of state, that sort of thing. Then prioritize in terms of degree of violence and whether a woman was involved."

"Watch the age," Hamme said. "Eleven years ago means we can eliminate a lot of teens."

"Right," Walsh said. "Okay, I'll get on this and let you know when the list is ready."

Morgan and the others left as Walsh went to talk with Bargan. Later, he and Hamme stood outside. It was Pennsylvania and spring but, being Pennsylvania, that meant they might be sweating by mid-day and it might snow overnight.

"You think this is a good idea?" Morgan asked his younger partner. Hamme shrugged.

"It's an idea," Hamme said, "and I don't hear a lot of new ones floating from our federal friends." He smiled. "This is mostly Walsh letting the feds know the Sheriff's Department is still involved. They're going to love it if we suddenly give them a long list of potential suspects. More work for everyone."

Morgan smiled. He was looking forward to doing something. Anything was better than doing nothing at all.

After all, that's what a cop was supposed to be about.

And it kept you from remembering.

Chapter 5

Ellen Parker hung up the telephone receiver and let herself have a bite from her very late lunch sandwich. Another call made, another bite. It was a thin reward system. She pulled the keyboard to the edge of the desk and typed her notes, her eyes on the flat, glowing screen. Around her, the late afternoon noise of people working on the upcoming edition was rising to a level suggesting chaos was sweeping through the floor.

The response from the prison shrinks had not been positive. More than one had bucked the responsibility to Department of Corrections, which effectively ended the effort – bureaucracies embedded within the Pennsylvania state government were not known for moving quickly in response to queries from the press.

Surprisingly, a pair of psychologists at two different prisons had waived away the idea and urged her to read one of a number of studies already completed. This was a surprise because neither was one of the authors of the studies. Ellen had already discovered the tendency of at least some Ph.Ds. to cite themselves whenever given the chance.

Finally, one had taken an unusual twist.

I don't think you know what you are letting yourself in for.

Ellen had explained it wouldn't be her doing the actual interview but the psychologist had not seemed to hear her.

These are still killers. If all they can do is kill your heart or mind, they will.

Very existential but not terribly helpful. She sighed, took another bite of her tasteless sandwich, and reviewed her notes. She shook her head. It felt like she wasn't holding up her end of the job. She wanted to do well but was getting nowhere. Maybe the project couldn't be done.

That wouldn't be all bad, she realized with a touch of relief.

Whatever possessed me to bring up the idea of talking with killers? She shook her head.

"What have you got?"

Ellen looked up, almost startled. Johnson stood near her desk, one hand on his hip, the other holding a cluster of papers. Though she was tempted to try to make it sound better than it was, she answered the question in her usual fashion.

"I've got nothing," she said. "They all said no. Two referred me up to Corrections but none were in the least supportive."

"How many did you talk to?"

"Six."

"Figured," Johnson said. "We may have to go to 'Plan B.'"

"We have a 'Plan B'?"

Johnson smiled in a faintly sardonic fashion and sat on the edge of her desk. He glanced across the aisle – interns did not rate cubicles – but the other desk was empty. He leaned forward slightly.

"I had an interesting conversation," he said. "One of the FBI folks and I have known each other for a while. I've got him running down some other information but he may have been able to help with your project."

Ellen did not let her pleasure at hearing the word "your" show on her face but Johnson's smile broadened anyway.

"I want you to go through the archives," Johnson said. "Look up a man named Michael Klemmer, that's spelled with a 'K'." He paused as her hands returned to the keyboard and then resumed. "First entry for him will be in 1985. Read up on him and any subsequent entries we have."

"Got it," Ellen said. She looked up. "What is he?"

"He *was* a shrink," Johnson said, still smiling. "Then he became a convicted felon. He did twelve years. My friend says he's shown some insight into the minds of killers."

"Because..?"

"Maybe because he is one." Johnson chuckled as he walked away and Ellen stared at his back.

Her heart felt cold.

It was three hours later that Ellen finally left the *Inquirer* building. She turned south on Eighth Street, her long coat catching an early evening wind that still had a touch of winter to it. She crossed Chestnut, tugging on the strap of her small handbag that she wore over a shoulder under her coat trying to adjust it. Both streets were heavy with cars and trucks. Philadelphia was a city on a wedge-shaped isthmus and the rivers flanking it seemed to condense traffic into a toothpaste-thick mass during rush hour.

Almost immediately after crossing Chestnut, just short of a collection of jewelry stores, Ellen turned into Westy's, a bar that had a nice, informal restaurant. As usual, there was a mix of students, young professionals, and Inquirer people. Already karaoke had started and Ellen winced as she turned away from a woman who was doing a very bad ABBA impression.

Ellen saw a hand rise above the crowd and made her way to a table. The other three interns were there, carefully guarding a fourth chair for her. There was a chorus of greetings; it was Friday night and it seemed appropriate to celebrate the end of the week even though at least three of them would be putting in time over the weekend.

Jay Enfield was the oldest of the group; he was from Columbia School of Journalism and was the informal leader. He was of average height, ordinary white male looks, but wore a finger-thick mustache that seemed pretty natural on his face and bridged between two pronounced smile lines. His blue-gray eyes were very clear and always suggested he was thinking two or three steps ahead of whomever he was talking to and sometimes, Ellen noticed, he was. He had been in the Navy, someone had told Ellen, though Enfield never made reference to it.

Like Ellen, Clay Stewart was from Temple. A tall black man, he had a ready smile and a narrow nose that gave him a raven-like aspect. He had gotten through his undergraduate studies on an athletic scholarship but had a brain that was as fast as his sprints. His area of interest was city politics and he always had a handful of stories ready on the foibles of Philadelphia pols.

Jackie Tolas was from New Mexico State and her smile was broader than Stewart's. Tolas spoke three languages and could disarm most of the men she encountered with a smile and a toss of her black hair. Ellen envied her ease with other people, something Ellen felt she had to work at. She also envied her stunning good looks and mentally kicked herself for it from time to time.

It was not much of a secret that Tolas and Stewart had developed a relationship that went well beyond that of intern friendship. Ellen was mystified as to when they found the time.

"The last of the Four Horsemen!" Stewart said, raising his glass of beer in a mock salute. The Apocalyptic reference was the nickname someone had bestowed on the four journalism interns during one of their first briefings at the Inquirer.

"Just one more survivor," Ellen said, shrugging off her coat and sitting down. Enfield raised his hand to get the waitress' attention. "That's *Horseperson* to you, bub." She smiled. "Long day."

"You look it," Tolas said, patting her hand. "Johnson kicking you around the building?"

Ellen's smile broadened. Everyone thought Johnson was terrible as an intern supervisor but she thought he was all right. In the past, Tolas had rolled her eyes when Ellen had tried to explain what it was like working for him and Stewart had made comments about "Stockholm syndrome," so she stopped.

"We may be doing an idea I had," Ellen said. "A sidebar on killers' minds with insight from a murderer." The fear gave her a small twinge but she ignored it; besides, reporting, even when the subject was murderers, helped shield her from it. *Why is that so?* She did not find an answer before Stewart spoke.

"Sounds good," Stewart said. "Who will you be talking to?"

"It's a big maybe," Ellen said. She turned and pointed at the beers in front of the others and the waitress nodded. "Johnson wants me to see if Michael Klemmer will talk to us."

"I remember him," Stewart said. "Years ago. Shot a guy, didn't he?"

"Peter Lang. Klemmer found him with his wife," Ellen said. "Had no idea, apparently. Didn't mount any kind of a defense but the prosecution didn't push too hard. He served twelve years. He's been out a few years and lives near Kennett Square."

"Doing what?" Tolas asked.

"Carpenter of some kind," Ellen said. "Some odd stuff. He was a Ph.D. psychologist, had a great reputation. A lot of *pro bono* work, helped out with some critical incident stress teams, that kind of thing."

"He was a nice man," Stewart said, his voice faintly mocking "Kind of quiet. Kept to himself."

"Be quiet," Tolas scolded. "What was the odd stuff?"

"He was eligible for parole at ten but for two years didn't put in for it."

"That *is* odd," Enfield said. "Any idea why not? And how did he get out?"

"He saved a man's life," Ellen said. "Two men, actually. He was present when a prisoner attacked and killed a guard and took another hostage. He talked the prisoner into giving himself up. At that point, they really pressured him to put in for parole and he did."

"That is odd," Tolas said. "Trying to do something like that, he could have ended up dead, even if only caught in the crossfire when the SWAT people stormed the place."

"It's happened before," Stewart said. He didn't think much of police.

38

"The *real* odd thing," Ellen went on, "is, while he was still in prison, Klemmer opened a correspondence with one of the FBI profilers down at their Behavior Analysis Unit in Quantico. Kept sending him notes he was taking on the 'habitual violent offenders,' his phrase. Apparently, he studied his fellow inmates."

"No shit," Tolas said, shaking her head. "Now *that* will really get you killed."

"The Fee-Bee," Ellen continued, "ignored but saved his letters for a couple of years. Finally, Klemmer sent him a study with data. He found a way to talk to whites, blacks, Hispanics, right across dividing lines. Gang bangers, pedophiles, all kinds. Quantified analysis. Did the statistics by hand. Ran tests against various hypotheses about predetermining variables, recidivism predictors, all kinds of stuff." She paused and took a sip of her beer.

"Klemmer didn't tell them a lot that they didn't know," Ellen said, "but getting the information from the subjects' own mouths was unique. He had seventy-three people in his database. His discussion of the subjects was enough to get the profiler to send him a letter back. They continued to correspond and are still in touch."

"That's incredible," Stewart said.

"Some of his data," Ellen said, "has been used by a couple of the prison reform groups that are trying to do away with the 'life without parole' statutes." She looked at Tolas. "Pennsylvania has over 4,000 people in prison for life without parole. A lot of them are old, still there from something they did when they were legally children. Some of them never killed anyone. A number of people think the law needs to be rewritten."

"Interesting," Tolas said. "I'm guessing a large proportion of those people are currently serving life sentences." She grinned.

"Cynic," said Stewart.

"Alright, he's an informal expert on murderers," Enfield said. "Has he ever explained *himself*?"

"I don't know," Ellen said. "He doesn't do anything public, at least not that we know of. It's all been with the one FBI agent."

"When are you going to talk with him?"

"I don't know," Ellen said. "I imagine with everything going on a lot of people want to talk to Michael Klemmer."

Chapter 6

Actually, only two people wanted to talk with Klemmer and both climbed out of their Chester County Sheriff's car the day after Ellen talked with her friends in Westy's.

Hamme, wearing the sunglasses he always wore when outside during daylight hours, got out on the passenger side and looked around. There was not much to see.

They parked in a broad, circular, gravel-covered area behind a two-story farmhouse. An old barn, its large door slid back to the cold spring air, was opposite the house. Bordering the parking area was a newer building made of cinderblock from which came the high-pitched scream of a band saw. The building connected to the barn with a covered breezeway.

Crop fields and fenced-in lots filled with trees stretched beyond the buildings. The effect made the place seem like it was miles from civilization rather than just a few miles from Kennett Square and US 1. Hamme looked around and shrugged, unimpressed.

Morgan believed that where and how a person lived told you as much about them as anything else, short of a long biography. The house, at the end of a straight, rutted drive nearly three hundred yards long, had been invisible from the state road. The black mailbox, a typical farmer's mailbox, had only white numbers on the side, no name.

The barn was old but well maintained. Some boards making up the wall had been taken out and replaced with new wood, judging by their flatness and uniform width. Oddly, they were painted to match the color of the old paint. *Why not just go ahead and paint the whole wall?* The house, though also old, was well looked after and he had not missed the television cable draped in with the power and telephone lines.

The new cinderblock building was white with a gray roof. It looked like every other Pennsylvania farm utility building and, from the sound of the band saw, was where Klemmer did most of his work. A metal roll-up garage door and a pair of windows, whose views were partially blocked on the inside by wood and shelves, punctuated the white wall.

"I'm going to check out the barn," Morgan said and Hamme nodded.

"Got your back," his partner said and Morgan felt a small warmth.

Whatever else you said about Hamme, he was anvil-reliable. Sure, he liked to strike a pose with his sunglasses and meticulously prepared uniform but he always did what he was supposed to and always carried his share of the load.

If he had been with me…

Morgan pushed the thought from his mind. It was not the first time it had come but there was no point in losing ground to "what might have beens." The trick was to keep on going. At least, Hamme never questioned him about *the incident.*

Morgan walked to the barn, his heavy shoes grinding the gravel and looked in the broad doorway. It was dark inside but he saw a variety of lumber stacked on six-by-six timbers lying across the ancient, dark wooden floor. It all was neatly organized, though there wasn't much of it. Morgan started to leave and saw to his right other wood. Again, carefully organized, these were stacked by types. He recognized cherry and white oak but there were perhaps a dozen different varieties, all hard to identify in the dim light. In the back of the barn, almost hidden in the shadows, were a dark, heavy table on curling legs and a tall cabinet, what Morgan recognized as an armoire. One door of it was closed and the other lay on a pair of sawhorses.

"It's 18th Century, French," someone said from one side and Morgan started. "Probably the middle of the century." A man walked over from the shadows and Morgan saw a door behind him that was half-open and in shadow. It looked like it opened onto a path to the workshop. "Gadrooned cornice, original brass except for some screws, and all oak."

Out of the corner of his eye, Morgan saw Hamme was close behind him, watching the man carefully, his right hand resting, fingers spread, on the grip of his holstered Glock. He nodded very slightly and Morgan turned to the man.

"What the hell is a gadrooned cornice?"

The man smiled slightly. He was taller and older than Morgan and wore a white-flecked mustache. His hair was pulled back into a rough ponytail and, like his mustache, his hair was streaked with white and gray. His broad, lined face held eyes that looked at Morgan over half-sized reading glasses. He wore an unbuttoned Levi jacket with the sleeves rolled up to his elbows; underneath it, he had a black John Mellencamp t-shirt captioned "Summer Work Tour, 2002." Faded jeans and heavy work shoes completed his dress.

41

"See the stuff that looks like leaves and flower petals up at the top, forming a wrap-around accent? That's a gadrooned cornice. Repeated design so well done that you can walk around and not know where they started or ended, no sudden realizing they needed to adjust the size of the in-and-out carving to make it all fit." He looked at Morgan.

"My name's Michael Klemmer, but I suppose you know that." He did not, Morgan noticed, offer his hand and his eyes flicked back at Hamme and to Morgan's badge before settling on his eyes. Then they seemed to study Morgan from the inside out.

"What's wrong with it?" Morgan asked. "The armoire, I mean."

"Brass hinges worked their way out on the one door," Klemmer said. "Someone had replaced the original screws maybe a century ago and they came out of the wood. We have to set something for new screws to get a hold of."

"I'm Deputy Sheriff Morgan. This is Deputy Hamme." Hamme nodded and his hand lowered.

"I got the call from your office," Klemmer said. He had a low voice and his eyes were cautious. "What do you want to know?"

Morgan had a prearranged set of questions to ask but he did not go into them directly. That was why he had asked about the armoire. He liked to circle his questions and then bring them in slowly, not too fast.

He knew it made his partner impatient but Morgan took Klemmer to be a bright, intelligent man and there was no sense triggering all of his defenses by a frontal assault. On the other hand, Klemmer had a slight smile that suggested he understood exactly what Morgan was doing and didn't mind. He followed Morgan attentively and responded fully.

Yes, he did more restoration work than straight-forward carpentry. No, he wasn't sure he could verify his whereabouts for all the dates not covered by his imprisonment but he would consult his journal of jobs. No, he didn't do much else beyond work.

Morgan followed Klemmer as they walked to the man's workshop. Hamme, managing to look bored even behind his sunglasses, took up a position next to their car. The two used the barn's side door and Morgan found that it was just a few steps to a door to the cinderblock workshop. The slanting roof of the breezeway, attached at either end to the two buildings, covered the short path. There was even a light, though it was off, keeping the path in shadow.

42

The workshop was a long and well-lit space. Shelving bordered the walls on both sides and a pair of work tables stood in the center. Beyond them, Morgan saw a variety of woodworking tools hanging from the far wall. Powered tools, including the band saw he had heard earlier, stood in a semi-circle.

The building had the scent of wood and stains and Morgan stifled a smile as a memory from his childhood came into his mind. It was a good smell, the kind of honest smell of a place used by a craftsman.

Including one who happened to be a murderer.

Beneath the tools an ancient, small desk stood equipped with a chair that looked like it needed massive restoration work of its own. A few neatly aligned papers lay on it next to a telephone receiver – Morgan guessed the parent unit was in the house. Klemmer walked to the desk and took a book from a drawer. It was a ledger complete with a green felt cover.

Klemmer opened it and quietly examined it for a moment. Then he looked up. Klemmer said, turning the ledger so Morgan could read it.

"Here you go," he said. "Date, customer, type of job. And notations for when I worked or talked with the customer." He smiled slightly. "A lot of my work is by the hour so I have to keep good records."

"I see," Morgan said, making notes on his own small pad. He paused. "What's a Pennsylvania spice box with Quaker locks?"

"A chest with small drawers," Klemmer said. "That one actually had a pair of secret ones with locks. The locks are just thin strips of oak on the bottom of the drawers – push it in and the strip snaps down making pulling it out impossible unless you open the drawer below it and push it up. That's the simple version. With this chest, the two drawers were hidden. You got to them from behind the chest."

"Clever," Morgan said. "More sneaky than I'd have thought of Quakers." Klemmer smiled. "And this Quaker chest of drawers...?"

"Full sized," Klemmer said, holding out a hand to show the height.

"Line and berry inlay?"

"Walnut for the drawers," Klemmer said, "and the inlay work was very geometric, using a compass. Thin strips of holly inlaid into the walnut. The berries are solid, inlaid circles, about the size of the tip of your little finger. Cherry. Front of one of the drawers split and they were afraid of losing the inlay."

Morgan nodded as he flipped his pad closed. He handed the ledger back to Klemmer.

"I think I'm covered for some of those dates, deputy," Klemmer said, putting it back in the drawer. "Sorry I can't come up with something more specific for others then just recalling that I was probably working."

"I doubt that it means much, Mister Klemmer," Morgan said. "We're pretty certain all of those dates belong to one man."

"Your serial murderer, you mean," Klemmer said, folding his arms and leaning back until he was half-sitting on the desk edge. He shook his head. "Clearly I don't fit any reasonable profile of your killer."

"What do you know of his profile?"

"White male, probably not younger than 20 when he started," Klemmer said, "strong, quick, clean shaven, though he may have a neatly trimmed mustache. Neatly trimmed hair. And he…"

"Wait a minute," Morgan said. "Why not younger than 20?"

"There have been seven murders in this round," Klemmer said. He frowned. "He's not been caught, even with the resources of two states and the FBI. So he's not leaving anything behind for you to work with. That suggests he's had some practice and that he's been at this for a time. He's not likely to be older than 40, since some of the women he's killed are prostitutes and they would be on their guard and able to physically resist. Some probably had weapons, like blades. To deal with them he has to be quick, strong, young, and, again, practiced."

"And clean shaven?"

"Again, the prostitutes," Klemmer said. "They may be desperate, but they learn to size up a customer pretty quickly. An edge will be his physical appearance. Clean-cut, all-American." Klemmer smiled as if he had said something amusing.

"That's not bad, Mister Klemmer," Morgan said. "Or do you prefer to be called 'Doctor'?"

"Mister will do," Klemmer said, "if you don't mind." Something moved through Klemmer's eyes but Morgan did not decipher it before it was gone.

"I don't," Morgan said. He looked around. "Nice workshop."

"Thank you."

"How did you afford all of this?"

"The lawyers didn't get everything," Klemmer said. "Was there anything else?"

"No, not really. Do I go out the way I came in?"

"Here," Klemmer said and walked over to the roll-up metal door and touched a button on a box. The door rose with a clatter.

Morgan nodded and walked to his car. He wasn't to it before the door descended.

"Get anything?" Hamme asked.

"Not much," Morgan said, waving his notepad as he stepped into the car. "Just some people to call and check. One odd thing, though."

"Just one?" Hamme's eyes were on the workshop.

Morgan started the car and carefully backed up, remaining silent as he thought. As they rolled down the driveway, he grimaced.

"He seems to have alibis for a few dates," Morgan said.

"Too bad," Hamme said. "There's something about him that's sour."

"You may be right," Morgan said. He looked both ways and pulled out onto the road. "He said that he financed his operation with money the lawyers didn't get. That's something I'd like to check."

"What are you thinking?"

"According to the file," Morgan said, "he didn't have 'lawyers,' just the one, and that fellow didn't do much."

"Right," Hamme said, nodding. "He pled out."

"Exactly. Maybe he had more money than he implied."

"Why lie?"

"Exactly," Morgan said. "Why lie?"

Chapter 7

Klemmer stood at one of the worktables, a piece of carved European beech in front of him though he did not see it. His lips were tight and he did not breathe deeply until he heard the police car's tires grinding gravel as it slowly left.

He stretched, easing the tension in his back and shoulders. As he turned to the beech, the telephone buzzed obnoxiously. He picked it up.

"Yes?"

Michael, it's Paul. How're you doing?

"Just finished talking with one of your minions," Klemmer said, a tinge of anger in his voice. "Was it necessary to have them...?"

Whoa, Michael. Who was it?

"Chester County Deputy Sheriff Morgan," Klemmer said, the anger slowly settling away. "His partner's name was Hamme."

I know them but they weren't there as a task force assignment. That's all I can say.

"I see," Klemmer said and shook his head. Someone was doing independent work?

I called on something else. You remember my telling you about the Inquirer reporter.

"Jefferson Johnson." Klemmer did not particularly care for reporters but Callahan had vouched for this one. He had agreed to talk "on background" to the reporter after a long discussion. At least it would be somebody to talk to but he already felt regret about giving in.

He and I go back a few years, as I said. You said you might be willing to talk to him. I just wanted to let you know that I gave him a green light to make a call. He's going to have his intern get in touch to see if it's worth doing.

"Paul," Klemmer said slowly, "as long as they understand it *won't* be about me. I don't want any questions, I don't want to see my name in print, none of that."

I've made that clear and will again, Michael. What did Morgan ask you?

"Where was I at various times," Klemmer said. He paused. "I gather you agree he's been at this for some time."

I always agreed with you on that one, Michael. Quantico finally dug up some data that supports our position. Some of it happened while you were away.

"I am reassured," Klemmer said sardonically. The FBI profiler laughed.

You were suspecting yourself? Too much introspection can be a bad thing.

"I'm not so sure of that." He paused. "I did talk about the case a little, I'm afraid."

Oh, that may not have been a good idea.

"I know," Klemmer said. "Stupid. I was irritated with being questioned and started pointing out differences between me and the target."

Ouch.

"I didn't say anything that he probably hasn't gotten from the task force."

We haven't given everyone everything. And we haven't broken my promise. Only the Behavioral Analysis Unit people know your name.

"Well," Klemmer said, shrugging slightly, "that's good. Besides, you people are doing all the real work. I'm just throwing out the occasional, off the wall idea."

It's always good to have another person's ideas, especially when working on a serial case. You know how fixated investigators into this kind of thing can get. That's why we talk to outsiders we trust. You've got good insights, Michael. I'm not expecting you to have some sort of made-in-Hollywood flash and solve everything for us, but you do provide a perspective that's damned useful. Is that reasonable?

"Agents make the best profilers," Klemmer said. "Remember? I'm happy that it's your responsibility. If I can help, fine." He paused. "Are you becoming a real shrink? I think you were working to make me feel better?"

Did it work?

"I refuse to reinforce your behavior," Klemmer said and chuckled. "All right, send in the intern. Have him call first."

Her. Twenty-first Century, Michael. Will do. Have a good one.

"One other thing," Klemmer said quickly before the agent could hang up. "Can you get me a count as to how many prostitutes were killed by edged weapons prior to these latest seven and the dates they were taken?"

There was a pause as the FBI agent thought the request over. Klemmer was guessing what Deever's data showed.

Yes. I'll email it to you today. Something up?
"Just an idea," Klemmer said. "Likely it's wrong."
Ah. All right, then.
Klemmer hung up and looked out the window towards the parking area. His eyes were cool, as calm as a sniper's as he thought about his conversation with Deputy Sheriff Morgan. He had said, he knew, too much. He shook his head; spilled milk over the dam or something. Besides, he was glad to get some company, even if it was a police officer.
He smiled and went back to work.

Ellen Parker stood in the doorway of Johnson's cubicle and waited while the reporter finished his telephone conversation.
"Got it, Paul," Johnson said and paused to blow his nose. "Damned allergy. No, really, I got it. She's here with me now. I'm the one who will be doing the writing. Klemmer remains on deep background. Just information for the sidebar." He winked at Parker, rolled his eyes and mouthed the initials "FBI" and grinned.
"Thanks again, Paul." Johnson's expression settled and he nodded. "You, too." He hung up the receiver. He looked at Ellen as he pulled another tissue from box incongruously decorated with a printed flower and butterfly design.
"Appears our Doctor Klemmer," he said to Ellen as he wiped haphazardly at his nose, "is really concerned about his name appearing in print."
"That may be understandable," Ellen said. "What does that do to the story?"
"Better to have a name," Johnson said, "but we can make this work. How far did your background work on him go?"
"Found an oddity I'd like to check out," Ellen said. "Has to do with money."
"Money?"
"You saw my email about what he did with his savings after the trial." Johnson nodded and Ellen continued. "He took his sizeable savings and put them into an annuity for Concerns of Police Survivors Incorporated."
"Scholarship fund, you said."
"Right. Specifically earmarked for education."
"I suppose that was guilt," Johnson said slowly, "though no cop was hurt."

"Well," Ellen said, "Peter Lang, the man he killed, had no next of kin. Maybe he just wanted to do some kind of payback." She shook her head. "The interesting thing is who staked him after he got out of prison."

"Shall I produce a drum roll, oh minion of mine?"

"His wife," Ellen said. "To be more exact, his ex-wife."

"Well now," Johnson said. "Ain't love grand? I wonder why she did that?"

"I suppose that was guilt," Ellen said, echoing Johnson's line.

"What's your source for the info?" Johnson asked.

"Public record," Ellen said. "When Klemmer finally agreed to attend a parole hearing, his ex-wife's attorney was present. He promised that Klemmer would be set-up as a carpenter; technically, a cabinetmaker. They always ask about employment prospects at those hearings. He also presented a signed letter in support of Klemmer's parole from his ex-wife."

"For the guy who killed her boyfriend?" Johnson smiled. "Once again, I say, ain't love grand?"

"I don't think it was love," Ellen said. "She gave no indication of ever wanting to see him again and the parole board stipulated he was not to go near her. He agreed on the record."

"Be interesting to get her insight on him," Johnson said. "Do we know where she is?"

"Here in town," Ellen said. "The Ayer."

Johnson made a low whistle as he raised his eyebrows.

"Not the low-rent district." He paused. "All right, make a call. Time to see if you can work without water wings."

"What do you mean?"

"I mean give her a call and see if you can't get an interview." He held up a hand. "Let her know it is *not* for publication. You can tell her that her ex has agreed to supply us with some insight from his studies, I guess that's the word, and we just want to have as complete a picture of him as possible."

"All right."

"'All right?'" Johnson leaned back in his chair and folded his arms. "This is an *interview*, a field assignment. Aren't you ready to jump up and down?"

Ellen looked at him and smiled slightly.

"I'm glad to get it," she said. "Thank you."

"You don't seem to rattle," Johnson said and, in response to Ellen's questioning look, he added, "I'm being serious."

"You may be right," she said and paused. "But it's mostly just not letting things show."

"Where does that come from?"

"I suppose," Ellen said slowly, "from how I was raised. That's where most of those kinds of traits come from. You know, don't show how anxious you are, that kind of thing. I think if anything negative shows, it's probably that I'm pissed. You saw that." She shrugged slightly. "Better with fear, things like that."

Johnson, his lips pursed, nodded. One thing Ellen did not do was show her anxiety.

"Listen," he said. "Reporters always have to be careful that they don't drag their own business into the story. Sometimes, sure, it can be the source of their fire about something but it can be a problem. It can set you up to see things, interpret things, in a certain way. And then it can hammer you if you have old stuff hanging around in the attic."

"What do you mean?" Ellen asked but Johnson read her eyes and thought she knew exactly what he was talking about.

"You lost a cousin to murder," Johnson said. "You mentioned that before. There was a lot of death near you around that time."

Ellen said nothing. Her golden-brown eyes were giving nothing away.

"An FBI agent was killed," Johnson said. "Steven Johnson. Same last name as me. Did you know that his partner at the time is working our serial killer case? Special Agent Karen Deevers."

"I knew Agent Johnson's name," Ellen said. "My aunt Catherine had a friend, a nurse, who treated Deevers after the ambush where Johnson died. But most of our police contact was with a Butler County deputy named James Jeffers."

"I know," Johnson said. "He married Deevers a year later. He's a lawyer nowadays, by the way. They've been separated for a few years."

"Have you been researching me?"

"Not really," Johnson said. He hid the lie well. "Hooked up some of the Ohio stuff when I did background on the task force members like Deevers. But what I want to point out to you is this story may drag up a bunch of old things. I want you to monitor yourself and think about how you might handle things if things do get stirred up. After all, almost a dozen deaths are a lot to dump on a child. Things like that can have repercussions."

50

"I appreciate your concern," Ellen said slowly, feeling her heartbeat. "But there won't be a problem. That's all old business, dealt with a long time ago." The lie came smoothly but Johnson's impassive face did not reveal if he believed it or not.

"So, you don't have a problem talking to a convicted murderer?"

"No," Ellen said. It was her turn to lie. "Besides, I'm just preparing the ground for your interview of him."

"All right, back on topic. Have you even known anyone who's killed another person?"

"Yes." Ellen did not anything at first but Johnson waited, his eyebrows raised and his arms folded.

"I had uncles who served in Vietnam," Ellen said. Her speech was careful, precise, as if steps through a minefield. "And my grandfather, Tom, served in Korea."

"They ever talk about it?" Johnson's tone was conversational but the guarded look in Ellen's eyes did not fall away. *What is she hiding?* The thought came to him suddenly.

"Not really," Ellen said. "My Grandpa Tom was decorated." She paused. "Uncle John was in the Marines, what they call Force Recon. Uncle James was an advisor to mountain people."

"The Montagnard," Johnson said.

"Degars," Ellen said. "That's their real name. But, no, they didn't talk much about it all." She paused, thinking. "Grandpa Tom really didn't. Uncle John did, a little. Maybe because he was a history prof at Indiana University."

"Go Hoosiers."

Ellen smiled slightly but there was no humor in her eyes.

"When they referred to it," Ellen said, "it was part of the job, doing what needed to be done." She shrugged slightly. "At least, that's what I remember of any of them talking about it. I know people in war have all kinds of ways of dealing with having to kill and I imagine that was true for them as well."

"My older brother is a colonel," Johnson said. "Served in the Gulf and then Bosnia." He grimaced. "Now he's with some Polish group in Iraq. I keep waiting to hear Saddam has thrown gas at them." He seemed to wrench himself back to Ellen. "He told me he's known people who've gotten into it."

Ellen said nothing but an image flashed into her mind.

It is an old military footlocker and she has opened it. It belongs to her Grandpa Tom who she loves. She reads a book of clippings prepared by her grandmother, sees citations, medals and metal military insignia and then finds an ancient bayonet. It comes out of its scabbard with a noise like the warning hiss of a poisonous snake. On the back edge of the blade, there are five carefully cut thin lines. One of the citations mentions five Chinese soldiers killed. Hand to hand...

"Ellen?" Johnson's voice is soft.

"I was just thinking about what you said," Ellen said, covering. "The men who killed my cousin were mostly about greed, I think. Lives didn't mean much to them. Maybe not even their own. Klemmer killed, I guess, out of passion and anger."

"Maybe betrayal."

"Maybe," Ellen said. "I can't imagine killing anyone. It would be a lot to bear." Her voice, Johnson noted, had the solid ring of truth – whatever else she might be hiding, this wasn't it.

"No one knows what they might do," Johnson said. "Not really. If they did, we'd be out of our jobs. Except for the comic strip writers."

"Except for them," Ellen agreed. She turned away and walked back to her cubicle, a remembered picture of an old bayonet in her mind and the thought of the dark farming soil of southern Ohio made darker by blood.

Chapter 8

The Ayer Building offered highly up-scale condominiums near Independence Park. Though crowned with what they called penthouses, Katherine McDonnell, ex-wife of Michael Klemmer, lived on the twelfth floor in one of the four condos that took up the floor's entire space.

Ellen sat on the edge of couch in the living slash dining room – she had read a brochure for the Ayer Building and the phrase had stuck in her mind – and held a cup of barely touched tea in her hands and looked at McDonnell.

Ellen had been very surprised when McDonnell agreed to the interview, though she stipulated that it was off the record and she was not to be referred to when talking with Klemmer.

The room they sat in had incredible views of Penn's Landing and the Delaware River. Light poured into it and lit up a kitchen, whose appliances would have been comfortable in an excellent restaurant, and the superb furniture of the living slash dining room.

Impressionist paintings hung on the walls and the high polish of the heavy wood furniture attracted the eye. A few carefully arranged shelves held a television and stereo system and a handful of glass sculptures. It was if the entire room was filled with things designed to hold the visitor's attention.

But Katherine McDonnell dominated. Everything else, no matter how impressive or attractive, was simply the setting for the jewel. She was the jewel and she knew it.

She was not as tall as Ellen, even in her pumps, but her carefully styled hair added a few inches that seemed to compensate. Her presence, her serious eyes and careful gaze, her erect carriage, made her seem taller than she was.

She was not beautiful so much as handsome. When she was younger, undoubtedly she had been considered beautiful – never 'pretty' – but the years had added lines of character and strength to her face. No, not beautiful, but her cool gray eyes, firm full mouth and slender nose held the viewer's attention.

"Do you like your tea?" McDonnell had a deep and clear voice with just a touch of music in it; Ellen remembered from her research that the woman had studied music in college.

"It's fine, thank you," Ellen said. She took another sip. It *was* fine.

"Explain again, please," McDonnell said as she raised her own cup, "why it is you wish to speak with Michael."

"It is in regards to the recent murders," Ellen said. "Doctor Klemmer has a reputation for having studied such people…"

"Killers," McDonnell said. "And never call him 'Doctor.' I hear he hates to be referred to by that title."

"Killers," Ellen said. "Thank you. We want to get some background from him about the killer. There's all the published material, of course, but every case has its own nuances."

"I see." McDonnell took another sip and then cocked her head to one side as she studied Ellen. "You know how he developed that expertise, of course."

"While he was in Graterford," Ellen said.

"Why do you think he studied the men around him?"

"I don't know," Ellen said. "He was a trained and experienced psychologist. I suppose professional curiosity or even boredom led him to it."

"Not quite," McDonnell said. "He was trying to understand himself."

"For what he had done?"

"Yes," the older woman said. "He was given to introspection." She smiled slightly. "I suppose he still is. That probably comes with being a psychotherapist. In our years together, I think that is one of the things that seemed a constant. The whole idea of 'knowing yourself' was something he never let go of."

"He must have been shocked to find himself doing what he did."

"I won't talk about that," McDonnell said. "He probably won't either." Her tone made it clear she would say nothing else about the murder of Peter Lang.

"You supported him during his parole hearing and afterwards," Ellen said, putting her cup down. "What led you to do that?"

"It seemed like the right thing to do," McDonnell said, "if that is not too much of a cliché. You know about the incident in prison?"

"The basics," Ellen said. "The news account, mostly."

"It is incomplete," McDonnell said. "One of the prison psychologists gave me the details." She took a final sip from her tea and then put her cup down on the table. For a moment, her eyes remained on the table as if studying the fine, dark grain. Then she looked at Ellen.

"The prisoner, a man called Ramer, was a convicted murderer. He was angry at one of the guards, the man he took hostage. He had managed to get a piece of metal and sharpened it over time. The guard he killed tried to intervene." She shook her head slightly. "A valiant effort. But it was the trigger for Michael." She smiled her quiet smile again.

"He did not like the guard, the hostage, either," McDonnell said. "Something of a bully, I gather. When the brave guard died trying to save the other, Michael, who was in the same area, intervened. The newspaper account you probably read referred to talking Ramer down. That's not precisely what happened. The prison psychologist said Michael told the man he had won." She paused and sipped her tea. "He told him his actions guaranteed the guard would be investigated and probably fired. Now was his chance to demonstrate that he was in control of himself and the situation by using his power, power that no one else in the room had, to grant the guard his life. Letting him live would give him disgrace that would haunt him for the rest of his life. That was the basic theme. I cannot imagine why but it worked. Ramer tossed the knife in a corner and let go of the guard." She smiled.

"Michael grabbed the bully-guard and pushed him down before he did something very stupid. The other guards rushed in and seized everyone and had them all in cuffs for a while until they sorted everything out. The psychologist said Michael told them to treat Ramer with respect, which none of them understood. But Ramer told Michael that everything was all right." She shook her head.

"Michael's lawyer was a friend of my lawyer," McDonnell said. "He told me the prison administration wanted Michael to put in for parole. He had been eligible for two years but had never requested one. I had my lawyer meet with Michael and urge him on my behalf to take the parole."

"That must have impressed him," Ellen said.

"Not immediately," McDonnell said. "It took both lawyers, the prison psychologist who had told me the story, and an unofficial and probably illegal call from a representative of a member of the parole board before Michael agreed to it. He studied carpentry in Graterford. It had always been a hobby of his. But he had no money."

"I know about the annuity for COPS," Ellen said.

"Not many people do," McDonnell said. "I promised to get him on his feet. I got him a small property near Kennett Square, some equipment, and had a friend find him a few clients. Not much."

"His studies," Ellen said, "are used by a number of prisoner rights organizations, particularly those trying to change the state's life imprisonment statutes. On the other hand, the same data has been referenced by the FBI's Behavioral Analysis Unit and he has corresponded with one of their profilers."

"He has a very active mind," McDonnell said. "Very insightful."

"Smart, knowledgeable, insightful," Ellen said. "What else do we need to know about him to understand him?"

"I may not be the best judge of that," McDonnell said. "I do care for him, still, but I do not want him near me."

"Because...?"

"He is a very dangerous man," McDonnell said.

"You mean that he might…"

"Kill again? Oh, no, I did not mean that. But he is dangerous in other ways." She paused and part of her seemed to collapse a little, like a cluster of trees losing their leaves and revealing something beyond them. "He sees too much. Much too much." She leaned forward as if passing on a secret. "I don't think that's good for anyone he's with." Then she sat upright.

"And I don't think it is good for him."

Ellen walked back to the Inquirer building, enjoying the chance to stretch. One might have thought she had the usual country girl's fascination with cities, a phrase she had read somewhere. The reality was, beyond the range of places to eat and the museums, there was little about a city that attracted her.

Especially Philadelphia. Everyone seemed to be, what was the phrase one of the other interns had used? *On the muscle.* You saw it in the surly responses of clerks in stores, the way people didn't bother to make room for you on the sidewalk, and the way people seemed to be looking for a fight. Or at least a disagreement.

But not Katherine McDonnell. Ellen had expected distance, possibly condescension, from a woman who was so Main Line the commuter rail service had to have a crossing named in her honor.

All right, SEPTA really didn't name crossings after anyone, Ellen grinned to herself, but if they did…

McDonnell had readily agreed to see her, a lowly intern. Surprise number one. She had been willing to talk about everything. Surprise number two. Well, wait, she wasn't willing to talk about Klemmer's murder of her lover. That really was to be expected and Ellen had not felt any need to press the issue.

What else was surprising? There was something about her tone. It was as if she was trying to warn Ellen about Klemmer.

Warn her about what? She didn't seem to think he was capable of doing anything violent. Then... *He sees too much.*

Ellen found the description made her a little uncomfortable. First Johnson obviously had pried a little into her history. That had stirred old memories, things from the past that she found intruding into her thoughts with greater frequency.

She had not told Johnson everything there was to say about Thomas Luther Parker and never would. What would Klemmer learn?

"How sure about that are you?" Johnson asked into his telephone receiver.

How sure can you be, Jeff? We were never able to account for all those Steel Riders that ended up dead. For a while, as I said, the hypothesis was the Dragons had brought in some outsiders, maybe from another allied gang, maybe from their drug connections, some heavy hitters, pros. But there was nothing, zip, that ever corroborated that idea.

"Big leap," Johnson said, leaning back in his chair, "that some old grand-dad had picked up a gun and was hunting down the accidental killers of his granddaughter." He raised his eyebrows. "Hell, don't you profilers have data on that?"

No. I'll tell you, get some of us alone in a bar and loosen our tongues and we'll admit it could be happening a lot more often than we think.

"Yeah, but no data, no cases."

Because they don't get caught. We think these are people who are very deliberate, very cool. People with backgrounds in things like police work or the military. People who are doing what they regard as justice and stop when they're done. Because we don't see them doesn't mean they're not there.

"And it doesn't mean they *are*."

There have been cases where you could reasonably suspect a relative but no conviction has resulted. I'm talking about situations where someone has made a move so well disciplined, we never even had a whiff.

"Come on, Paul," Johnson said. "There has to be a reason you suspect Tom Parker of killing a bunch of biker outlaws a decade ago beyond an *absence* of data."

Hey, I don't suspect him of anything. You asked about what happened back then. I asked some questions, read the reports, and got some informal information that I thought I'd pass on.

"Sorry, sorry," Johnson said. "Didn't mean to sound sarcastic."

No offense taken. You're a reporter; I have to make allowances. Come on, Jeff. Have you forgotten? This here's America. Violence is in our mother's milk. When we come, we come hard. Go ask Saddam.

"I regret you ever learned French," Johnson laughed. "Those stereotypes must get in the way of your police work."

There is one other piece of the equation. You remember my mention of the Butler County deputy?

"James Jeffers," Johnson said, remembering that Ellen, too, had referred to the man. "Married your Special Agent Deevers."

That's the one. The head of the Ohio task force was an old-time DEA-type. A conversation between him and one of the FBI people ended up in a debriefing report. Seems the task force leader thought Jeffers might have covered something up about who was killing those Steel Riders.

"He was bought?"

The straightest arrow in the Midwest, married to a straight arrow FBI agent? No, not even close. Jeffers was working on an independent project checking likely places for a big meth lab. Guess what? He showed up when the leader of the Steel Riders and the last of his command group were taken out and the lab blown up. Had a bad radio battery and couldn't call for help. What he didn't know was the TF leader had exchanged batteries – he had good ones.

"Oops," Johnson said.

Roger that. Shortly after that, Jeffers got out of the county mounty business and went to law school. And married Special Agent Deevers.

"It's just hard to picture," Johnson said. "Some old man wandering the county shooting members of an outlaw motorcycle gang."

Who killed his granddaughter. Who got off on a legal technicality. And an old man who happened to have been one of Uncle's best in Korea. And had a small history of violence back here in the world. An old man who, back in the day, had been a dangerous man. Hell, I know it's full of holes. I'm curious about it just because we think it does happen but we can't profile it beyond speculation.

"Listen, Paul," Johnson said, leaning towards his telephone. "I appreciate you doing all this digging. I was just curious about what might have gone on back then."

I think it's one of those things we'll never know the truth about, Jeff. But I sure would like to know more about it.

"Me, too, partner."

After he hung up, Johnson sat and stared out the window. Sometimes you asked questions you already knew, or thought you knew, the answers to. Sometimes you asked questions that gave you answers that jumped up and slapped you in the side of your face.

Johnson sighed. It was simple curiosity that had led him to tap his source. What had he learned about Ellen Parker? Nothing – she was just a kid back then. None of this had anything to do with her.

It didn't, did it?

Chapter 9

"There's something not right about Klemmer," Hamme said in greeting as Morgan walked into the central Sheriff's office, a Dunkin Donuts bag in one hand and a tall hot coffee in the other.

"Mind if I put my breakfast down?" Morgan asked with a smile as he put the bag on his desk. Around them, several other Deputy Sheriffs, all in their brown and yellow uniforms, prepared for the day.

"I've been thinking about it all weekend," Hamme said. "I know he doesn't match most of the dates. This isn't about that." His lips tightened. "But he's sour about something."

"You usually have good instincts," Morgan said, sitting down. *Sour* was the word Hamme used when his instincts told him someone was a bad guy. "Suggestions?"

"We need to keep an eye on him," Hamme said. "This is a guy who gets into a lot of peoples' homes."

"Theft?" Morgan raised an eyebrow as he opened the bag. "That would explain where he got his money to set up his business."

"Maybe," Hamme said. "Anything new from the task force?"

"Since Friday? No. I talked with Bargan and Callahan yesterday about our meeting with Klemmer."

"I hope you talked with the Sheriff first," Hamme said, grinning. "She can be a little turf conscious."

"She called *me*." Morgan shook his head. "Somehow Bargan learned of it and called her and so she told me to call him." He sipped from his coffee. "I think the entire law enforcement community was organized by the telephone company to boost their profits."

"That's interesting," Hamme said, sitting on the edge of Morgan's desk. "The Fee-Bees are already watching Klemmer?"

"Not exactly watching," Morgan said. He opened the bag, took out a sandwich and slowly unwrapped it as he gathered his thoughts. He never fixed breakfast, always bought it and lunch, and about half of his suppers; the bachelor life had not resulted in Morgan becoming a good cook.

"Callahan didn't have a lot to say. He wanted to know how it went and seemed to already know what Klemmer said. He did say they, and he was referring to the task force, didn't think Klemmer was good for any of the killings, including the ones from Deever's historical record."

"What do they base that on?"

"Dates and times, mostly," Morgan said. "He was in prison during some of those deaths. At least, that was the impression I got. They probably think he's a real outlier in terms of the profile they've worked up."

"Profiles," Hamme said and shook his head. "Guessing the obvious. All their profiling doesn't seem to have helped much. You got to wonder if those people are as bright as they think they are."

"Are any of us?" Morgan asked. "Hey, I meant to ask. How's your mom? You saw her yesterday, right?" He put his sandwich down.

"Not great," Hamme said. "Yeah, every Sunday. But she seems to have leveled off."

"Any improvement at all?"

"No," Hamme said. "The doctors don't expect any. That kind of stroke, it just blows out so much of the brain." He shook his head. "She can't move, can't speak. If it wasn't for her eyes moving when I talk to her I'd doubt she was still there, you know?"

Morgan nodded silently. He had never met Hamme's mother and did not even know she was still alive until his partner brought her to a nursing home close to West Chester. She had had a massive stroke over in Paoli. Morgan guessed the two had not been close but it was like Hamme to step up to his obligation as a son and take care of his mother.

"We've got two more to check out today," Morgan said. "Both near Coatesville. If you want to swing by and see her…"

"Maybe," Hamme said.

He was not eager and Morgan thought he understood. It could not be a good thing to see someone significant in your life slowly falling to pieces. Whatever the sense of obligation, there would also be the small horror encountered every time he was with her and unable to help her. It had to be incredibly frustrating.

"What do we have on the next two?"

"One's Donald Perdan," Morgan said, reciting from memory. "Long list of offenses for assaulting women. Likes to slap them around. He's had some minor jail time and a restraining order." He picked his sandwich up and took a bite. "Some juvenile offenses. Coatesville PD has been called and they will have an officer on-site with us."

"Understood."

"The other damn near killed a woman about sixteen years back," Morgan said. "His name is Jack Toomey. Did five years."

"But has been around for the latest seven," Hamme said.

"Blocked on some of the historical ones."

"*If* they are related," Hamme reminded him. "And there's always the copy-cat possibility."

"That's why we're talking to him."

"Hey, Ellen." The clear voice of Jay Enfield carried across the cubicles from which the low murmurs of conversations floated up as reporters and staff caught up on the weekend news and assignments. Several people looked up in annoyance but their heads dipped back down to their voice mail and computer screens.

Ellen Parker stood beside her desk, one arm in her coat turning off her computer while the other arm struggled to pull on the coat while the strap of her handbag tried to catch her arm. She looked towards Jay who was moving quickly down the aisle and smiled.

"Hey," Enfield repeated as he stepped up to her. "Johnson told me you were going over to Kennett Square."

"Near there," Ellen said. "The man Johnson wants to interview is out there and I'm setting it up."

"Great," Enfield said. "Can I go along? We're doing a piece on the mushroom business and I wanted to take a look around Kennett. I won't hold you up much."

"It's all right with me," Ellen said as she led the way to the elevators. She hid her relief – being face to face with a killer… "You're probably going to be bored sitting in the car."

"Story of my life," Enfield said as they entered the elevator. He pushed the button.

"Mushroom story?" Ellen asked.

"Regional and local," Enfield singsonged. "Regional and local." He grinned. "That's what the Inquirer does."

"Mushrooms?"

"Biggest agricultural business in Pennsylvania," Enfield said as they walked out of the elevator and crossed the lobby. "And the biggest mushroom growing area in the United States. But they've got some problems."

"Workers?"

"That's one of the biggies," Enfield said. They turned down the street, walking with the wind, and heading toward a parking lot. "Since 9-11, it's been hard for a lot of workers to get up here and mushroom growing uses a lot of labor."

"Are they having trouble hiring local people?"

"Not a lot of people," Enfield said, "who want to work in the dark and be kept in shit. Not everyone is cut out to be an intern."

Ellen laughed.

In theory, the fastest way to Kennett Square would have been straight out US 1. But Philadelphia's road net was built around Indian trails and cow paths and the direct way was seldom the fastest way. Though Kennett was southwest of Philadelphia, they first went northwest until they came to an interstate. They took that south until it cut across US 1. Then they followed it southwest as it changed back and forth between a limited access four-lane highway and an ordinary broad boulevard that seemed to serve as a display center for manufacturers of traffic lights.

Ellen maintained silence until she was on the interstate; she was not fond of Philadelphia drivers and their somewhat arbitrary skills. On the other hand, she was a very skilled driver, remembering everything she had ever learned about good driving. She continuously checked around them and her hands gripped the wheel at the old-school, "ten and two" position.

"Now," she said, "tell me the truth. Did Johnson ask you to come along?"

Enfield paused before answering. He liked Parker. Though she was younger than he, she wasn't like the others in their small group of interns. Sure, she could get as silly as the others; a symptom of their age. There was something else about her, something that reminded him of many of the veterans he knew. She was like the others in some ways but there was this... He struggled for a word. *Maturity.* Like some of her development had been accelerated so there was a part of her much older than her years. Like a vet. Like him. He made a half smile.

That's damning with faint praise.

"Sort of," Enfield finally said. "But we really are doing a story about mushrooms."

"Did he say why I needed an escort?"

"That's not the word he used," Enfield said. "He's not sure about Klemmer and thought it might be a good idea to have someone else along with you."

"Why didn't he say anything to me?"

"I guess it occurred to him late," Enfield said. "Target fixation."

"What do you mean?" Ellen turned down the heater.

"That's when a pilot gets so locked onto hitting the target, he forgets he's flying into the ground." Enfield looked out the window for a moment and then back at Ellen. "I get the impression he's a lot like that."

"He is." Ellen did not like the idea of someone thinking she needed protection but she understood the reasoning. Klemmer was an unknown quantity.

And it helped the fear.

"Johnson said you talked to Klemmer."

"To set this up," Ellen nodded. "He was polite. I briefly described the kind of sidebar we were looking at doing."

"How did he react to that?"

"Called it 'filler.'" Ellen smiled. "He said he'd be willing to discuss whether or not he'd do an interview. 'Hear you out,' he said."

"But no commitment."

"Nope." She glanced at Enfield from the corner of her eye. "Do you think he will do it?"

"I have no idea. He seems like an unusual man from what little I know."

"Well, yes, he is," Ellen said. "At least on paper. He is a killer."

"That doesn't make him unusual."

"What do you mean?"

"Almost everyone's a killer," Enfield said. "Most people don't realize it."

"What are you talking about?"

"Oh," Enfield said, smiling without humor, "I was just being a sophomore philosopher. Ignore it."

"Seriously," Ellen said, "what did you mean?" She paused. "I know you were in the war."

"Which one?" There was a touch of bitterness in Enfield's voice that Ellen had never heard before. "Sorry."

"If I offended you by referring to it, I apologize."

"You didn't," Enfield said. "I'm an asshole."

"I can't argue with you," Ellen said and smiled.

"Yeah, well, thanks for the recognition." Enfield was grinning. "That's everything in the news business." He said nothing for a moment and Ellen let the silence go on.

"What I meant was," Enfield said slowly, "is that we all do things to other people, things that damage, even shorten, their lives. Sure, Klemmer is obvious. He shot that guy. But, hell, how much does it cost a mother when her baby is born, how much does it take away from her own longevity? Some it kills immediately. Others are going to be worn down by the wear and tear."

"It's not the same."

"Didn't say it was," Enfield said, frowning in concentration. "What I'm trying to say is that life requires death, right, but that's not all. I'm not just talking about food. I'm not a born-again, shrimp-saving PETA fanatic." He grinned. "I like cocktail sauce too much."

"What *are* you talking about?"

"What we do to other people. By omission or commission. Yeah, it's obvious when someone shoots someone. But what about the times when we don't do something and how that affects someone?"

"I'm not clear…"

"Say you're a sergeant," Enfield said, "and you give an order. And someone dies following that order. Or you have a loved one who's desperately sick and you don't visit them, maybe because you can't stand seeing them like that. What does that isolation do to them? And doesn't it translate into shortening their lives?"

"I see. It might."

"In the Gulf," Enfield said, his voice low, "I never shot anyone. I was a corpsman, a medic."

"I know what a corpsman is."

"I had Marines die," Enfield said. "A real doctor could have saved them. I didn't know enough. I knew everything they taught me, sure. I did everything I was supposed to do. Obviously, they couldn't make me a doctor but they could make me a corpsman."

"Omission."

"Exactly." Enfield was silent again. "And it's not about the circumstances. I never murdered anyone, I understand that, but because of my inadequacies, they died. Not my fault in the usual sense, but it *was* my fault. I was the last person who had a chance to save them and I didn't."

"I think I understand what you mean," Ellen said. "It's really about the harm we do others, whether intentional or not. So what do you do with that understanding?"

"I think you do two things," Enfield said. "First, you try to be aware so that you keep the unintentional suffering down."

"Yes."

For a moment, Enfield said nothing. Finally, Ellen took a quick look at him. He was staring out the window of the car.

"Jay?"

"And the second thing is," Enfield said, "you only kill when you have to."

Chapter 10

They were early for Ellen's appointment with Klemmer so they stopped in Kennett Square. Enfield, who seemed to know the town well, directed her to a small coffee shop called Harrington's on the slope of a shallow hill and, miraculously, a parking place was open almost directly in front. An ugly four-story red brick office building was across the street as was an old, out of business fire department garage.

"I'll get something when I come back," he said. "I shouldn't be more than ten minutes."

"The clock is ticking," Ellen said and went into the shop.

It was a two-roomed place with padded chairs and couches in one room and tables and chairs in the other. The menu was large and Ellen paused for a moment, reading the chalkboard, before asking for a coffee blend she had never heard of.

A moment later, she sat in front of the plate glass window, watching people walk up and down the low hill.

Killers? Ellen sipped her coffee; it was surprisingly good and she tried to remember the name of the blend. *I had enough of that kind of thing. Eileen, all that happened, it left me with... I'm not a killer, not even by Jay's broad definition.*

Then she heard Enfield's response in her mind as clearly as if he was sitting at the table.

Not yet.

Enfield was back within his ten-minute promise and they followed State Street out of town. With both of them looking, they still managed to miss their turn but quickly realized their mistake.

Ellen did a quick turn and they were soon deep in the rural, rolling hills southwest of Kennett Square.

"He said there was just a black mailbox," Ellen said, looking ahead and trying to spot the drive to Klemmer's home. "I don't see any on this side."

"Blue with a yellow newspaper tube on this side," Enfield reported. "They'll all be over here. Next one is pretty dark, might be black. Yep, there it is."

It was. The hand-painted white numbers matched and Ellen turned into the driveway. Tall trees serving as a windbreak lined the drive on the west side and blocked any view of the house, though short telephone poles on the other side carried long lines of black cables that led to it.

When they could see it, the white-painted, two-story house had a green roof and a broad porch in front. It looked well-tended. The drive continued past and Ellen followed it.

Ellen pulled into the parking area behind the house and parked at the edge beside a Saab sedan. Next to the house was a pick-up that was easily a decade old.

"I'll wait here," Enfield said. "Better privacy in case I have to change into my Superman costume."

"Oh, right, humor," Ellen said. "Very good." The tightness in her voice surprised Enfield but before he could say anything she was gone.

She got out of the car as two people came out from around the workshop. One was a woman wearing glasses and an L.L. Bean down vest and jeans that were just a little too tight for her age. The other was a man and Ellen recognized him as Klemmer. She held back as he walked the woman to the car. He smiled as he saw her but said nothing.

"Well," the woman said as she opened the door to her car, "thanks again. It really looks like it's coming along."

"It is a very nice piece," Klemmer said. "I'm glad the water damage was less than it appeared. Tuesday, then." He closed her door for her and then stood to one side as she started her car and drove away. He turned to Ellen.

"Ms. Parker?"

"Yes," she said, walking forward. She held out her hand and he took it. "Thank you for seeing me." Ellen felt for an instant her body go rigid as their hands touched but Klemmer did not seem to notice, his expression not changing.

Klemmer was a little above average height and white haired. His complexion was rosy. A large nose stood over full lips. His eyes were brown and cautious and he looked at Ellen with his head turned slightly aside as if he did not want to look at her full on.

Killers

Ellen's dark blue coat and khaki slacks seemed almost formal compared to Klemmer's jeans and brown and green flannel shirt.

"Do you and your companion wish to come inside for a cup of tea?"

"He'll wait here, if that's all right," Ellen said.

"That will be fine," Klemmer said, smiling for a second as he waved at Enfield who made a small wave back.

He led the way into the house, pausing to hold open the door.

"I drink regular tea in the morning hours," Klemmer said. They entered the kitchen and he gestured to a table with a pair of chairs. He slid one out for her and then walked to the stove, talking over his shoulder. "After lunch, it's all herbal. What's your preference?"

"Regular is fine," Ellen said, looking around. The kitchen was a strange mix of old and new. Most appliances were old, though very clean. An exception to the age standard was the refrigerator, a two-door monolith in stainless steel. All of the cabinetry was custom made for the room and she assumed it was Klemmer's work. Ancient linoleum covered the floor but the table was circular, all pine, and looked like it was made yesterday. It was perfectly proportional for its place next to tall windows.

The windows let light come into the kitchen but Klemmer had not bothered to turn on the overhead recessed lighting so shadows lay in heaps in the corners. Despite the shadows, perhaps in part because of them, Ellen liked the room immediately. It had the feel of kitchens she had known in her childhood; they seldom had recessed lighting and stainless steel but rather the warmth of yellow lights and worn surfaces made so by lives spent in them. She shrugged off her coat and took off her handbag, hanging both on the back of her chair.

"I can hang that for you," Klemmer said as he worked.

"This is fine, thanks."

Klemmer heated water on an old gas stove and in a moment put a large mug down in front of her. He had a mug of a different style that he used to point at a small caddy on the table as he placed a saucer on the table. He undid the two buttons holding his shirt closed and it opened to reveal a Bon Jovi t-shirt that was captioned, "Livin' On A Prayer."

"Honey and brown sugar if you like," he said. "Give the tea a few minutes and then take it out by that chain you see." He saw her looking at his cup. "Local potter," he said. "Had a show in Kennett. They have a regular affair, what they call an 'Art Crawl,' in town and I try to see as many of the local artists as I can. Do you like it?"

"That's a nice glaze," Ellen said. "And I like a broad handle." She hefted her own mug. "Same artist?" She was happy to have something to talk about that distracted her from the anxiety that crawled up from her stomach from being so close to Klemmer.

"Yes," Klemmer said as he sat down. Ellen noticed that he had given her the chair closest to the door and wondered if he was trying to reassure her. "From a few years later. It's interesting to see how her work has changed and remained the same." He reached for the honey and squeezed some into his cup. He took a spoon from the caddy and stirred it for a moment.

"So, what is it that your Mr. Johnson hopes to accomplish?"

"The idea has evolved a little," Ellen said, focusing on the subject. "As I said when I spoke with you, most of the reporting that has gone on so far has been simply a rehashing of what information has been released. We haven't spent a lot of space on talking about how the mind of a serial murderer works."

"Why aren't you talking to one of the state or FBI profilers?" He idly stirred his tea. The spoon hit the metal ball holding the tea and the side of the mug in a gentle tinkling sound. "They are pretty good, you know." His eyes were on her face and his head was no longer slightly turned away. Ellen had the sensation that he was catching every nuance of her expression and cataloging it.

"They aren't talking," Ellen said, "because they don't want to say anything that might affect the behavior of the killer."

"Understandable," Klemmer said. "That has happened."

"There are people who've written books," Ellen said, "but they are either journalists who have recounted what other people learned or they are professionals and they are reluctant to speculate."

"I'm all that's left?" He smiled and pulled the chain of his tea ball, held it over the cup, and then placed it on the saucer. Ellen copied his movements. "I don't think that's why I was selected."

"Well," she said, "you were the name Agent Callahan mentioned to Mister Johnson."

"You want to talk to me," Klemmer said, "because you want to get the perspective of a killer, not just a psychologist or profiler." He took a sip of his tea.

"That was part of the original idea," Ellen said, quickly deciding that trying to bluff her way through was not going to work. "In fact, we wanted to interview captured serial killers and do a sort of personality profile."

"Good luck on that," Klemmer said, smiling. "Most of them are anything but honest. What they say is usually designed to carry on their battles in a different arena." He paused and his smile faded. "Sometimes they even tell the truth as a way of maneuvering." He put his cup down. "I would think the Commonwealth prison psychologists would have blocked that effort pretty quickly."

"They did."

"Then you turned to Mister Johnson's friend in the FBI."

"Yes," Ellen said. "We want your expertise but we don't want *you*. This isn't going to be about you, your background, any of that. I understand there's a real difference between a serial murderer and…" Ellen stopped.

"And an ordinary, run of the mill murderer," Klemmer finished for her. "And what got you involved in this effort?" He seemed remarkably at ease in referring to his own crime, something that seemed odd to Ellen.

"The original idea was mine," Ellen said. "I thought it would be a good sidebar."

"Do they pay much attention to the ideas of interns at the Inquirer?"

"No, they don't. Mostly, we're just there to learn by doing."

"Mostly you do the scut work? Setting up interviews, doing background research, going through the files?"

"Pretty much."

"Do you think you are learning a lot or just a little or nothing at all?"

"A lot," Ellen said and then paused. "Lots of nuts and bolts specific to the Inquirer and more generally to newspaper work and lots about the news culture."

"What's the most important thing you've learned?"

Ellen thought for a moment.

"To be a good reporter," she said, "it isn't necessary to be an expert on every subject you cover but it *is* necessary to be an expert on learning. You need to how to learn from the experts, yes, and then how to organize what they teach you so you can present it to the readers."

"That's an interesting observation," Klemmer said. "Most of the journalists I see on television simply allow two experts to present opposing points of views but don't do much in the way of organizing it so anyone can make a reasonable judgment without being an expert themselves."

"We have a little more freedom in print journalism, I think," Ellen said. "Not every story has to be pushed out the door as fast as on television. But we still fall flat at times."

"Indeed," Klemmer said. He waved a hand. "This war…" He shook his head. "But back to the issue at hand. All right. I'll be your background source. My conditions are as I have already explained. My name does not appear and there is no allusion to me, not even obliquely. I will not comment on anything that is not presented publicly by the police. If Mister Johnson thinks I might be a conduit to some of the workings of the task force, he is mistaken. I wouldn't do that and, besides, they're not sharing anything with me."

"You do talk to Agent Callahan, right?"

"I throw ideas at him," Klemmer said. "I'm not sure he is always grateful. I occasionally ask for data but never for the crime scene specifics that they want to hold onto."

"I see."

"Anything I might say about the case I will clear with Callahan first."

"Understood."

"Finally, I want you to be my interviewer."

"Doctor Klemmer…"

"*Mister* Klemmer."

"Mister Klemmer," Ellen said, cringing internally at her mistake. *Damn, I was warned!* "That's probably not possible for all sorts of legal and ethical reasons."

"You ask the questions," Klemmer said. "Johnson can write it up. If he has questions, he asks them through you. If he needs to confirm what I've said, you may tape the session or sessions. We'll do it here. No long telephone conversations." He sipped from his mug and then looked at Ellen.

"Take my conditions back to Mister Johnson and let's see what he says."

"What do you think is going on?" Johnson said, leaning back in his chair and Ellen stood in the doorway of his office.

"I think," Ellen said, "he feels like he was pressured into doing this, maybe by your FBI friend, and this is his way to jerk someone's chain in retaliation."

"I suppose that's better than shooting someone." Johnson sat up in his chair. "How do you feel about it?"

"I can handle it," Ellen said. "The sessions will be taped, so the lawyers won't have to worry about an intern being responsible for his behavior at some point in the future."

"I meant," Johnson said, "how do you *feel* about it? Happy, sad, excited, scared, indifferent? What?"

"Excited, sure," Ellen said. "It's a good opportunity, conducting an interview under supervision. A little uneasy – I don't want to screw up. And one other thing." Ellen's eyes were level as she looked at Johnson. "I'm a little angry that you didn't check with me before sending Jay along."

Johnson said nothing for several seconds. He was seeing something in Ellen Parker's eyes that he had not encountered before. The yellow-brown flashed, as if reflecting the light of something deeper inside. A thought came to Johnson suddenly: *You are Thomas Luther Parker's granddaughter whether you know it or not.*

"I should have," Johnson said. "I was just being cautious."

"I'm not objectin' to the escort," Ellen said. As if confirming Johnson's thought, for a moment Ellen's voice dipped into a soft, Ohio twang. "That's your call to make as my supervisor. But you should have asked me about it."

"I apologize," Johnson said, faintly surprising himself with the words. "All right?"

"Yes, sir," Ellen said. "It's all right." The eyes were their usual clear golden-brown and the twang faded. "How do we do this?"

"Do you have a recorder?"

"Yes, sir."

"I'll write up the questions," Johnson said. "The first ones will be pretty general. You can do a follow-up on them for clarification. But don't take off on a new tack." He leaned back. "I read a copy of his study that the prison-for-life people are using. It's not the data analysis he sent the FBI. He's a good writer. How does he sound?"

"He listens two steps ahead," Ellen said. "I had the feeling afterward that he anticipated my request and already had determined what he was going to do in response." She shook her head. "He could have done it by phone."

"Maybe he wanted to size you up," Johnson said. He grinned. "Hell, he's a shrink. Maybe he wanted to analyze you. Or maybe he just wanted to show off."

"Maybe," Ellen tentatively agreed. "And maybe there was something else."

"Like...?"

"I think he just wanted someone to talk to." She paused and then smiled. "We might be able to use that."

"The key secret of journalism," Johnson said. "Everyone wants to tell their story."

Ellen paused again, remembering her fear as she sat next to Klemmer, and then, still smiling, replied.

"Not everyone."

Chapter 11

Hamme backed the white Sheriff's car into the parking space as Morgan flipped through the pages of his notepad. As they stopped and Hamme put on the parking brake, Morgan shook his head.

"Nothing," he said.

"Well," Hamme said, "at least we're doing something. That's more than the task force can say."

The two deputies stepped out of the car. They were in the parking area of a small pizza place near the sprawling campus of Coatesville Area Senior High School and they paused as an AMTRAK train hurried past on its tracks across the road. Morgan gave his utility belt a tug upward; he noticed that Hamme didn't need to adjust his uniform. As always, his partner looked sharp.

"Be careful you don't say anything like that in front of someone from the task force," Morgan said as he slipped his pad into a shirt pocket and buttoned it. "You know what the politics are like. The Sheriff would probably have to pull you. And I would find things pretty damned boring." He smiled but Hamme did not seem to notice as they walked into the restaurant. The younger man seemed stuck on the theme.

"They're supposed to be knowledgeable," Hamme said. "They are not impressive."

The *They* he referred to, Morgan knew, were the FBI profilers. In Hamme's view, they had not added anything to the work of the state troopers' profilers.

"Let's eat," Morgan said. He didn't want this conversation overheard by anyone else.

They ordered slices of pizza and sodas and paid. Lebanese immigrants making American versions of Italian tomato pies; Morgan smiled. Secretly, this kind of swirl of culture was one of the things he liked about his country. The two deputies sat at a table in a relatively isolated corner and waited for their food.

"That's four off the list," Morgan said. Hamme nodded. "I suspect we did some good just letting a couple of those bad apples know we have our eyes on them."

"That may be true," Hamme conceded. He seemed off his rant as he took out his own notepad. "Two Coatesville, one South Coatesville, and one Sadsburyville." He looked up. "We could see the fellow over in Thorndale today and then get the Downingtown people tomorrow."

"We need to call both Thorndale and Downingtown P.D.s," Morgan said. He paused as their pizza slices were brought to them. "They already know we're coming but they don't know the times."

"Right." Hamme ignored his pizza slice for a moment as he flipped through his pad. He looked up. "Did we get anything more about Klemmer?"

"No," Morgan said. He took a bite of his pizza – white, nothing on it. Working with Hamme encouraged him to lose a few pounds and look better. He raised his eyebrows. "You still think he's good for something?"

"Can't shake the feeling," Hamme said, putting away his notepad. "I mentioned it to one of the state people but he didn't seem very interested." He shrugged and picked up a slice, one of two – red with sausage and pepperoni. "I supposed I can't blame them. I don't have any *data*." He bit and then spoke with a mouth still chewing. "Just a cop's hunch."

"Sometimes that's all you have," Morgan said.

Special Agent Paul Callahan looked at the sheet of paper in his hand and frowned. He had followed Klemmer's request and then passed the information around. Everyone who saw it agreed that the killer, if the historical data was added to the seven recent killings, had shifted to killing primarily prostitutes very early in his career. No question of it.

But what did it *mean*? He shook his head. The explanation most of the people he talked to thought it might be a greater focus by the perpetrator; prostitutes could be the target of someone working under a moral imperative to punish the sinners. On the other hand, Callahan and a few others thought the shift represented the learning curve of the murderer. He had come to understand that these women would not be missed as readily as his first victims.

Klemmer had not been a great help. He had agreed to both hypotheses almost impatiently.

Of course, Paul. Those can certainly be threads in the weave. But what else? What is this telling us about him?

Then Klemmer had had to hang up; a customer had arrived. Callahan wanted to know what else was in the numbers. What did Klemmer see that he didn't?

"Still working on it?" a woman asked.

Callahan looked up and saw Karen Deevers stirring her coffee in a Styrofoam cup. Unlike the other members of the task force, she had not yet gotten her own coffee cup.

"I dislike appearing ignorant," Callahan admitted, something he found easy to do with Deevers. "Especially with Klemmer."

"I read your bio of him," Deevers said and sat on the chair beside Callahan's desk. "Very interesting man." She blew on her coffee. "He has a unique perspective."

"True enough," Callahan said. "It's been good to have someone from the outside to listen to. I wanted to have him come in as part of the guest lecturer series."

"J. Edgar would spin in his grave."

"Right out of his dress," Callahan said. Thirty-two years after Hoover's death FBI agents still were reluctant to make jokes in public about the man who had built The Bureau but between two in private, especially two who had not served under him, that reluctance was far less prevalent.

Deevers smiled and held out her hand. Callahan passed her the sheet with the table. She studied it a moment and nodded.

"It's definitely a shift," she said, "especially if the cases I brought up are valid." She looked up. "The first two weren't pros, but after them they all were. What does Klemmer say? Anything different than how we read the data?"

"Nothing *different*," Callahan said, taking the paper back. "But he seems to think there's something else going on as well."

"Well," Deevers said, picking up her cup, "there's the nature of the prey, of course."

"You mean that they are easier to disappear? We covered that."

"No," Deevers said. "Think about it for a moment. What makes prostitutes different from other women, and no jokes, please."

Callahan smiled and thought about what the killer would see about a prostitute that would be greater than an ordinary woman. Right, less likely to be missed. Right, a sinner. What else?

She would look different, probably. Dressing for the role, dressing to advertise perhaps. What else?

Callahan pictured walking up to a prostitute and contrasted the image with walking up to an ordinary woman.

"The prostitute," Callahan said, "is a harder target in one regard." Deevers nodded.

"Right," Deevers agreed. "A pro is much more alert to what's going on around her. She's in the business of making judgments about who she goes with. She's not hesitant about striking out to protect herself. All generalities, of course." She smiled slightly. "We could be saying the same about a female FBI agent."

"Now who's making the jokes?" Callahan thought for a moment and nodded. "He shifted targets because they were more exciting."

"A bigger emotional payoff," Deevers said. "Maybe on more than one level."

"He's a hunter," Callahan said, "looking for ways to get more enjoyment out of the hunt."

"Exactly." Deevers took a drink of coffee. "I wonder what he'll do next to boost the thrill."

"Yes, Paul," Klemmer said. "I think that's correct. I think he's going to be looking to increase the rush. After all, other than the first two, he's been doing prostitutes for nine of the last ten..."

It's ten, Michael. We have the identity of the woman in Cumberland County.

"Where was she from?" Klemmer's eyes swept around his workshop as if using it as an anchor, a way of holding himself in place while discussing madness.

West Chester.

"West Chester?" Klemmer frowned. "He took her all the way across Chester County, across *another* county, and to the far side of Cumberland County to kill her? That was an incredible risk."

I know. This may be an effort to throw us off and maybe to get more of a thrill out of it. All that additional danger of transporting her so far, had to have been a hell of a rush when he pulled it off.

"He's been doing that," Klemmer said. "Moving them away from where he picks them up, but there's something else about this. Paul, he's arrogant.

78

He has to know you are looking for him and he's trying to show you that he has contempt for you. The task force is based in West Chester."

That occurred to us. And there aren't that many prostitutes in this town for him to target. They're pretty discrete. To a certain extent, he was sacrificing the anonymous factor. The local cops know her pretty well. Part-timer, worked in one of the college bars. There was even a missing person report.

"He's local, we knew that," Klemmer said. "Maybe even local to West Chester." Another thought crept into Klemmer's mind but he let it sit while he slowly considered it. "The longest distance he has ever taken a victim. He really wanted to rub your noses in it."

He's succeeded. We're working on methods of transport.

"He's careful," Klemmer said, distracted. "Something without a trail. Nothing rented, nothing borrowed. Look, Paul, I don't think this was just for the thrill. Yes, it was for that, but this was mostly thumbing his nose. We haven't seen the escalation that will produce greater thrill for him. He probably thought of this as no more than an extended taxi ride, taking the trash to the dump. He's arrogant, confident. He never believed there was a chance of him being stopped or having an accident."

He's got his blinders on. They all do, one way or the other.

"Target fixation," Klemmer agreed. "Part of the pathology. Listen, Paul, I've got to go. Thank you for the data."

You're welcome – thanks for the input.

Klemmer hung up, his thoughts elsewhere. Almost automatically, he stood and went to his worktable. A piece of new wood lay next to a very old and very dark piece that he was trying to match. His hands moved to the new piece and hefted it. Right now, it was crudely cut to the general shape of the piece it would replace. Now he would use his knife, files, and sandpaper to make it match exactly. The hard part would be staining, of course.

If it did not look exactly like the rest of the cabinet, it would draw the eye. The human eye was excellent at…

Klemmer paused, the wood in his hands. His eyes were on what he held but he did not see it, for the image his mind held was a dark shadow vaguely in the shape of a man. The only clarity was the glint of the knife's blade he held.

What would *not* draw the eye?

Morgan backed the sheriff's car carefully down Hamme's driveway. His partner, standing beside his white van, watched him and finally waved as the car turned onto the street. Morgan waved back.

It had been a long day in which little was accomplished. The Sheriff's idea was worth checking out; Morgan still agreed to that. So far, though, all the people on the long list of men using violence involving women had alibis for at least some of the last seven killings.

Morgan shook his head as he turned out of the housing development and onto the main road. Some of the men looked like the kinds of men who beat women. There was something ugly about their faces or in their eyes and Morgan had difficulty imagining how any woman would let someone like them ever get close them.

It happens. They know how to use camouflage.

Of course, there were the men who looked, well, like anyone else. How could you tell?

...Camouflage.

The word came back to Morgan but he could not pin down why. He knew better than to try to force it. A cop learned to accept such things as an indication that part of his mind was working through information, perhaps extracting something that might prove to be valuable.

Or maybe just spinning my wheels.

He smiled at himself and slowed for an intersection. He turned north, towards his home and let his mind wander.

Camouflage. Letting his mind drift, the word took him to an image of a Mossy Oak hooded jacket he had seen in a hunting magazine ad. Nice jacket, though he really couldn't justify getting a new jacket; his old one was in pretty good shape.

Another image; something from the news. Marines in the Iraqi desert in tan, camouflaged uniforms made superfluous by all of their equipment and gear being dark olive drab. And that led to...

The image of David Plant, wearing an old field jacket splotched with green, brown, and black. *The incident.* David Plant, on his back in the middle of the street, arms moving slowly as if he was underwater and drowning. The red pool around him grew and slid towards the gutter, though it looked like it did not have the strength to get there.

Morgan bit his lip and gripped the steering wheel hard enough that he half expected it to crack.

"Enough of that," he said aloud. "It's done, it's over."

But he knew he was lying to himself.

Twenty minutes later Morgan stood in his small kitchen. His utility belt hung in a closet and his Glock was locked in a safe bolted to the floor of the trailer's bedroom. He opened a can of soda, walked into the almost as small living room and used the remote to turn on the television.

He punched up ESPN but watched without seeing. Instead, he thought about camouflage.

Chapter 12

The task force used the second-floor office space above a bank across the street from the county courthouse. Callahan had an office, as did the lead representative of the Pennsylvania State Police. Everyone else shared common space in what were the conference room and three smaller offices. It was not as great a handicap as it sounded, since the Chester County Sheriff Deputies most of the time used their own offices just across the street. As a result, there was even space for a coffee urn that tended to be fired up on weekends and evenings only; there were too many good places in downtown West Chester to get a morning cup of coffee.

Karen Deevers rapped on the doorframe and Callahan motioned her in. She shut the door as she came in. It being morning, she had a cup of coffee in one hand and Callahan noticed she had finally gotten a personal mug for it.

"So," she said.

"So," Callahan replied. "What do they think?"

"They agree," Deevers said. "The perpetrator knows West Chester extremely well. He may live here or nearby. And he has probably made use of the prostitutes here or, at least, has had contact with them."

"I'm guessing he's a john," Callahan said. "That would give him plenty of opportunities to see how the girls work. He might even have been taking ones he has used."

"They were going to suggest that," Deevers said, smiling.

"We've got some of the locals working that line," he said, returning the smile. "Yesterday I had a meeting with the chief of police. He has a small file of men busted as johns and is giving us the list. In the meantime, his people are continuing to run down leads they've developed from people who knew Dana Kerr, victim seven. A couple of her co-workers are helping with that. What else does Quantico think?"

"They are not so sure that Klemmer is right about the need for greater thrills. The predator has been very well controlled to this point." Karen frowned. "After all, he's been disciplined and very careful."

"I'd agree that he's been squeaky clean," Callahan said. "But…"

"Yeah, 'but.' He has sat on the sidelines from time to time, maybe because he's had to."

"Jail, you mean."

"Always a possibility if you're involved with working girls," Deevers said. "But he may have simply benched himself for other reasons. That's control as well."

"He has control," Callahan said, "but he cannot stop. He keeps coming back. Three waves, remember. A shift in victims early on."

"Discipline or thrill seeking like Klemmer thinks?"

"If he is going to escalate, where do they think he might go? What might he do?"

"Lots of guesses," Deevers said. "Quantico is a bit hampered in that regard because they don't think he needs more thrills than he's getting by killing and dumping." She hesitated. "I have an idea or two."

"So do I," Callahan said. "You first."

"All right. First, about escalation. It might be accomplished by frequency. Instead of every other month, more often."

"He might," Callahan said. "I suspect that would force him to rush and his need to be careful would act as a constraint on that."

"I'm not so sure he would have a choice," Deevers said. "We're talking about deep-seated needs but you might be right. Let me give you a second escalation scenario."

"Hit me."

"He shoves it in our faces. I agree with Klemmer about this guy's arrogance. He must hold us in complete contempt. I think he's going to dump the next one in our laps."

"And that I agree with," Callahan said calmly. He glanced at the door and then looked back at Deevers. "Now, let's talk about another hypothesis I have. And this stays in this room."

Hamme's phone beeped as Morgan turned onto Strasburg Road, heading for West Chester. Hamme listened for a moment.

"Yes," he said. He turned to Morgan. "It's my mother. Her blood pressure has suddenly dropped. It could be bad. Can we go to her nursing home?"

"You got it," Morgan said.

He pressed down on the accelerator and turned on the car's flashers. Hamme was silent, his eyes staring straight ahead through the diffuse morning light of the valley.

Their route took them through the countryside, following roads that rose and fell with the rolling hills. Morgan turned onto the road leading to the nursing home. Weed-covered fields bordered them on both sides while tree lots stood in the distance, darkly framing the approach to the nursing home's driveway.

Morgan swung the car in front of the main entrance and killed the flashers. Hamme was out of the car quickly. He paused and stuck his head back in.

"She's in the DCC Unit wing," he said, then he was gone.

Morgan found a parking space in the nearly empty lot and called in his location. He secured the car and followed after Hamme.

The nursing home was a single-story, modern looking building. Two sliding doors opened as Morgan walked down the covered walkway. He stepped into the lobby, well-lit with broad, various-colored lines on the floor. Bright prints were on the walls. A young black woman wearing a dark blue sweater over her shoulders stood behind an information desk.

"Hi," Morgan said. "Looking for the DCC Unit."

She pointed down a hall to the left. "You're with the other deputy," she said. "Follow the blue line. Room One Four Seven."

Morgan smiled his thanks and followed the line. Around him, occasional nursing home staff, usually wearing a variety of multi-colored scrubs, scurried past along with a smaller number of residents.

Only a few residents moved about; several used walkers and one was in a wheelchair pushed along by a bored attendant. He glimpsed people in beds as he passed rooms. Some showed no signs of consciousness.

Morgan saw they were old, their ages carved deeply into their faces. Milky eyes blinked at him, little of their focus still present. A passing woman, an attendant holding her hand, looked at him and smiled from beneath thinning white hair.

Morgan sighed. He didn't need the sign on the hall wall that identified the blue line as leading to the Diminished Capacity Care Unit. The people around him were living evidence of the brutality of strokes and Alzheimer's. He thought about what Hamme must have gone through putting his mother into a place like this.

Room 147 was on the left and Morgan looked in the open door. Hamme was talking to a woman doctor – she had a white lab coat on while everyone else wore scrubs – and made small gestures as she talked quietly. Morgan stood across the hall as the two carried on their conversation.

He could see Hamme's mother. She seemed almost too small to have ever had a son as big as Hamme. Her arms were above the covers and Morgan saw an IV attached to her while a variety of medical instruments stood in a rack delivering their stories in green and yellow displays.

She, like the others, was white haired; short white curls hung from her head without any style, other than "long-term hospital patient." Her face was lined though, perhaps because of being asleep, the lines were not terribly deep. Her ears and nose seemed larger than for someone who was so small. Her thin lips were held in a curved line that, even though she was unconscious, seemed disapproving, almost bitter. Morgan looked around, taking in the nursing home.

That's all right, Mrs. Hamme. You've got a lot to be pissed about.

After another minute, Hamme came out. He nodded silently to Morgan and the two men walked out the way they had come. Morgan said nothing until they were in the car. As he started it, he turned to his partner.

"How is she?" he asked.

"Stable," Hamme said. "They don't think it was another stroke." He looked around and found the shoulder belt and then carefully attached it. He put on his sunglasses. "The doctor says she's stable," he repeated and Morgan nodded.

They drove back out onto the road and turned towards West Chester. Morgan called in that they were moving.

"She's not doing well," Hamme said as they paused at a stop sign. "They don't expect her to improve."

"That's rough," Morgan said.

"They don't know what her real level of awareness is." Hamme scratched idly at his jaw. "She was out the whole time I was there but when I've been by in the past, she seemed to follow my voice. Not much expression, so I don't know if she knows it's me."

"No way to be sure?"

"Not really," Hamme said. He smiled slightly. "She's had a rough life. My father died in an accident and I know that was a tough time for her. She blew through a bunch of relationships but seemed to drive off any man worth a damn."

"Sounds pretty hard on both of you." Morgan had never heard Hamme talk so much about his mother or his childhood and felt like he was being allowed a look into someone's secret diary. He wondered when the cover would close.

"It wasn't pleasant," Hamme said and shrugged. "Some of her friends were pretty nasty. They weren't very supportive. She was angry a lot." He was silent and Morgan thought he was finished talking. "But she was always in charge, always controlled things. I never missed a meal, always went to school." He smiled oddly, as if seeing something that he wasn't sure was amusing or not. "It was just after school that things could get a little bad."

Morgan nodded, not sure what to say.

"It did give me an appreciation of law and order," Hamme said and the strange smile returned. "I guess it did. I don't know. Maybe that was just something that was inside me all the time." His smile became regular. "We've been hanging around profilers and shrinks too much. I'm starting to become analytical."

"That's dangerous," Morgan joked.

"I try to tell her," Hamme said, "what I do, what I've achieved. Just to let her know, you know?" Morgan nodded again. "She deserves to know what the outcome of all those years was."

"Maybe she does know," Morgan said. "Maybe she takes a great deal of satisfaction, of pride, in you. Hell, in spite of everything, she must have doing something right. Look at you."

"You might be right, Morg," Hamme said. He smiled slightly. "You might be right."

Chapter 13

All of his moves are well thought out, organized around a carefully constructed plan. But he understands that the unexpected can always occur and so he has contingencies already considered and ready.

He does not move until everything is perfect; it is not about numbers. He does not keep score. It is about the act. Discipline is necessary for the act ever to take place.

He reads almost everything available on serial murderers and uses the information to evaluate his own performance. He considers most of those he has read about as fools, unable to control their appetites. That lack of self-discipline is something he despises.

Above all, he is disciplined. He does not allow himself to vent the powerful feelings, The Excitement, he carefully contains until the very end, when he is completing the act. Then, and only then, does he let the rage sweep up through him like a violent storm.

He does not see himself as some angel of vengeance; Hollywood metaphors he finds ridiculous and faintly clown-like. Yes, there is vengeance in his actions. He knows this is true at a deep level. But it is more than that.

He does what he does because he likes it. It does not have to be any deeper than that, though he knows it is. There is always, her... He moves his mind away from the thought and focuses on what he is about tonight.

He knows he is hunted. He views the police with contempt. They do not see, they are hamstrung by their own procedures, weighed down by bureaucracies to the point of immobility, and more concerned with jealous guarding of their turfs and reputations than in catching him.

He does not want to be caught, he is not leaving clues, and he is not playing games. He is killing.

The woman is trading herself for money to trade for drugs. She is obviously cold in the small hours of the night, pulling on her cigarette as if drawing heat from it.

She stalks her street corner near a house used by crack addicts, willing to trade herself for cash or drugs. Earlier in the evening, cars would slowly cruise by, the driver's hand holding money, looking for drugs or sex or both. She would look through the passenger side, out of the driver's reach, and negotiate terms. He watched all of this from five blocks away from within his vehicle; his binoculars are more than powerful enough to see her and his position is a good one; slightly elevated, he can see her and the area surrounding her clearly.

She knows about him, of course, but no one from Coatesville has ever been taken and she needs to feel as safe as she can. She has not understood that he has never taken a woman from the same place twice.

And her need is so great that she would be out on her corner even if he had been there before, even if he had taken someone she knew.

It is late, well past midnight. The intermittent stream of customers appears to have dried up and he can see she is close to ending it for the night. She glances again at her watch. He nods to himself and starts his vehicle, far enough away she doesn't hear it.

She glances in his direction as his lights come on. He lowers his window and takes a twenty-dollar bill out of his jacket and holds it between two fingers, his elbow on the window frame, the money in the wind like a pennant.

She sees the money and when he stops opposite her, lowering the passenger window she looks in, careful not to touch the door and be close enough that someone inside might grab her wrist.

"Hey, baby," she says.

"Hey," he says. He lets the street light play on his face and smiles while keeping both hands on the steering wheel. "I'm just looking for a quickie," he says.

"I can go for a blow," she says and smiles vacantly at her phrase. "It's thirty."

"Seems fair," he says. He looks around and then points at the intersection. "Can we pull around the corner? I don't want to go far." He motions to the back of his vehicle. "There's room in back." He looks around, checking for traffic but there is none.

"Sure," she says, deciding, and opens the door and gets in, still facing him. "Just go around the corner. I'll do you right in your seat." She smiles again. "Money up front, baby."

"Right," he says, and reaches behind him.

He moves so fast, so violently, she does not realize what is happening until she slams onto the vehicle's floor. It is metal covered with a plastic tarp. She tries to rise but he has a knee in the small of her back. Then she feels the point of steel at the side of her throat.

"You don't want to move," he says, "unless I tell you to move. You don't want to yell. You want to stay alive."

She cannot think of doing anything other than nodding and does not resist as he pulls her hands behind her back. She hears the sound of duct tape and her wrists are bound. He does her ankles. Then her mouth. He loops the tape around an elbow and forces it close to the other and then tapes them so close together her chest and back hurt.

She feels his hand in her blond hair and he pulls her head up. His other hand pulls her face towards his and she can smell the latex of the gloves he wears.

He says nothing and that raises her terror.

She does not know where they go. She is not even sure how long they drive. Suddenly they stop. He steps out of the driver's seat and walks past her to the back of the vehicle. She hears the doors open. She looks but there is only darkness outside.

He drags her out and carries her no more than ten feet before dropping her face down on the ground. As he walks, he makes an odd noise and it is a moment before she understands he has pulled on something over his clothes.

She feels him tearing at her clothing. His breathing is hoarse, panting as if exerting himself to his physical limits. He uses a knife to cut clothing away and she feels nicks and slices where the razor-like steel touches her flesh.

Then he attacks her hair, pulling at it viciously and slicing, hacking, at it with the knife. She feels pain again as the knife cuts her scalp. She is just forming the question of why he is attacking her hair when he stops. Then his hand clutches the remains of her hair and savagely jerks her head back.

"Now," he says and there is pure hate in his voice.

Then she feels the edge of the steel touch her throat.

Chapter 14

"They have another," Johnson said. "The body was found two hours ago in Hibernia Park."

Big Sam frowned as he looked up from his desk; he had just sat down and his coffee was untouched.

"That's north of Coatesville, right?"

"Correct," Johnson said. His own coffee was in his hand and already was half-gone. He didn't bother to look at his notes that he held in his other hand. "Our guy says they are keeping it close to the chest but it looks like it's the same perpetrator. The body was found by a pair of park employees swinging through to empty some of the trash cans."

"The park wasn't locked up for the night?"

"Not at all the entrances," Johnson said. "It's bordered on the north by Cedar Knoll Road," looking at his notes to get the name right. "He came in through there. One curve and you're invisible because of the trees." He looked up. "Our guy says there's not a lot of traffic on the road anyway and this took place, he guesses, somewhere between two and three AM. Anyway, he pulled over onto the shoulder and took her to one of the picnic pavilions."

"And you...?"

"I'm going out there," Johnson said. "I'm taking Parker."

"All right," Sam said. "Stay in touch." He shook his head. "Eight, now. Hey, let's get moving on that sidebar."

"We're talking with Klemmer and I have a rough outline already set," Johnson said. He did not explain that Ellen would be serving as the conduit for questions. "Already have some of the information we've picked up from research."

"Good," Sam said and turned to his coffee as Johnson left.

"Don't take off your coat," Johnson said as he intercepted Ellen on her way to her desk. "There's been another killing, maybe fifty minutes away north of Coatesville. I'll drive."

Fifteen minutes later they were on the Schuylkill Expressway, I-76, and Ellen discovered that Johnson was an almost insane driver.

Still holding his coffee in one hand and steering with the other, he described the situation to Ellen.

"One of our people, Daryl Jennings," he explained, "covers the Coatesville area. He lives in Wagontown, just north of there but south of the park. Heard the sirens and went over. He's on my speed-dial," he said, pointing at his cell phone sitting in a recharger plugged into the dashboard. "He got to the park employees and got some information from them before the police told them to shut up."

The car, a late model Ford, picked up speed as they raced northwest, paralleling the river, and Ellen resisted the temptation to close her eyes.

"We think this is our guy why?" Ellen asked.

"No clothes," Johnson said. "Hair ripped off. Dirty blond, by the way. Throat cut."

"That's him."

"They may have the park closed off," Johnson said. "There's a map in your door." He waited while Ellen pulled a thick book of Pennsylvania maps arranged by counties. She flipped it open and, in a few seconds, looked at him.

"Got it," she said.

"As I recall," Johnson said, "there are two main entrances for people coming from the east."

"Cedar Knoll Road," Ellen said. "Borders the park on the north. And it looks like Wagontown Road comes in from the south."

"We'll try Cedar Knoll," Johnson said. "Wagontown entrance is 82 to 340 to Wagontown, right?"

"Correct," Ellen said. "Stay on 82 after it crosses 340 and then we'll hit Cedar Knoll." She looked up. "What if they have both entrances closed?"

"If they do, they do," Johnson said. "But Cedar Knoll we can park on and walk on in. I hope you're wearing sensible shoes."

"Always," Ellen said. She smiled.

"Big Sam asked about the sidebar," Johnson said, maneuvering around a semi tractor-trailer and then taking the exit for US 202. He decelerated rapidly on the exit and then picked up speed again. "I haven't gone into a lot of detail about how you'll be asking Klemmer questions."

"I see."

"If it falls apart for any reason," Johnson said, glancing at his review mirror and then at Ellen, who wished he would just look ahead, "don't worry. We have enough for the sidebar already. In fact, I've written a draft that I'll want you to review after we start talking to Klemmer."

"Why after?" Ellen threw out the question while she thought about what Johnson had just said. *...Falls apart for any reason...*

"I want you to really hear Klemmer," Johnson said, "without what I've written filtering anything."

"I understand," Ellen said. She looked at Johnson. "Why do you think it might fall apart?"

"Klemmer may be totally fine with the questions," Johnson said. "But he's a little bit of an unknown quantity to me. I don't like hanging a project on someone I don't know." He smiled. "We've got plenty of information sources. We can do it without him. But if he jerks us around anymore, then we'll drop him and move on." He looked at Ellen from the corner of his eye.

"This isn't an investigative piece," Johnson said. "It's background, explanatory. We've got plenty of information and don't need multiple sources. There are a lot of things we can have you involved in so if Klemmer doesn't work out, then I don't want to waste time with him. Better to get you over into something you can get your fangs into." He paused. "Clear?"

"Got it," Ellen said. She felt a little relief at the message she might not have to work with Klemmer. *Not a great attitude for a reporter.*

She looked out the window. Pennsylvania streamed by. The further west they went, the more the ground filled with trees, as if the undifferentiated towns were a long isthmus through a sea of trees, a sea that, in the old days, formed a barrier few could cross. Pennsylvania was settled in the east from the sea and in the west by way of the rivers and lakes; the interior was too difficult. The trees said the interior, mountains made dark by trees, would, if it could, reclaim every step people had made across this ground.

Ellen blinked. *Where did that come from?* But there was something about Pennsylvania that seemed to begrudge the presence of people, something still dark and wild that pressed in close and watched the traffic on the four-lane highways and counted the years. She shook her head.

Too many late hours, too much reading about murderers. Too many bad dreams.

She deliberately turned from the view and looked at Johnson. She was torn in her feelings about the man. On the one hand, his comment that he wanted to make sure she had something rewarding to do was appreciated. On the other was the prying – that word kept coming to Ellen's mind – into her background.

There were things that had happened in Ohio that she did not anyone looking at too closely.

Grandpa Tom is gone. And Uncle John is happily teaching away in Indiana and is not about to talk about what happened back then. What could anyone possibly learn?

Ellen smiled with a touch of sourness. One thing the news business had taught her quickly, if she had not already known it, was it was not always about learned facts. Implications were enough to destroy reputations, even lives. The news was a machine whose primary purpose was to make money and that meant getting people to buy the product. The greater the flash, the greater the sales. No one had ever said to her, "If it bleeds, it leads," but that was the ever-present pressure as reporters and editors wrestled with getting words onto paper.

And yet... Ellen shook her head. It was what she wanted to do with her life. In spite of the bad side of the news business, she wanted to be a part of it. She smiled at her faint reflection as she turned to the car window again. She just wanted to *know*, to know whatever there was to know, and she wanted to write about it, and she wanted people to read what she wrote.

Some days she felt like she was selling a small piece of herself to become a reporter; other days the desire to write, to gain the understanding of things and to put that understanding into words, seemed to be all she could bear.

"Do you have your identity?" Johnson asked and Ellen turned toward him, her eyes questioning. "Your Inquirer I.D.," he said. "Make sure it's visible."

Ellen nodded and looked back out the window as they turned onto an exit.

Do you have your identity?

Chapter 15

"The scene's closed off," Daryl Jennings said, leaning against Johnson's door. "You can park here," he added, gesturing at a grassy area that already had a cluster of vehicles including two trucks with satellite antennae pointed slightly above the horizon. People were standing around in small groups.

The road was blocked by a police car whose red and blues kept up a steady, flashing rhythm. A pair of gray-clad officers sipped coffee from paper cups and watched with mild interest the gathering reporters.

"Have they announced a time for a briefing?" Johnson asked.

"No," Jennings said. He flipped open a notepad. "The local senior police officer has been superseded by a detective from the troopers."

"He won't be in charge long," Johnson said. "The task force probably already has people here."

"Helicopters, two, landed in the park more than an hour and a half ago." Jennings smiled at Ellen but said nothing. He was an older, stout white man with a reddish complexion, gold-rimmed glasses, and vaguely yellow hair that the morning breeze played with.

"All right," Johnson said. "We'll park." Jennings nodded and stepped back.

Johnson swung onto the clear area and maneuvered so that the car was facing back the way they had come and was close to the road.

"In case we have to beat a fast retreat," he joked as he opened his door.

"We may have something," Jennings said as he approached, his cell phone held against his ear. "They're going to let us in, escorted. They have removed the body." He put away the cell phone.

"Must have gone out Wagontown Road," Johnson said. "Escorted?"

"No cameras," Jennings said and motioned with his head towards the television trucks. "That should piss some people off." He glanced at Ellen. "Pardon my French."

"No problem," she said.

"How long before we go?" Johnson asked.

"They have sent a trooper. We can go to the car," Jennings motioned with his head toward the police car. "'Thus far you shall come, and no farther.'"

"Sounds familiar," Johnson said. He walked toward the police car and the other two followed.

"It's Job," Ellen said. "I think."

"Very good," Jennings said and smiled. His teeth looked artificial. "Don't ask me for chapter and verse. It's about the only biblical quote I know."

"Odd one to know," Ellen said.

"Used it in a story once," Jennings said and winked. "Editor cut it and we had a fight about it. Only reason I remember it."

"Good enough." Ellen said, liking Jennings.

A Pennsylvania State Trooper stood at the police car. He was a young man and wore his dark gray campaign hat pulled low so that none of his forehead showed. His uniform shirt was gray with black epaulets and he wore a black tie – Ellen remembered that troopers wore their ties year-round. His trousers were a darker gray and had a black stripe. His trousers matched his hat in color. Both his shoes and leather belt gleamed. On his shoulders was the black and gold keystone-patch of a trooper and a single, gold-outlined chevron. He did not look happy.

The trooper, who seemed older close-up than he had from a distance, was patiently explaining to a television crew that they could not bring their cameras. The television people were obviously unhappy but finally the camera and sound people hoisted their equipment and slowly walked away while the television reporter from their competition grinned.

"Told you," the reporter, a neatly dressed black man said to his opposite number who grimaced and shook his head.

"I am Trooper Morrison," the trooper said. "Here is how this is going to go. You will follow me. I am going to take you to the crime scene. You will stay close to me as we walk. You will not take pictures. This is an active crime scene. Forensic investigations are still being conducted. You will remain behind the yellow tape. You may observe until I take you to a detective who is going to provide a briefing. She may be able to provide you with details. Are there any questions?"

"How 'close' is close?" the white television reporter asked. "How much can we wander?"

"You can't," Trooper Morrison said. He made a fleeting smile. "Is everyone ready?"

He turned and led the way into the park. Directly behind the police car there was simple, swinging steel pole gate. It had been hidden from sight because of the police car. Ellen saw black smudges on the yellow paint. Someone had taken fingerprints? The trooper did not look at it as they passed. She touched Johnson's arm and pointed. The reporter nodded back.

Morrison kept them on the road. It curved quickly and it was only a moment before they could no longer see Cedar Knoll Road and not much more than that before the television trucks and crews were hidden.

"Good place for dumping," Johnson said, nodding and looking around.

The road came to an intersection. Morrison took them to the right, towards a parking area. Off to the left, Ellen saw a two-story building.

"Park building," Jennings said, seeing her glance. "It's generally not occupied at night." He gestured with his arm. "Behind us and up there are picnic pavilions and there are individual picnic areas off most of the roads."

"No one camps here overnight?"

"You're not supposed to," Jennings said. "The park people do a sweep before they lock up."

There were police and emergency vehicles everywhere. Over by the house a pair of helicopters sat, one in a parking lot, the other on grass.

They walked up on the murder scene almost abruptly. They came around a large, white-colored van with state markings and suddenly Morrison stopped. In front of him, yellow police tape stretched to either side.

For a moment, it appeared to Ellen that there was little to see. The yellow tape formed an irregular circle perhaps forty feet across at the widest. It was looped tightly around saplings and trees and enclosed a strip of grass that gradually faded away where the trees became denser.

Small markers, wires with white and yellow pennants on them, were stuck into the ground, some scattered close to the road and others in a tight cluster about half way into the circle, close to where the trees started. Someone was using a laser device and a GPS to record dimensions. The body was gone. All in all, it looked like there wasn't much that made the area enclosed within the yellow tape significant.

Then Ellen saw the blood. It was a reddish darkness that resembled no other and she bit her lower lip. She forced herself to take a breath.

"Those markers," Johnson said, his voice low and pointing towards the cluster near the dried blood. "There's nothing there now but I'm guessing that's where her clothes were."

96

"Clothes and hair," Jennings said. He spoke quietly, as if not wanting to disturb someone. Or something. "The park guys said her clothes were scattered but all on one side and her hair was in the same place."

"This is our guy," Johnson said.

"Folks," Trooper Morrison said, "they're ready for the briefing. We're going to be over by the support vehicles."

Ellen had no idea what 'support vehicles' were but it turned out they were a series of trucks and vans flanked by a pair of large, black SUVs. A cluster of well-dressed people waited for them. Slightly behind them, a pair of Chester County Deputy Sheriffs, one older, one young with sunglasses, impassively watched the small group approach.

Ellen recognized none of them but they all had the probing eyes of police. The woman among them looked a little familiar.

Introductions were quickly made. The man speaking was from the State Police. He called himself Tayson and then nodded to the people to his left. "These are Special Agents Paul Callahan and Karen Deevers," he said. Ellen looked closely at Callahan, Johnson's FBI contact and the man who knew Michael Klemmer.

Karen Deevers... Ohio, 1994. She was an FBI agent there. They had never met but this was another deep echo to the bell of her memory. The two FBI agents nodded and stepped away from Tayson and stood together while Deevers talked quietly on her cell phone.

Tayson was not a dynamic speaker and there was not much he said they did not already know. The killing resembled earlier killings. The victim was yet to be identified. He would not comment on specifics. They believed the killings were the work of one man. He would not comment on leads. He would not comment on evidence gathered.

The only question Johnson asked came quickly.

"How did he get into the park?"

"Had to have been from Cedar Knoll Road," Tayson said. "The Wagontown entrance was locked. Where you came in, the bar was in place but the lock for securing it was broken. The perpetrator opened it and came in. He left it open and it was found that way by the maintenance workers when they entered this morning."

Johnson nodded and glanced at Ellen. So they had been trying for fingerprints.

The television reporters had questions but Johnson leaned over to Ellen. "Why don't you get with Agent Callahan and ask him about Klemmer. Find out what he thinks of our ex-shrink."

Ellen nodded and walked away from the group, half expecting the trooper to intercept her. Callahan and Deevers were still together, talking quietly. Deevers looked up as she approached.

"Special Agent Callahan," Ellen said, holding out her hand. "I'm Ellen Parker."

Automatically, Callahan took her hand and shook it while Deevers looked at her impassively.

"Right," Callahan said. "You're working with Jeff Johnson. This is Special Agent Karen Deevers."

"I'm glad to meet you," Ellen said. She held out her hand. "I heard about you when I was a girl."

"Ohio," Deevers said. She took Ellen's hand and shook it, studying Ellen carefully. For her part, Ellen remembered that Special Agent Deevers killed three outlaw gang members in an ambush that killed another FBI agent and wounded a county deputy.

"You know we're going to talk to Michael Klemmer," Ellen said to Callahan. "I've met him once. He's asking us to have all questions be brought by me."

"That's Michael," Callahan said.

"What do you mean?"

"If he feels he's being pushed," Callahan said, "he pushes back." He tilted his head. "I think he agreed too quickly to talk to you people and it left him thinking he needs to assert himself. Control things a little."

"I see," Ellen said, though she wasn't sure she did. "What can you tell me about him?"

"What do you want to know?"

"This is all off the record," Ellen said quickly.

"So, what do you want to know?" Callahan said, smiling.

"What's the best way to work with him?"

"Let him go at his own pace," Callahan said. His expression turned serious. "He's not a full-time psychologist any more. He has other things to do. If you're too demanding, he's likely to ignore you."

"Is he really any good at this?"

"At profiling?" Callahan looked at Deevers and then back at Ellen. "He's not a cop, he doesn't have a cop's instincts. But he's pretty sharp, damned sharp."

"Would you regard him as a consultant?"

"No," Callahan said. He smiled. "We pay our consultants. Contracts, government paperwork, the whole nine yards. But, no, he's not a consultant. Technically, he's just an interested citizen who shares his thoughts. We don't give him access to any information regarded as confidential. On the other hand, he was a psychologist who has had an opportunity to see habitually violent offenders over time and we welcome input from whatever source."

"How long have you been practicing that?" Ellen asked and smiled.

"Since the second letter I got from him," Callahan said. "That's my story and I'm sticking to it." He smiled again.

"Well," Ellen said, "thank you for your time. Agent Deevers." Ellen nodded and turned and walked away.

Callahan and Deevers watched her walk back to Johnson.

"So that's Thomas Luther Parker's granddaughter," Callahan said. "She doesn't seem like someone related to…"

"Acorns," Deevers said.

"Acorns?"

"They don't fall far from the tree."

Morgan walked back to Hamme after using the bathroom in the park house; the nearby latrines were sealed while the forensic people checked them out on the off-chance the killer had dumped something in one of them. Some people, Morgan thought, had jobs much worse than his.

"The reporters are leaving," Hamme said as Morgan stopped beside him. "Callahan said we're all going to meet back in West Chester. They may already have an I.D. on the victim."

"All right, Bobby," Morgan said. He led the way to their car.

"Heard something interesting," Hamme said. "One of the reporters got next to Callahan. Guess who she questioned him about?"

"Bart Simpson?" One of Morgan's nephews had taken to wearing an "Under Achiever" Bart Simpson t-shirt.

"Michael Klemmer."

"What about?"

"I couldn't hear," Hamme said, opening the car door and slipping inside. "I'm telling you, though; there is something sour about that guy."

"You might be right."

Chapter 16

"It is our guy," Callahan said to Deevers as she walked into the task force office. "He left the bracelets and took the earrings and rings."

"Autopsy is a match," Deevers said, holding up a manila folder holding a copy of the examiner's report. "But there's something here I want to review with you."

Callahan waved her to follow him and he took her into the small office that he used. She closed the door and handed him the report.

"Congratulations, by the way," she said.

"Ugh," Callahan replied as he walked back to his desk. "I'd like to know what strings Bargan pulled to get out of here."

"They're short-handed," Deevers said. "With that situation in Florida, someone had to organize the new task force and you know the situation here. He's good at team forming."

"He is that," Callahan said, opening the report. "They've promised us more people if we need them, though I have no idea where they'll get them." He raised an eyebrow. "I will only require you to bow as you enter my office henceforth."

He sat down as he read and Deevers took one of the other chairs. She waited patiently and watched him as he read; Callahan gave nothing away. Finally, he put the report down and lifted his eyes to her.

"That's not good," he said.

"The examiner," Deevers said, "Doctor Maire, has seen other victims of our perp, as I understand it."

"He's the lead medical examiner for the county," Deevers said. "The state has been happy to let him do his thing. Long history of work in Philadelphia. Our people report he is very thorough and has left nothing to chance."

"He gets good evaluations, then?"

"Doctor Bennert thinks he's one of the best there is," Callahan said.

"Floyd Bennert said something nice about another doctor?" Deevers smiled wryly. Bennert had a reputation for brilliant forensic autopsies, superb testimony in trial, and an almost complete disdain for any other medical professional. His work with the FBI was legendary.

"He's agreed with everything Maire has come up with," Callahan said. "He was not so complimentary of some of the other examiners who have been involved."

"The results are on their way to Bennert," Deevers said.

"Good," Callahan said. He tapped the open folder. "This will bring him up here in a hurry."

It was late afternoon before Doctor Floyd Bennert arrived in West Chester. He went directly to see the body and confer with Maire. An hour after that he took the stairs two at a time – his usual practice; he ran six miles every morning and looked like a human version of a whippet – to the task force offices over the bank that faced the county courthouse.

"You have a problem," Bennert said as he walked through the open door of Callahan's office. He offered no other greeting.

"Good afternoon, Doctor Bennert," Callahan said as Bennert sat down and flipped open his ever-present laptop. "Let me have Special Agent Deevers join us." He picked up his telephone and pushed a button. Bennert, his eyes on his computer's screen, ignored him.

Deevers walked into the office and Bennert barely glanced up. He was tapping something on the screen.

"Violence," Bennert said. "Escalation. He almost lost control."

"As evidenced by…" Callahan said.

"Wounds," Bennert said and Deevers nodded at the confirmation to what Maire had found. "He barely had himself under control when he attacked her hair and stripped her clothes. There were more wounds, deeper wounds, and blood spatter *not*, I say again *not*, from the throat wound. They found droplets on top of clothes that matched the directions of knife wounds; the trajectories are a good fit. And the hair…" He glanced at Deevers. "He hacked and sliced the hair but she has scalp wound from where the point of the blade made contact." He looked back at Callahan. "Have the state profilers been told of this?"

"We briefed all the profilers right after I called you," Callahan said.

"Do any of them have ideas about what is going on?" His tone made it clear he did not expect much.

"He's under pressure," Callahan said. Bennert all but rolled his eyes.

"Do you remember the killings in the Eighties?" Bennert asked slowly, as if trying to teach a not very bright person something basic. "Along the Mississippi-Alabama border."

"I do," Callahan said.

"Four women,'" Bennert said. "Escalation in violence as indicated by wounds." He looked at Deevers. "*He* used a knife, too," he said.

"Escalated the violence and the risks he ran," Callahan said. "An Alabama trooper killed him at a traffic stop for no brake lights."

"His fifth victim," Bennert said, still looking at Deevers, "was alive and in the trunk of the car." He turned back to Callahan. "He had taken her from her home in the middle of the day. Escalation of risk, certainly, he had been a night stalker, meticulous planner. By the time he was killed, all that was out the window. He was going for his second kill in two days."

"He had an apparent history."

"Twelve," Bennert said, half smiling as if pleased that Callahan remembered the case. "That we know about. Three in eight months, then nothing for four years."

"Prison." Callahan thought for a moment. "Receiving stolen property."

"Very good," Bennert said. His new dog could do clever tricks. "Then four in the same eight months, nothing for two years."

"He was employed as a pine woods logger. Isolated for a great deal of the time."

"And then five. Stretched out over six months."

"I recall," Callahan said. "We never were able to definitively pin those on him, either."

"Bodies were too old," Bennert said. "And the last four were over three months." He leaned back in his chair. "He was escalating the frequency."

"Needed more and more thrill," Deevers said. "That's not uncommon."

"Right," Bennert said. "Addiction. He was also losing control. Even some of the old remains that were found before and after his death showed that the later in the group you looked, the more likely there would be injuries consistent with increased violence." He smiled. "The bones don't lie."

"Look," Bennert said, "I'm a forensics man, not a shrink." Callahan raised his eyebrows at the admission of any kind of limit and Deevers smiled slightly. "I can tell you that what we see for this latest victim is increased violence. The interpretation of that is straightforward: he is having greater difficulty with control." He hesitated and Callahan frowned.

"This has been," Bennert said, "one carefully controlled predator. If he is escalating…" He shook his head. "This could become very ugly."

"I agree," Callahan said.

"It already is," Deevers added.

"Anything else you can think of?" Johnson asked Ellen who studied her legal pad, flipping the yellow pages back and forth."

"You have kept things in pretty general terms," she said.

"Background," Johnson agreed, nodding. "I want to bounce off Klemmer some of what we've researched and see if he can't pull it all together for us."

"You don't want specific analysis of our killer?"

"He's not *mine*," Johnson said, grinning. "*You* can have him if you want." His expression turned serious. "But a specific analysis is not something he can do inasmuch as he is not working the case. I don't think Callahan has shared any of the forensic evidence with him. Besides, it would be unattributed speculation. We can do that ourselves if we want. No, I just want to give readers an insight to the kinds of ways someone might end up a serial killer. 'The killer's mind,' that's the focus of the sidebar."

"All right," Ellen said.

"You want more," Johnson said.

"I'd like to know who he is," Ellen said and smiled. "Background is needed, of course." She stopped.

"Sources can surprise you," Johnson said. "You think someone only has a limited amount of information and it turns out they know more. You go into the interview ready to follow the branching tree, if it's there." He nodded. "That's how a good reporter works. But you have to watch the expectation that someone knows more than they do. Then you may put words into their mouths, over-interpret what they are saying, get them commenting beyond their competence, and find yourself taking yourself into dead-ends."

"A balancing act," Ellen said.

"A balance," Johnson said. "Needing isn't always wanting. Reporters always *want* things and they are not always the facts. I *want* to believe Saddam was hand-in-glove with the 9-11 terrorists since we've invaded Iraq. I *need* the facts that clarify that relationship and whether or not it exists." He frowned. "It's a balance, all right, between what you need to know with what you want to know."

"I see," Ellen said. "Well, there's a question I would like to put to Klemmer not on your list." She smiled slightly. "We can keep it in generalities, one pertaining to all of the killers."

"Which is...?"

"How do we stop them?"

Chapter 17

The morning sun had difficulty evaporating the mist lying across the fields and shallow valleys west of Kennett Square. Klemmer enjoyed the play of the light as he drove his pick-up on the road returning him to his home. Rising and falling, the road took him through the light fog a little like a dolphin leading a ship.

He smiled; he did not have much of an artistic view of the world around him despite his profession. He had shared morning coffee with a potter and he suspected that was the only way she saw the world. He glanced at the newspaper-wrapped object on the seat beside him; he had purchased a cup from her show at one of the Kennett galleries and, with the show over, she had delivered it to him.

Would she have done that if she had known you had killed a man?

Probably she would, Klemmer answered his own question. They had run into each other at the coffee shop often enough to know each other's first names; he knew her full name, of course. With others sitting at one of the planked tables, they had talked about art, books, movies, and a dozen other subjects.

The small group accepted him; besides the potter there was an architect, a rich fellow heavily involved in *pro bono* work, an antiques dealer, the daughter of the owner who frequently showed up with her new baby, and a cluster of others. Including the potter's husband, a man who usually had a book and, to judge from a glimpse made when his jacket had slid up, a large-caliber handgun in the small of his back.

Klemmer shook his head. He had no firearms in his home; over the conditions of his parole were the repercussions from his past that still echoed. He did not want ever to touch a gun again.

Besides, he joked to himself, he had a band saw.

Ahead, Klemmer saw a white sedan parked on the shoulder next to his driveway. Though the windows were dark and it was otherwise unmarked, the several small bumps on its roof identified it as a police car. Klemmer sighed; the deputies were back. He pulled into the driveway and stopped.

Getting out of his car, Klemmer walked to the police car. As he approached, the driver's door opened and Deputy Morgan got out.

"Did you wish to see me?" Klemmer said.

"Yes, sir," Morgan said. "I drove in and found you weren't home."

"You saw my sign." Klemmer had, in his back-door window, a cardboard clock-face sign on which he could display when he expected to return, a device he had gotten into the habit of using for his customers.

"Yes, sir," Morgan said. "And you are on time." He glanced at his watch. "Precisely."

"Follow me in," Klemmer said. He walked back to his truck and drove down the lane. Morgan followed and when he got out of his car Klemmer, holding his still-wrapped cup in one hand, used the other to gesture towards his house.

"Come on in," Klemmer said. "I want to try out my new cup."

Morgan appeared slightly puzzled but followed. Klemmer noticed that the other deputy, Hamme, was not present.

Morgan said something into the microphone hanging from his shirt's epaulet and Klemmer assumed he was checking in with his dispatcher. He held the door open for Morgan and then entered the kitchen.

Putting the cup on the table, he took the teapot on the stove over to the sink and put fresh water in it.

"I have instant coffee," Klemmer said. He noticed that Morgan was still standing. "Please have a seat," he added. "I'm having tea. I have several different types. I'm having an orange pekoe."

"That sounds fine," Morgan said. He did not drink a lot of tea, preferring coffee, but instant coffee never did much for him. He watched Klemmer work over the stove and then come to the table.

Klemmer unwrapped the cup. It was large and had a smooth gray and green glaze on it. Klemmer turned it around and Morgan saw it had an owl on one side and a squirrel on the other.

"I know the artist," Klemmer said, handing it to Morgan.

Morgan looked at it. It was a good cup, large enough for his hands. He liked the smoothness of the glaze. He handed it back to Klemmer.

"Nice," he said.

"So," Klemmer said as he went back to the stove. "What can I do for you, deputy?"

"I've done a little reading," Morgan said. "About you. You gathered some information while you were in prison that people are using about the sentencing guidelines issue."

"Yes," Klemmer said. "I had some time on my hands."

"I also found out," Morgan said, "that you did a study on habitual violent offenders. I'm told by people who know about such things it was a pretty good job."

"Thanks," Klemmer said. He looked over his shoulder as the teapot began to bubble. "There's sugar and honey on the table."

"Thanks," Morgan said. "I take it straight."

"Best way," Klemmer said. He poured water and Morgan heard the tinkle of metal tea balls lowered into the cups. He walked back to the table and put a cup in front of Morgan. "It'll take a few minutes." He sat down. "And what else brought you out here, Deputy Morgan?"

"Well," Morgan said, idly turning the cup as it rested on the tabletop, "I also read about your case."

Klemmer said nothing for a moment and then he leaned back.

"Am I 'a person of interest'?" He frowned slightly. "I thought I was clear of…"

"No," Morgan said. "No, you are not a suspect in the killings." He paused, considering his words. "No," he repeated. "Your case, something about it didn't hold together."

"You think I didn't kill Peter Lang?" Klemmer's voice was tinged with sarcasm. "I'm pretty certain I did."

"That's not it," Morgan said. "Everyone was happy to take your plea." He leaned back in his chair. "I don't think it was him who you tried to kill that night."

Silence pressed into the kitchen and Klemmer did not move, his fingertips touching the handle of his cup. He did not look at Morgan.

After a moment, he slowly took the tea ball out of his cup and put it in a saucer. He took a careful sip, still avoiding Morgan's eyes.

"What are you talking about?" Klemmer finally said. He studied his cup as if he was reading something important.

"Angle of passage of the slug," Morgan said. "No one spent a great deal of time on it since you immediately admitted your guilt. It doesn't work if you shot him while he was standing upright. It only works if he is leaning or falling to one side, his right."

Klemmer looked at Morgan.

"What's the point of this?" he asked.

"Mister Klemmer," Morgan said slowly, "I don't think you were trying to kill him. I think you were trying to kill your wife. He put himself in the way trying to protect her."

Klemmer covered his mouth with one hand and finally looked at Morgan. His tear-filled eyes showed nothing but sorrow. The sharp gaze was gone, swept by a wave of emotion that Morgan thought would have dropped Klemmer to the floor if he had not been sitting. Klemmer said nothing but his hand muffled a short, sharp cry.

With his elbows on the table, Klemmer covered his face with both hands as if trying to hide. Morgan saw the fingers press into the thin flesh of Klemmer's forehead. The man froze in position, held like a butterfly on a pin.

Morgan looked around, finding it hard to stare at Klemmer. The kitchen – this was not the room for this. How long had this kitchen been here? A hundred years? How many families had lived here? What grief had come to them in this room? He sighed and turned back to Klemmer.

The other man slowly lowered his hands. The lines in his face now looked as if they went to the bones of his skull. He wiped at his eyes with his hands and then got up. From a rail in front of the sink, he took a brightly colored kitchen towel and wiped his face. Then he ran some water and used it to wash off his face. He used the towel again and then carefully folded it as if it was part of a ritual. He laid the neat rectangle on the counter and turned around, folding his arms. He leaned against the counter.

"Why are you here?" Klemmer asked. His voice was small, almost distant.

"People," Morgan said, turning in his chair towards Klemmer, "have questions about you. Some things about you have, let's say, generated attention. I did a little investigating on my own."

"'People.'" Klemmer's voice was still very quiet, as if speaking from another room. "That would be your partner, Deputy Hamme."

"It would," Morgan said, nodding. "He has good instincts."

"At this point," Klemmer said, his voice a little stronger though he kept leaning against the sink counter, "what does it matter?"

"You mean in terms of prosecution?"

"No," Klemmer said. "I meant, what does it matter to *you*? Why bring this to me? Investigate my history, yes. I imagine that happens periodically when there's a killing in this county. But why bring it here to me?"

Morgan said nothing and Klemmer looked at him for a moment and then shook his head, smiling without humor.

"You just wanted to see if you were right," Klemmer said. He looked at Morgan, his head tilted to one side. "You looked at that old report, searching for some tidbit that you could put in front of your partner, something that would build you up."

"That's not it," Morgan said.

"You're not thinking of prosecution," Klemmer said. "That opportunity is gone."

"No," Morgan said. "You killed Peter Lang and admitted to it. You had a lot of money and should have had a strong defense going. But you didn't bother. You pled out. Then you gave your money away." He shrugged. "It didn't make any sense to me, so I dug up the old records. I had to know the answer."

"Peter Lang," Klemmer started to say and then stopped. He grimaced. "Peter Lang was a good man. I think he genuinely loved my wife. I knew him, knew him for years." Klemmer ran his hand across the top of his head, pressing his hair down. "I knew Katherine had someone else. I had been depressed for a long time, frustrated with my work, and I simply wasn't good to be around." He took a breath. "I didn't know the degree of involvement. I found them together." He paused, again studying his cup. Then he looked up.

"I tried to kill her," Klemmer said. "I was enraged. Pete threw himself in the way. He saved her. When I saw what I had done… It snapped me back. I put the gun down and tried to revive him but he was gone. I sat and waited for the police."

"Your wife," Morgan said, "was the target."

"In that moment," Klemmer said, "yes, she was. All my suspicions, all my frustrations about us, about everything else in my life, suddenly had a target. And I had a gun. In that moment, I just wanted to hurt her severely enough that she would understand how badly I was hurt." He shook his head. "I wasn't thinking about her death, only her pain. It was reasoning in an alley; no looking left or right or even ahead."

"She helped you get out of prison," Morgan said. "Set you up here."

"Not because she loves me," Klemmer said.

"Guilt, then," Morgan said. "About what happened to you and Lang."

"Yes," Klemmer said. "As far as she's concerned, she destroyed two lives." He snorted in bitter humor. "She thinks of herself as a more accomplished killer than me." He shook his head. "I should have left the two of them alone. If I cared about them, then I should have let them find some kind of happiness in this… life."

"It can be a bitch," Morgan said. The clichéd phrase was said with a tone of warmth and understanding and, among men, tone is often more important than the words themselves. It seemed to touch Klemmer, who slowly nodded.

For a moment, neither man said anything. Finally, Klemmer looked across the table.

"How's your tea?"

Morgan took a sip. It was lukewarm.

"Good," he said and smiled.

Oddly, in the kitchen that held the ghosts of generations, Klemmer smiled back.

"Do you want to see what I've done with the armoire?"

"Yes," Morgan said, standing up. "I've done a little woodworking."

"I thought you might have," Klemmer said as he led the way from the kitchen.

While Morgan visited Klemmer, Bobby Hamme sat in an unmarked county sheriff car and slowly sipped hot chocolate from an insulated cup. The car, sitting in a driveway and bracketed by carefully groomed shrubbery, was largely hidden from the road but offered Hamme a good view of the northern entrance to Hibernia Park.

It was a well-known practice of serial murderers to return to where they had disposed of their victims' bodies and it was routine for those who hunted them to put surveillance on those sites. Several such killers had been caught in that fashion.

Where there were multiple sites stretching back many years, one theory held that the killers would tend to go back to the most recent dumping ground to get a taste of the thrill. The task force, now led by Special Agent Callahan, had set up the surveillance of as many sites as they could making use of local law enforcement. Sometimes there were gaps in the coverage – most local police departments were very small and were hard-pressed to provide eyes for surveillance. Bobby Hamme volunteered to fill in.

While he *knew* such surveillance would not amount to anything, it did score points with the task force and the Sheriff. That didn't hurt a deputy's career path, and it did result in overtime hours. The extra pay helped with the nursing home bill. In fact, with a little left over, there was a chance at getting one of the new high-definition televisions that he had admired over at Circuit City. But there was zero chance of catching anyone this way.

What no one in the task force could seem to understand, Hamme thought, was that serial killers read the same damned books as the cops. Only an idiot, and maybe a crazy idiot at that, would return to one of the sites. He shook his head. He had read all the books, attended all the briefings, and even prowled the internet sites that held information on tracking down serial killers. Why didn't Callahan and the others understand that there was little that was terribly secret or sophisticated about catching killers?

What the cops mostly did was gather evidence that was used for trial *after* the killer was caught. And the killer was seldom caught as a result of brilliant police work. There was chance; a bad brake light gets the killer pulled over and a tired cop at two A.M. sees something that isn't right, like a bound and gagged terrified woman in the back seat.

There was a chance of witnesses; a killer who was so poor in impulse control that he can't stop from grabbing a kid from a playground with an entire Little League team and their parents watching. The victims themselves, running for their lives, meant the end for a sloppy killer. That's how they got Dahmer. And only after the cops returned one victim to him.

Sometimes the killers themselves blabbed about what they had done. The killer-arsonist Toole, arrested for setting a fire, could not keep his mouth shut and admitted to a murder. Sure, he was crazy, schizophrenic, but Hamme found it unbelievable that anyone would voluntarily tell the police what they did.

No, the trick was to keep a low profile. No visiting of dump sites, no mistakes, no witnesses, and no talking. Hamme nodded. The task force was underestimating this killer. He was not like all the others. Hamme thought for a moment, trying to find the right word. Then he nodded again.

They didn't realize this killer was a *professional.*

Chapter 18

Later that day Morgan walked into the Chester County Sheriff's Department that resided within the County Court House. He passed through the narrow, yellow-lit hallway and turned into the communications office. Several people were inside, including Hamme.

"They let me know you swung by to check on your mother," Morgan said and Hamme nodded. "How did it go?"

"The doctor isn't hopeful," Hamme said. "He said he's surprised she's hung on this long. He gives her a few more weeks at the outside."

"I'm sorry to hear that."

"Thanks," Hamme said. He did not appear to want to talk about it and Morgan moved on.

"While you pulled your observation shift," Morgan said, "I ran out to Klemmer's."

"I saw that's where you were logged out to," Hamme nodded at the ever-present clipboard beside the dispatcher. The older woman looked up and smiled at the two deputies. "What happened?"

"Not much," Morgan said. He paused, gathering his words. "I don't think he's into anything. He's a little long in the tooth to be up to something. Besides, he seems to prefer to stay out of sight and out of mind." He nodded. "I think you may have been picking up on his desire to isolate himself."

"You might be right," Hamme said. He shrugged. "The people across the street," he said, referring to the task force, "haven't done much except cash in their per diem, so I guess I might have been clutching at straws, trying to find *something* that would help us."

"It's been damned frustrating," Morgan said. He didn't share Hamme's views of the task force members – the FBI people seemed pretty sharp and the State Troopers were all solid investigators. There just hadn't been much to work with, other than the patterns of the killings. That helped the profilers but it did not seem to take them any closer to the killer.

"The Sheriff has more names for us," Hamme said. He tapped a sheet of paper on the counter he leaned against. "More violent offenders. She called a bunch of us in just as I got back from the home."

Morgan picked up the paper and narrowed his eyes.

"Only two names?"

"They re-did the filtering," Hamme explained. "After talking to the state profiler, they set up a priority. You make the list if you've attacked a woman and there's no apparent blocking on any of the dates."

"You don't get counted if you were around for any, you have to be around for all."

"Exactly," Hamme said, nodding. "And you have to have attacked a woman. The old list included those where women were involved but not necessarily the target."

"Klemmer wouldn't qualify under this new system," Morgan said, raising an eyebrow.

"Yeah," Hamme said. "Talking to him was a waste of time." Hamme was willing to ignore his initial instincts about the man and now was dismissive, having moved on. "Maybe this approach will get us to something faster."

"Maybe."

"These are our two," Morgan said. "Are there others?"

"About seventeen," Hamme said. "They've been rank ordered by degree of violence and number of incidents. The Sheriff said that the detectives were involved in the checks as well as the deputies. When we get through with these two, we can check back and see if there are any others still outstanding."

"All right," Morgan said, nodding. "Do we have the sheets on these two?"

"Summary sheets are upstairs," Hamme said. "A couple of bad apples, for sure."

"Another sunny day in Chester County," Morgan said.

"Another day in which to excel," the dispatcher chimed in with part of the old phrase.

"You two…" Hamme said, shaking his head, smiling.

Morgan winked at the dispatcher and led Hamme from the room.

Klemmer's insistence on talking with Ellen was not a problem for Johnson; it would slow things down but the questions would still get asked. Besides, and he did not mention this to Ellen, the sidebar had evolved conceptually. The added dash of talking with a serial killer was gone. Time and bureaucracy had blocked off that approach. Now it was simply going to be short piece on how serial murderers come into existence.

Johnson already had enough information to write the piece up. He doubted that Klemmer would say anything that would be much different from what he and Ellen had found in the articles by various authorities on the subject.

For Johnson, letting Ellen talk to Klemmer was part of Ellen's education. Slow with praise for his interns, Johnson always tried to bring the good ones along by giving them tasks that would sharpen their skills and, in his phrase, "broaden their horizons."

Talking with a convicted murderer might do both.

Johnson nodded to himself as he worked his keyboard. Ellen Parker was good; there was no question about that. She did not seem to rattle, could absorb massive amounts of information like a sponge, and wrote very well, but those things didn't make a good reporter.

What made a good reporter was a desire to find out things, a desire so strong everything else took a back seat, everything else was sacrificed. It ate at you, pushed you, and became all that you were aware of. Johnson shook his head. Years ago, his almost sacrificed his marriage to that desire. Many of his friends had not been so fortunate.

There was one thing about Ellen that Johnson wondered about, a piece of the jigsaw puzzle that did not fit. Ellen had been around violence as a child, from what she had said and what Johnson had learned. Could she handle a profession that would expose her to the aftermath of violence on a regular basis? Not everyone could handle looking at the dark side of things. Some got out of the business entirely, while others moved over to subject areas that were, for lack of a better word, safer.

Agent Callahan's comments, the newspaper reports of the time, and Ellen's own remarks built a picture of a 13-year old girl from rural Ohio whose family was visited by ugly violence. Ellen's cousin Eileen had been killed during a drug gang fight. That incident, though not the girl's death, was the trigger for a full-scale war. The Steel Riders killed their rivals in towns and cities throughout Ohio.

During the war, right when it seemed the Steel Riders had won, their leadership was hunted by someone who knew how to do it. Maybe an imported professional, but maybe not…

There was no way to prove it, as Callahan pointed out, but there was an implication that her grandfather, Thomas Luther Parker, and maybe at least one of her uncles, took out those who killed the girl.

Johnson rubbed his chin; on his computer display was an archived picture of Tom Parker. In the picture, he was not old; the faded picture, scanned from an old newspaper during the archiving process, showed a general pinning a medal on the pajamas of a man lying in a hospital bed. It was not a great picture – the photographer was more interested in the general than the sergeant.

Tom Parker, expressionless, looked at the general with black eyes. He had an Indian-nose, a slightly forward-jutting chin, and almost gaunt cheekbones. The cheekbones seemed to be part of the Parker genetic package and Ellen's face echoed them.

If Parker and one of his sons went after the gang members, what had that done to Ellen? If it happened, had she known? Even if it didn't happen, what kind of an effect had her cousin's death had on her? Johnson shook his head. There were lots of children in Philadelphia who had been traumatized by the deaths of their relatives and the effects could be long-lasting.

Ellen was a little emotionally distant, a little cool, compared to most of the interns he had worked with. Was that some result of the killing of her cousin? Johnson didn't know. She had talked with Klemmer before and nothing seemed to have happened.

All right, too much analysis. Johnson smiled at himself. Talking with Klemmer, asking the prepared questions, that would be a good work experience for Ellen and that was probably all it would be.

He touched his keyboard, the old picture of the Korean War sergeant disappeared and Johnson moved on to other work.

Chapter 19

Ellen steered her ancient Honda into Klemmer's driveway and took a breath. Klemmer set up the time for the interview, noon, easily enough but he was abrupt on the telephone as if distracted by something. He wanted a copy of the questions in advance, which she had provided as an email attachment after checking with Johnson. Her supervisor suspected he wanted to be sure that the questions were not going to be about him. She hoped he would not turn out to be perfunctory in his answers.

After parking parked her car, she paused to look around. Klemmer was not in sight. It was turning into a warm day and she slipped off her coat and put it back into the car. As she closed the door, Klemmer appeared at the foot of the stairs going into his house; she had not heard him emerge from the house.

Quiet customer.

"Have you had lunch?" Klemmer asked as Ellen approached.

"No," she said. She held out her hand and he shook it.

"I fixed something," he said. He led the way into the house.

Ellen liked the kitchen. It had the look of kitchens from her childhood, places that had been at the center of families and acquired appearances that reflected that use. Modern kitchens that were part of houses in developments, "ticky-tacky houses," seemed cold and soulless.

Of course, this is the kitchen of a convicted murderer.

Ellen smiled as she sat down. She liked the kitchen anyway and focusing on that pushed the anxiety back a little.

Klemmer walked over to the refrigerator and opened it, talking as he did.

"Thanks for emailing the questions," he said, bending over and reaching for things. "I went ahead and typed up my answers. I thought," he turned with a platter and a bowl in his hands, "we could focus on amplifying my remarks."

Ellen's eyes opened slightly in surprise. Klemmer put the platter and bowl down and folded his arms. "Cold cuts and cheese, both local," he said. "The onion and tomato slices obviously aren't. The tuna fish is made with low-fat mayo. I have to watch my cholesterol." He nodded. "And I have two kinds of bread, a local rye that I picked up this morning and a whole wheat."

"Wheat will be great," Ellen said. "I'll do the cold cuts."

"Good idea," Klemmer said. He brought to the table the two already sliced loaves of bread. He snapped his fingers and went back to the refrigerator. "Forgot the mustard." He looked over his shoulder. "It's locally made, but I do have more of that mayonnaise, if you prefer."

"No," Ellen said. "I prefer mustard."

"Good," Klemmer said, reaching into the refrigerator. "That's a healthy position to take in life."

Ellen smiled but was not sure what Klemmer meant.

"Stone ground," Klemmer said, putting the jar with its home-made label on the table. "I have root beer, iced tea, and a couple of cans of diet Pepsi. I can make coffee."

"Is the root beer local?"

"You've identified a common theme," Klemmer said, smiling. "Yes, right over in Lancaster County. Amish."

"I'll try it."

Klemmer nodded his approval. He took two cold brown bottles from the refrigerator and put one in front of Ellen. He scooped paper plates from a shelf and a handful of silverware. He sat down and the two busied themselves with building sandwiches.

"You are wondering," Klemmer said as he put slices of cheese on top of his sandwich, "why I bothered to have you drive all the way out here if I went ahead and wrote my answers." He put the top slice of bread – he was using the rye – on and squeezed the sandwich together. He smiled in a gentle fashion as if embarrassed.

"Frankly," he said, not looking at Ellen, "I thought it might be nice to just talk to you." He looked up. "And, no, it's not what you think."

"What do I think?" Ellen asked. She took a sip of the root beer. It was very good, far more flavorful than any of the national brands.

"You are concerned it might be that I am attracted to you," Klemmer said. "I am, but not in *that* way. No, what I found attractive was that you did not show fear. You were sitting in a room, alone, with someone you knew was a murderer and you could have been talking to a Philadelphia city councilman."

"*That*," Ellen said, "would have been cause for fear." She smiled and so did Klemmer. "I notice you did not say that I did not feel fear, only that I did not show it." *How much can he see?*

118

"People, psychologists, often confuse the two," Klemmer said. "I've learned to differentiate. As to what you were actually feeling, I think it probable that you were and are feeling some anxiety." He waved his hand, holding his bottle of root beer, dismissively. "What caught my attention was your presentation. Tell me, was that part of what you've learned as a journalism student or is keeping things hidden something you learned while growing up?"

"I haven't thought about that," Ellen said. It was a lie. She took a bite of her sandwich. Klemmer said nothing, just looked at her. For reasons she could not have said, she answered.

"It's probably from my childhood," she said finally. "I think it's pretty common for girls to learn to be careful what they reveal and to whom." She smiled. "I had a good teacher when it came to learning to put on a face of confidence when you might feel a different way."

"That's a good thing to learn," Klemmer said. "It can scare the wolves away. Who did you learn it from?"

"My grandfather, I think," Ellen said.

"He was a brave man?"

"He was a farmer."

"So the answer is yes," Klemmer said, smiling. "I've gotten to know some farmers and that's a job that takes courage."

"He had that," Ellen said.

"Let me get the answers before I forget," Klemmer said, getting up. He disappeared deeper into the house and was back in a few minutes. He put several sheets of paper stapled together down next to Ellen.

She saw her questions were in italics, each followed by several paragraphs of Klemmer's comments. Ellen read while she ate; Klemmer even put in references and she recognized some of the authors of research and study he mentioned.

"Thank you," she said, looking up. "This is impressive."

"You're welcome," he said. "Now, what are your questions about my answers?"

Ellen hesitated. The questions were supposed to come from Johnson and Big Sam had explicitly said that she was not to conduct an interview. But if she stayed within the context of the questions and their answers, then she was just getting clarification. Right?

Right.

This was an opportunity and, for the moment, her anxiety faded.

"You mention," Ellen said, "the neurobiology of serial killers. Genetics, injury, and addiction. The genetic issue...?"

"Is still very much in the air," Klemmer said. He picked up Ellen's empty bottle and his own and put them on the counter next to the sink. He brought out two fresh bottles from the refrigerator and opened them as he sat down. "No definitive genetic markers have as yet been identified but keep your eye on the investigators. I think that's where the next action is going to be."

"Why?"

"Well," Klemmer said, taking a swig from his bottle, "sure, damage to the frontal lobes can result in a decrease of inhibition, making control of anger, for example, more difficult. A large number of serial murderers have frontal lobe damage, especially the ones who tend to be very unorganized in their actions."

"But not all."

"Not all," Klemmer agreed. "So, we look for other things, multiple causal agents of the same behavior. Is there a genetic profile that does it? I think we are going to find that there is for sociopaths, people who are unable to bond with others, who have no empathy. But those people aren't necessarily killers. They simply don't give a damn about anyone else but that's not the same as running the risks entailed in murdering. They might kill if it gets them ahead but they are not compulsive."

"What does that mean for genetic markers?"

"Everyone is a potential killer," Klemmer said. "Not everyone kills. Almost no one kills in a serial fashion. What does a person get out of that behavior? That's where the addiction model has something to offer. Such a person is getting stimulation similar to what an addict gets."

"A rush of some kind."

"A rush that can be addictive," Klemmer said. "For at least some people," he added and was silent for several seconds. "And for those for whom it is addicting, perhaps that's the genetic predisposition."

"And they discover they have the disposition..."

"Gradually, usually," Klemmer said. "They hurt something as a kid. Other people are scared or appalled or have some kind of negative reaction and they notice, 'Hey, that was not so bad, that was all right. In fact, I liked it.'" He shrugged. "Repetition at that level leads to desensitization through habituation. They have to increase the stimulation. They go from shooting a neighbor's pet with a bb gun to killing something. The prey item increases in value and meaning, as does the act. One day they find humans are a good target for what they want."

"All of what you've said," Ellen said, "doesn't rule out the role of life producing a monster."

"Absolutely," Klemmer said. "But not everyone subjected to the classic kinds of circumstances, like abusive parents and those sorts of things, ends up killing people. Likewise, not everyone with frontal lobe damage starts killing people. It's the combination of ingredients. That's why, while everyone has the potential to kill, not everyone can be a serial killer."

Ellen nodded but remained silent for a moment. She looked at Klemmer.

"I have a friend," she said, "who agrees with you."

"About serial murderers?"

"About everyone being killers." She hesitated before speaking. "He thinks that our lives require us to kill."

"You think he's just using a metaphor?"

"He didn't seem to," she said. "He was in the Gulf War."

"I see," Klemmer said. "What I mean is, I don't see. But he might."

"What do you mean?"

"I've never studied veterans," Klemmer said. "But what I've read leads me to believe that they know reality with greater clarity than the rest of us. When he says something like that, he might be right." He smiled but his eyes looked sad. "I never imagined I would ever kill someone."

"I can't imagine myself doing something like that," Ellen said.

"Have you ever thought," Klemmer asked gently, "that perhaps you are limiting your imagination?"

Chapter 20

Ellen returned to the newspaper and wrote up her notes, adding them to the printout of Klemmer's answers to the questions. She discovered in her email that, on her way back to Philadelphia, Klemmer had sent his answers electronically. She turned in the pile of paper to Johnson who seemed distracted. She was almost out of his office when he called to her.

"Wait a minute," Johnson said, quickly scanning the pages. He looked up. "He had prepared answers waiting for you?"

"Yes," Ellen replied. "He sent me a copy by email as well."

"And you then asked him questions?"

"Clarifying his answers, yes," she said. She felt a twinge of anxiety but looked at Johnson with calm eyes.

"You know," Johnson said, leaning back in his chair and putting his hands behind his head, "Big Sam is likely to view that as an interview. And that's a no-no for interns."

"It was just clarification," Ellen said. "Should I go and tell him about it?"

"That's a splendid idea," Johnson said, smiling. "After he keel-hauls you, we would end up with more desk space for the surviving interns." He leaned forward in his chair and motioned for Ellen to close the door.

"No," he said, "*you* will not talk to Sam. I will. Why did you proceed?"

"It was an opportunity," Ellen said, "one that, if I delayed, might be lost." She hesitated. "Klemmer lives alone but I don't think through his own choice."

"What do you mean?"

"I think he's lonely."

"And so he lives alone because...?"

"He doesn't believe he deserves to live among people," Ellen said, her voice firm. "What that means is, when he gets a chance to talk, he does." She nodded at the notes. "I know he said he would not talk about our killer but he ended up doing so."

Johnson picked up the papers and turned to the last few. He read for a moment and then nodded.

"Interesting stuff," he said. "How did you get him to talk about it?"

"We were talking about the act of killing," Ellen said. "When I said I had trouble imagining killing he suggested I was limiting my imagination."

"The man's a shrink," Johnson said, smiling wryly.

"I asked what he thought the role of imagination was for serial killers. I had read a paper about what such killers were seeking and thought to bounce it off him. He made a couple of general comments and then went specific."

"And you didn't interrupt him."

"No, sir," Ellen said. "I knew we were outside the boundaries of what I was supposed to be doing but he's been talking to the task force. This was a chance to learn something that the task force hadn't told us, maybe something important." She took a breath. "I wasn't asking questions, he volunteered information. I just listened."

"'Outside the boundaries' is right." Johnson read the last page. "But your instincts were right." He looked up. "All right, get out of here and do your voucher for travel miles. You've got a stack of 'to-do' things in your mailbox. Get hopping but get the voucher to me before I leave this afternoon. And don't talk to Sam."

"Yes, sir," Ellen said and turned away.

Johnson was right; in the small box that was a relic of the days before voice messages, she found several slips of paper for things that Johnson wanted done. Only two were for him. The rest were from other staff but that was an intern's life.

As she walked back to her desk, she saw the editor's office door was open. Big Sam, a big porcelain coffee cup in his hand, was listening to Johnson who stood on the other side of his desk. Sam looked at her but his expression was blank.

Ellen did not know if she was in trouble and decided to focus on the tasks in front of her. It had been too good an opportunity to let pass. After all, Klemmer *did* talk to the task force and apparently was a friend of the agent now in charge of it. That same agent had steered the newspaper towards Klemmer.

They were asking for it.

She smiled as she typed on her keyboard. Well, no, undoubtedly the FBI had boundaries of its own and it was Klemmer who had, from their perspective, crossed them, not her. No, her problem would be with Big Sam and...

"Hey," Big Sam said and Ellen looked up. He stood next to her, coffee cup still in hand.

"Hi," Ellen said. Johnson was not with the editor.

"I just had a talk with Jeff," Sam said. "You did some very good work out there today. I'm not sure how much of it we can use just now but it was good work." He nodded. "Keep it up."

"Thank you," Ellen said and watched Sam walk away. Her telephone buzzed. She picked up the handset and punched the button for intramural calls.

"Ellen Parker," she said. It was Johnson.

What did he say?

"He said I did a good job," Ellen said. "He said we might not be able to use it."

Klemmer talked too much. He said some things about the kind of person the task force was thinking about. If we publish that part, it could alert the killer. I'm going to talk to Paul about it. But Sam didn't keel-haul you?

"Not even a cat o' nine tails," Ellen said. "Thanks."

Don't mention it. Really, don't mention it. If he ever decides you've done a bad thing to the pooch, my butt will be fed to PETA right behind yours. Be sure to drop off your voucher before you go home.

"I will," Ellen said. She slowly hung up the handset and sat for a moment staring blankly at her computer screen. Then she let out a breath and went back to work.

"No," Callahan said, stifling a curse, "you *cannot* use that."

But it was Klemmer who thought of that? Just confirm it for me. We'll sit on it until you give us a green light.

"Jeff," Callahan said slowly as Deevers appeared in his doorway. He motioned her in and then signaled her to close the door. "Yes, he offered the idea on his own but Agent Karen Deevers and the Behavioral Analysis Unit in Quantico previously had suggested the possibility. You understand why we can't spread this around."

Let's start with panic in the streets, then move over to destroying careers, and somewhere along the line we'll be giving the killer the signal to crawl back into his cave and outwait us. Yeah, I get it.

"That's about it," Callahan said.

Hey, we're not totally irresponsible, my brother.

"Oh, hell," Callahan said, grinning, "you're going to the 'my brother' line. You know us white liberal bleeding hearts can't resist that. What do you want in return?"

Even if you give us nothing, we'll keep this off the page until you say okay. But, my brother, how about a token of your love for the Fourth Estate?

"Are you sure about the numbering?" Callahan shook his head. "I thought newspapers were the Fifth Estate or something."

Close enough for newspaper work. Anyway, how about if I have one of our staff have a background sit-down with you? Deep background, nothing for publication until you say "go."

"Who?" Callahan looked at Deevers who raised an eyebrow.

How about the reporter who Klemmer opened up to?

"It wasn't you?" It was Callahan's turn to raise an eyebrow.

No. A youngster you've met, Ellen Parker. It would be a good experience for her to speak with one of our crack experts in the federal law enforcement community.

"Stop," Callahan said. "You'll turn my head. All right, it's a deal. Have her give me a call tomorrow and we'll set it up."

Peace, my brother.

"Up yours," Callahan said agreeably and hung up. He looked at Deevers.

"Klemmer," he said, "had an interview with that Inquirer journalism intern. Ellen Parker. And could not keep his mouth shut." He shook his head.

"What did he say?"

"Only that our investigation was quietly looking at, and here I quote, 'Members of emergency services, such as police officers.'"

"Oh, no," Deevers said. "If that gets out…"

"I think he understands the situation," Callahan said, holding up both hands. "But I've agreed to let Parker interview me."

"Good opportunity to impress on her the problem this could cause."

"For all of us."

Chapter 21

It was a party, one of those events that graduate school seemed to force upon people. People came to them often motivated by a desire to support group solidarity in the face of whatever torments graduate student life dumped on said students.

At least, that was the explanation Enfield offered Ellen as they stood in the big living room with more than a dozen other people. Slightly more than half of the group were grad students; the others were spouses or significant others.

Ellen had forgotten about the party until Enfield called her; they had arranged for him to drive her to the party on Pine Street and then she had let the date slip from awareness. She thought she covered it well.

It was a typical graduate party. Everyone had brought something, with alcohol dominating. There were strange dips and chopped vegetables for dipping. There was a shortage of diet drinks. Small clumps of people who knew each other stood around in positions carefully selected to keep others from getting to the refreshments.

People gravitated to people they knew and few moved from clump to clump. Besides the Inquirer interns, which included two women from finance and advertising that Ellen had seen only during their initial briefings, there were people from local university programs of some kind or another. It would take a major genealogical investigation to determine all the relationships and who knew who. Some college friends of Stewart were the hosts; Ellen didn't know them but one of the keys of graduate student parties hinged on large numbers.

Ellen smiled at a number of people out of politeness more than recognition. She felt too tired to make the effort to engage with others. That did not seem to be the case with a couple of the males present. One, a fairly nice-looking guy who looked a little Hispanic with a broad smile, started a brief conversation with her but spotted a group of friends arriving and went over to say hello and never came back.

Another was a pushy guy who had started his gambit with observing she was alone. He wore one of those semi-beards that Ellen didn't understand.

What was the point? Insufficient testosterone to grow a real beard? Hardly a good advertisement. Ellen gave him all the signals she wasn't interested; she didn't look at him, responded in monosyllables to his statements, and half turned away while he was expounding on something. He didn't get it and when he touched her forearm, ostensibly making a point, she decided she was going to have to shake him loose. Her chance came when he decided, with a clumsy joke, he had to visit the little boy's room.

Looking around, Ellen saw Enfield sitting alone on a padded chair, a bottle of beer sitting on the table next to him. He was alone, if you didn't count the four empty bottles, and he was watching her.

Ellen mouthed the word *Help* and Enfield motioned her over.

"You are having a really good time," Enfield said. The noise in the room – someone had decided to turn on the radio and XPN was playing some sort of live concert – made her bend over to hear him. "Are you two going to announce your engagement?"

"Who *is* he?" Ellen asked. She sat on the floor next to his feet, carefully balancing her wine glass. It was only her second but she did not drink much and she was feeling the effects.

"No idea," Enfield said and took a drink from his bottle. "I think he came in with some English majors. Maybe they were colonels." He looked down at Ellen. "Sorry for the pun."

"Not a problem," Ellen said, smiling. It was the most entertaining thing anyone had said within hearing all evening.

Mr. Semi-Beard reappeared, looking around the room. He spotted Ellen and took a step but then saw Enfield. Ellen glanced up and saw Enfield was looking at him.

"Boo," Enfield said, though, with the noise, only Ellen could have heard him.

Mr. Semi-Beard grimaced and turned away.

"Thanks," Ellen said. "I could have dealt with him but it would have been very boring."

"You're welcome," Enfield said. He took a swallow. "I haven't killed anyone in thirteen years, four months, and three days and I was beginning to get a little itchy."

"You shouldn't joke about those kinds of things," Ellen said. Before Enfield said anything, she hurried on. "Sorry. I'm no one to tell other people what they should or shouldn't say."

"Not a problem," he said. "I probably shouldn't, you're right."

"I thought about what you said," Ellen said, watching the room.

"About what?"

"About all of us being killers."

"Ah. What do you think?"

Ellen sighed. Perhaps it was the wine but she found herself wanting to tell Enfield everything.

"I had a cousin," she said. "Her name was Eileen. We were inseparable. 'Ellen and Eileen.' It was almost one word."

"Sounds nice," Enfield said. His voice sounded as if he was drifting away.

"She was a little older than me," Ellen said. "She got to the teens a bit before me and we drifted apart a little."

"That can happen. Critical age."

"Right," Ellen said. "But we were connecting back." She took a sip of wine. "Then she was killed. Couple of cycle gangs fighting over the meth trade and a stray round hit her." She fell silent and Enfield said nothing. Ellen didn't look up at him.

"I dream about her a couple of times a month," Ellen said. "I see her shot down, even though I wasn't there. Or lost in the river and I can't help her." She shrugged. "The dreams started a few months after the trial, after all the killing that followed the trial." She sipped at her wine. "There wasn't really a trial. The case was dismissed. But that wasn't the end of it." For a moment, Ellen was silent and felt a little gratitude that Enfield did not rush in to say something.

"The men who killed Eileen," Ellen said, "all five were killed. One at a time. No one knew who did it. Part of the war, everyone thought. But no one knew." She took another sip. "I knew." She fell silent again. The noise from the others around them and the radio seemed to isolate her with Enfield and somehow made talking easier.

"It was my Grandpa Tom," Ellen said. "I found his notes and saw the Xs for those he had already killed. I didn't know what to do so I went to my Aunt Catherine. She talked to Uncle John." She shook her head. "Uncle John helped Grandpa Tom finish them off."

"So now," Ellen said, "I dream about Eileen. And I dream about my grandfather. And all the dreams are about killing." She shook her head. "I'm terrified." She grimaced. "Johnson's got me talking to a murderer. He has no idea." She finished her wine and sat silently.

"Killing, violence," she said slowly, as if using words that were best not spoken. "People talk about them so easily. Every time I hear, I want to throw up. Or cry." She smiled slightly but it faded with her heartbeat. "I don't know how you survived it or how people like Agent Deevers endure it. I never could, I never could handle it."

"This whole project," Ellen started but then stopped. She looked at her glass and then stared at nothing across the crowded room. "I'm terrified," she repeated. Without realizing it, she clenched her fist and pressed down on her thigh. "But I've got to stay with it. *Because* I'm scared. You know?"

After a moment without a response, she turned and looked up at Enfield. He was slumped to one side, his eyes closed, breathing heavily. Ellen felt a flash of anger and then grinned.

"I," she said, "am a doughnut. A cowardly doughnut." She carefully got up and walked into the next room, dropping off her wine glass and picking up a can of diet soda.

Back in the living room, Jay Enfield opened his eyes to a slit and watched her leave.

"I doubt that, lady," he whispered and then returned to feigning sleep.

Chapter 22

Part of Ellen expected it; her dreams responded to triggers and her half-conversation with Enfield was more than enough. So even as she found herself in it, she watched herself and thought, "What did you expect?"

The Ohio River, slate gray and moving with an almost sullen strength, flowed at her feet. Over her shoulder the bullies approached. Grandpa Tom was somewhere but, as in real life, she could not see him. She would have to stand alone.

Ellen knew how to keep them from her and reached down for the stone she would use to threaten them. But the rocks refused respond to her hands. They were like a sculpture of stones, all connected, all unbudging.

And the bullies kept coming. She knew they were more than bullies, that they were talking themselves into something more than tossing her into the river.

She tried and tried to lift a stone but none would come. Desperately, Ellen looked around for someone. Eileen... There was no Eileen.

Grandpa Tom was gone, not just out of sight, waiting for her back where their picnic was spread. He had left her.

She was all alone.

The part of Ellen watching her in her dream seemed to nod. "That's what it is all about," she said to younger Ellen and kept saying it even as the bullies closed in.

She was still saying it even as she jerked awake.

Craig Morgan sat up in bed feeling as if he was drowning. Only the red numbers of the clock lit the dark bedroom.

2:36

He did not have the energy to curse. He took a moment to gather himself and then made his way to his bathroom. After using the toilet, Morgan slowly walked back to bed. He knew better than to turn on the light – that would be enough to keep him up for the rest of the night.

He lay down, bunching the pillow under his head and rolled so he could not see the clock. Watching the minutes pass just made it more difficult to get back to sleep.

It had been months since he had dreamt about *the incident*. That was how he thought about it, when he thought about it. Or, at least, how he tried to think about it.

The incident.

Eleven, almost twelve, years ago, the Coatesville police had called for help. There had been a shooting in the projects overlooking the town and adjacent steel mill. Things were confused and unclear, including how many people were shot.

Coatesville police were in hot pursuit of the shooters, three young men in a red van. That much was clear and Deputy Sheriff Craig Morgan was sitting in a cruiser south of Coatesville, watching the sparse cars on Route 10 and looking for speeders.

He listened to the pursuit as it passed Cochranville; the red van didn't try to turn right or left onto 41. They wanted to get out of the state and the Maryland border was close, very close.

A state trooper joined the chase at 10 and 41 but Morgan was in front of them. He let the pursuers know he had spike strips and the trooper told him to use them.

With his car backed off the road, Morgan popped the trunk and pulled out the case of the Federal Signal Stinger spike strip. He stood by the side of the road, waiting until he saw the van's lights in the distance, closely followed by flashing red and blues. It took only seconds to open the case and extend the accordion-like strip its full ten feet. He held onto its rope and backed away from the road, his eyes looking north at the oncoming lights.

It was a clean hit. The van's front tires both hit the strip. Each element of the strip rocked forward, positioning the spikes as close to a right angle to the tires as was possible and the van's speed forced the hollow spikes deep into the tires. One of the rear tires caught the spikes as well.

Porcupine-like, the hollow spikes remained in the tires, letting air out gradually, just as they were designed. Morgan yanked the Stinger out of the road and turned to watch the van.

But the driver saw Morgan or the reflective on his car or the strip or something at the last second. He tried to swerve but his slow reflexes –

everyone in the van had been drinking and drugging all night – meant he did not initiate his move until the van hit the strip.

Trying to turn the van violently at close to 90 miles per hour would have been risky in the best of circumstances; doing it with rapidly deflating front tires was suicidal.

The van left the road twenty feet beyond Morgan and he ran towards it, flashlight in his left hand, his right hand on the butt of his Glock, before it finished tumbling. It smashed itself into a shallow drainage ditch bordering the road, a blur of light and sparks and dust with the sound of a hundred metal garbage cans slamming into one another. Pieces of metal flew and disappeared into the darkness as the van slid onto its side.

Morgan saw the state police car stop beside him as he ran and heard the trooper yelling into his microphone. Somewhere behind him other police cars, their headlights spraying in several different directions, braked, their discordant sirens still wailing in the night.

No one could have survived the crash but one had. He pulled himself up, standing half out of the van's sliding door and, less than twenty feet away, turned towards Morgan's light. Morgan skidded to a halt.

He was a man, a black man, and bright red blood covered half his face and spattered the old Army field jacket he wore. His name was David Plant, though Morgan did not learn that until later. He looked only at Morgan, though what he could have seen in the darkness with the police car headlights shining into his eyes was a question that would be raised later.

Morgan's gun was out and in his hand, crossing his wrist while his other hand kept the flashlight on the man. He started to yell at the man when he saw the gun. The man raised it, still looking at Morgan.

He did not think; there wasn't time. The Glock fired three times almost of its own volition. One nine-millimeter slug missed entirely and flew out into the darkness. The second hit Plant in his side, drilling a neat hole along his rib cage and exiting having done very little damage. The third smashed through the man's sternum and ripped through the upper half of his heart.

David Plant fell backwards out of the van, gone from sight. Morgan held his position while other officers circled the van. As if they had rehearsed it a dozen times before, Morgan covered the van door while the state trooper and the Coatesville cop circled to the front, each approaching the remains of the front windshield and trying to see inside without exposing themselves.

The trooper motioned Morgan forward to the front and only then did he see Plant lying in the road, next to a short stretch of concrete curb that held a storm drain. Blood had made its way into the drain as if a scene from a too-obvious Hollywood movie.

The two men inside were dead, killed by the crash. One had the gun used in the projects shooting stuck in his belt.

There was no other gun in the van or on the ground. David Plant had not had a gun.

The investigation determined, using the trooper's dash-mounted video camera, that the man had *something* in his hand when he emerged. The best guess anyone had was that it was a wadded, dark t-shirt found inside the van. Maybe Plant had tried to use it on his lacerated head. In the informal term used by police, the shooting was declared *righteous* and Morgan was cleared by the investigation.

But not by himself.

In the dream, the man stands in the van, braced on one of the seats, and, also as he did, he looks directly at Morgan. Except in the dream, even though it is night, the van, the ditch, and his hands are seen clearly. They are empty.

Morgan watches his finger pull the trigger again and again and again and again. The bullets, many more than he fired, all hit the man. The man just looks into Morgan's eyes.

It is nearly three hours before Morgan manages to go back to sleep.

Morgan walked into the small room used by the deputies as a locker room.

"You look like something the cat dragged in," a young deputy named Collins said. "Out partying last night?" The deputy grinned.

"I wish," Morgan said. He opened his locker and took out a yellow plastic can of powder and then took off his uniform shirt.

"Hey," Collins said, watching him. "You're not wearing a vest?"

It was a requirement of the Sheriff's Department that all deputies had to wear a ballistics vest; some of the old timers occasionally cheated on the regulation when assigned to desk duty but Sheriff Walsh was adamant about it and more than one deputy had found himself jerked out of the field for failing to wear his vest.

Morgan raised his shirt and began dusting his side with the powder.

"I was," he said. "But the strap seams irritated my skin. Rubbed me raw. I'm just giving my skin a chance to heal."

"Had the same problem," Collins said. "I know what to do." He left the room before Morgan could reply but was back in a moment with a folded t-shirt in his hand.

"Here you go," Collins said, handing the t-shirt to Morgan. The older man opened it.

It was one of the D.A.R.E. t-shirts the deputies gave to kids who completed the anti-drug program. Morgan looked at Collins.

"Put it on over your regular t-shirt," Collins said, "and see if it doesn't give you enough padding."

Morgan did as Collins suggested. The D.A.R.E. t-shirt was very high quality and was thick. Though the label said it was an extra-large, it was a snug fit. He reached into his locker and took out his First Defense vest. He opened it, slipped it on, and then carefully sealed the straps. He pulled at the oval neck opening, adjusting it. He swiveled his torso a little and raised his eyebrows.

"Not bad," he said. "I can still feel it a little," Morgan patted the side of the blue vest, "but it doesn't rub at all."

"Lenny showed me that trick," Collins said. "Just passing on a good idea." He smiled and left as Morgan finished getting dressed.

That was one of the best things about being a deputy, Morgan thought. Everyone really looked out for one another. Big and small stuff like how to get your Level IIA vest to fit comfortably. A few minutes later, he walked down the hall to the dispatcher's office to check his mail.

"You look like something the cat dragged in," the dispatcher named Carolyn said as Morgan checked for mail. The phrase was becoming repetitious.

"Stayed up too late," he lied. "Got into a movie and lost track of the time." He opened a letter that turned out to be from a travel bureau with offers of trips to Africa, South America, and the Caribbean. He shook his head, dropped it in the trash and opened the next one. "Has Hamme checked in this morning?"

"Not yet," Carolyn said. She was an older woman, reputedly a dispatcher since Indians had prowled the outskirts of West Chester. Her voice was deepened by age and too many cigarettes. "He got out of here late yesterday after going over his testimony." She shook her head. "It has to be rough."

Hamme was scheduled to go to a trial to testify; the case was a nasty vehicular homicide and the county prosecutor was determined to nail the man responsible.

"Well," Morgan said, leafing through a police equipment catalog from his mailbox, "Bobby handles himself well in court."

"I meant because it was a fatal TA," Carolyn said. "Those are always hard on him, I think."

"What do you mean?" Morgan was interested in her remark; he had never seen Hamme bothered by a trial, or for that matter, anything else.

"Well," she said, lowering her voice so much that Morgan had to lean forward, "you know that's how his father died." Morgan shook his head and Carolyn continued. "He was just a boy. His mother, well, she drank some, and she was driving. The two were returning from some society thing. She missed a curve."

"Damn," Morgan said.

"He was thirteen," Carolyn said. "He was very close to his father but," she shrugged slightly, "he was a VP over at Lukens Steel, always on the go, so they didn't get to spend much time together. And his mother…"

"How did he handle it?" Morgan asked in spite of his impulse to back away; he felt a little like he was violating Hamme's privacy.

"It was hard," Carolyn said. A disapproving tone came into her voice. "His mother was more interested in breaking into the Main Line, that kind of thing. Moved to Paoli. She spent all of her time in all kinds of charity things. Saving animals, whores, drug addicts, kids, everyone except Bobby."

"Damn," Morgan repeated.

"He pulled himself up," Carolyn said, smiling. "By his own bootstraps. Pushed himself into school, got that scholarship." She nodded. "Went from the rent-a-cops to here. The Sheriff thinks he's pretty sharp."

"I agree with her," Morgan said.

"Then she had that stroke," Carolyn said. "And the heart thing." She shook her head in mock sympathy. "But he's really seen to her. She can't speak or see but he's been a damned good son to her."

"Impressive," Morgan said, nodding.

"Deputy Hamme," Carolyn said more loudly, looking beyond Morgan, "good morning."

"Hey," Hamme said as he entered the office. He was folding his sunglasses as turned to Morgan. "The task force has a meeting at 1300. They have some forensic doc in to talk about the autopsies. We're invited."

Morgan raised an eyebrow; there was something in Hamme's tone.

"Something going on?"

Hamme shrugged. For a moment, he said nothing but finally he leaned on the counter.

"How much," Hamme asked, "do you think they hold back from us?"

"I don't know that they do," Morgan said, frowning. "Why do you ask?"

"Look," he said, "you remember that presentation Deevers did?"

"The early cases," Morgan said, nodding. "All the red dots."

"Right," Hamme said. "How long do you think they had that information before they decided to share it?"

"I had the impression it was given to us as soon as they got it."

"Hardly," Hamme said. "They have a computer program that produces it. You can read about it on the internet if you missed it in the journals. It takes elements of crimes and sorts out the ones that are similar. They've had it for years. It came available after Bundy was caught and it was able to identify killings that matched his movements across the country."

"You think they've known of the earlier cases long before Deevers did her briefing?"

"They would have had to know right away," Hamme said. "That's just like the feds to keep stuff from us."

"What does that accomplish?"

"And this forensics doc," Hamme went on as if he hadn't heard Morgan's question. "Bennert has been here three weeks and only now are we hearing what he thinks."

"If all that's so," Morgan said, feeling tired, "why do you think it's being done?"

"Trust. They don't trust us."

"What," Morgan raised his eyebrows in disbelief, "you think *they* think one of us did it?"

"No, no," Hamme said, shaking his head. "They think we'll go blabbing one of their precious insights before they're ready to reveal to the world how brilliant they are. It's about credit and getting the Bureau onto the six o'clock news."

Morgan thought for a moment and then nodded.

"You could be right," he conceded. "It does seem to me, now that I think about it, they were a lot more open back when all this started."

"They were just trying to ingratiate themselves then," Hamme said. He shook his head. "Like any of us want to have reporters chasing us."

"Been there," Morgan said, remembering feeling pursued after *the incident*.

"Don't want to go there," Hamme said. "Let's get some coffee."

Morgan nodded and followed his partner from the office. What were the feds up to, if anything?

Chapter 23

"The appointment's set," Johnson said to Ellen when she leaned into his office cubicle. "This afternoon, one PM. Don't be late. Callahan hates lateness."

"Got it," Ellen said. "Can I tape?"

"Hell, no." Johnson shook his head. "Idiot, imbecile, Childe Harold little one, are you daft? This is deep background, no attribution, no use until the source says so." He grinned. "Now, if we hear something we really like, we can always find a couple of other sources that we *can* use for attribution and then, bingo. No, and don't take notes. Nothing written. Keep it in that head of yours, such as it is."

"All right," Ellen said. She turned and walked back towards the interns' desks.

Jay Enfield was at the other desk, typing madly on a keyboard. He didn't look up.

"Hey," he said, his eyes still on the computer monitor, "thanks for doing the driving the other night. I think I was unsafe at all speeds."

"You looked like you needed the sleep," Ellen said as she sat down. "What do you remember from our conversation?"

"You had a problem with some guy," Enfield said. He rubbed his cheek as he re-read what he had written and then his fingers flew across the keyboard again. "But he went away." He looked at her. "He did go away, right? I can't remember."

"He went away," Ellen said. "Thanks."

"*De nada*," Enfield said. "What was the rest of the party like?"

"Pretty boring," Ellen said. "Taking you home was my highlight."

"Always entertaining with the women," Enfield said, still typing. "That's me." He paused. "And thanks again for getting me home. That's the most I've drunk in a long time."

"Me, too," Ellen said

"It can make me pugnacious."

"Just makes me a blabber mouth," Ellen said. "You didn't miss anything." She hid her relief.

Enfield nodded and didn't say anything.

No, I didn't.

"We're not up to anything," Callahan said to Ellen Parker. She sat in his office holding a paper cup of very hot tea, slowly discovering the insulated sleeve from the coffee shop was insufficient. "But we have to be very careful about what we are doing."

"I understand," Ellen said. "Even the smallest thing could be the piece that solves everything." She wondered if she sounded as nervous as she felt.

"That's how it works on television," Callahan said, smiling. "Some brilliant forensics tech or quirky detective picks up a piece of lint and determines that it comes from a silk weaving made only in Seattle in the '80s and only the relatively famous guest star could be the killer. While that can happen, most of the time it's not small things but big and obvious things – where someone was at the time of the killing, blood on their clothing that belongs to a victim, and so forth." He leaned back in his chair.

"What it is," he went on, "is that we look at *everything*. We have a crime scene in a clearing, we will line up officers shoulder to shoulder and sweep the clearing two or three times, picking up everything. If it happens in a town, we will check every, and I mean every, trashcan in four blocks in the off chance something was discarded. Gutters, storm drains, the whole nine yards." He paused. "That's *if*...

"If the crime," Ellen said, shifting the cup to her other hand, "warrants it."

"Exactly," Callahan said. "If *we* are brought into a case, then pretty much by definition it warrants it. That's the position we are in. We have lots of material but we don't know which of it is relevant. Some, most, of it will turn out to be just trash that happened to be there. Some may be connected to the killer but doesn't help make the case."

"How close to the killer do you think you are?"

"Not very," Callahan said. Ellen nodded; Johnson said the FBI agent was *straight*, his word for people who did not try to pretend things were other than they were. "With serial murderers, you sometimes see them learn from their experience and get better at it. We don't have much from the earlier killings we think were his but that's when he probably developed his technique."

"'Earlier killings?'" Ellen was surprised at the information.

"Five may belong to our murderer," Callahan said. "That's based on victim similarities, geographic locations, and some medical and forensic data. Special Agent Deevers will discuss them with you."

"How far back does he go?"

"Eleven years," Callahan said.

"To get away with it that long," Ellen said, "based on my reading," she paused and smiled in a self-deprecating fashion as she added, "for what that's worth, he must be a very controlled individual."

"To at least some extent," Callahan agreed nodding. "What we are seeing recently is that control may be slipping." He paused as he considered his words. "One of the reasons we are very sensitive to anything getting out is that we don't want to affect his behavior."

"I know some killers follow the press accounts of their crimes pretty closely."

"True," Callahan said. "Others appear to be oblivious of what's being said, even to the point of ignoring items that made identification of them easy. We assume our man is following everything closely. That's why all of this is on very deep background."

"I am surprised," Ellen said, "that you are willing to run that kind of risk."

"The penalties," Callahan said, his voice serious, "for violating trust are usually multi-layered. If a reporter breaks their word, the consequences usually include being cut out forever. And if some damage results, then there can be lawsuits. Usually the plaintiffs don't win but it ties up the reporter, sometimes for years, and can drain bank accounts while mounting the defense, including those of the reporter's employer." He smiled though his eyes showed a hardness that reminded Ellen that Callahan was not by accident an FBI Special Agent. "That tends to make the employer unhappy. Not a good career move."

"That's how Mister Johnson explained it," Ellen said. Her eyes were level and did not look away from Callahan's.

Did you take that for a threat, Ms. Parker?

"I'm not used to hearing 'Mister' when referring to him," Callahan said, changing direction. "What's he like to work for?"

"I'm learning a lot," Ellen said. "He took a little getting used to."

"You realize," Callahan said, smiling and lightly tapping his desktop, "you didn't get me to agree to keep *your* comments on 'background.'"

"I think he knows what I think," Ellen said, smiling.

"I suspect you're right," Callahan said. "All right, I'm going to put you together with Karen Deevers. She'll wrap up your briefing. What she says is covered by the same agreement."

"Understood," Ellen said. She stood and reached out to shake Callahan's hand.

Slightly surprised at the gesture, Callahan shook her hand. Ellen had a firm grip, one that hinted that there was more strength in reserve if she needed it. As she walked away, he watched her, rubbing his chin. The young woman seemed like, well, any other youngster her age and was obviously anxious when meeting him. Still, there was something else about her, some strength reflected in the handshake. In her eyes, too.

Almost idly, Callahan wondered if she knew of her strength.

"Lunch," Deevers said, pointing at the elevator as Ellen approached. "I'm buying."

Ellen fell in beside Deevers as the stood in the elevator. She glanced at the FBI agent out of the corner of her eye.

Karen Deevers seemed to have strength Ellen did not. How did she do it? It could *not* be "something you get used to." How could you get used to living within a world that was so filled with violence or its threat?

The elevator stopped and they walked out. Deevers turned her head slightly.

"Have you gotten used to it yet?" she asked and Ellen felt her heart stop.

"Used to what?" she asked as they stepped outside.

"Being a journalist," Deevers said. She smiled crookedly. "I can't imagine another profession that bounces you around so much. We get assigned to a case or to an office; we can be with it for years, sometimes your whole career. Journalists go from topic to topic, crisis to crisis, assignment to assignment. I imagine just trying to absorb it all is a major challenge."

"I'm just a newbie," Ellen said. "I still have learner's wheels on my keyboard." She paused as Deevers smiled while leading them down the street.

"It's fascinating," Ellen said. "Yes, you have to scramble, but you get involved in so many different things. I love the learning part. And I've always liked to write, so that part fits."

"The stereotype of a reporter," Deevers said, pausing on the corner and waiting for the light to change, "is of a cynic, one who only gets to see the dark side of things. Has that happened to you yet?"

"No," Ellen said firmly. "And much the same stereotype holds for police officers."

"Touché." Deevers grinned.

"But it's something I didn't think about before I became a journalism major." Ellen considered the question as they continued across the street. "I don't know if it will or not. I'm beginning to see a lot of that 'dark side.' But…" Her voice trailed off as they entered a small restaurant.

Deevers shrugged off her coat. For a second, her jacket was pulled to one side and Ellen saw the agent's handgun in its holster. Deevers waved at a woman in a dark green restaurant t-shirt who smiled in return as they sat down.

"The usual?" the woman asked. She had a Lebanese accent.

"For two," Deevers said. She turned to Ellen. "You eat meat, right?"

"Yes."

"For two," Deevers said and looked at Ellen. "So what's the 'but'?"

"I'm just starting," Ellen said. "Maybe it's too soon to say anything definite. The 'but' is just an early impression." She took a breath. "Yes, I'm getting to see some awful things but there are always awful things." Deevers nodded as she listened. "And I'm getting to see people who try to deal with the awful things. People, all kinds, who try to help, try to be decent, try to do what has to be done. People who do it pretty up and walkin' good." Her southern Ohio twang gently appeared. "I think there's more of that in the world than the awful things." She smiled. "I sound naïve."

"You sound," Deevers said as the woman walked over to them to get their drink order, "like you're a hell of a lot older than you appear."

After ordering, Ellen paused, considering how to frame her question. Deevers said nothing but seemed to know what was going on and smiled.

"Is it really possible," Ellen said, "that the perpetrator is an emergency service worker?"

"Good," Deevers said, putting down her drink. "You didn't say 'cop.'" She paused. "I may not be able to answer all your questions."

"You don't have the answers yet?"

"I love the 'yet,'" Deevers grinned. "Such faith. No, there are things I can't say. I'm going to keep things pretty general."

"All right," Ellen said. "What about my question?"

"It's a possibility, though I'm not sure it's likely."

"There've never been any serial murderers who were police officers?"

"Almost never," Deevers corrected her. "Hard to pull off, I suspect. Too many eyes who know what to look for around you. But we could be looking for someone who has knowledge of police procedures. That could include people who work alongside police. Ambulance people, for example, or forest rangers. Or maybe someone who has seen too many shows of 'CSI:'."

"He's very thorough." Ellen frowned. "The impression I've gotten from what *has* been said is that he hasn't left much behind you can work with."

"Well, he's not a disorganized killer. He isn't ruled by impulse, though all serial killers are driven by their desires. But you don't want to lose track of the fact that, even though he's not a disorganized psychotic, he's a gambler. There is always a moment of vulnerability in what he does. He takes a prostitute off the street. He may have reconned the area as thoroughly as he could, but there's always the possibility of someone coming along. His need is so great that, sooner or later, he *has* to act and therefore take those risks. This is not simply someone playing chess. You can walk away from a game. But he *has* to come back to his killing."

"What is the killing doing for him?"

"Everything," Deevers said. "But the specifics are unknown until we get our hands on him. There are obvious, general things. He's angry about women, or a woman. The hair suggests a particular woman. He humiliates them with what he does to their clothes. That means he wants to get back at a woman who humiliated him in some way." She shook her head. "There's no evidence of sexual behavior. That can mean he's impotent at the moment he gets a woman under control or, and I think this more likely, it isn't about sex." Deevers smiled briefly. "All of that has been in the news, though I'd preferred those earlier cases had not been talked about quite so much."

"Why do you think it's not about sex?"

"Because," Deevers said, "a man who is into that and sex is a part of it, even if he can't get it up, he finds other ways." She sipped her cola. "He'll attack the genitals of the woman with objects other than his penis."

Ellen nodded; her reading list from Johnson had included accounts of such things. Some of the reading had left her almost disoriented, opening a door into a room she had never known existed and even the brief glimpse provided by the printed page was powerful.

"Are you," Ellen asked, "at a point where you have a suspect?"

"No," Deevers said, shaking her head and smiling. "Even if we did, I wouldn't say so."

"According to the dates," Ellen said, "it looks a little like his attacks might be coming closer together. I read that kind of pattern reflects an escalation, a drive to capture the intensity of the first kills."

"That can happen," Deevers said.

"And trying to get that intensity might lead him to become more violent?"

"You have been reading," Deevers said. She paused. "Yes, that's possible as well."

"But you're not sure why?"

"Two theories are making the rounds among the profilers," Deevers said. "The first is, serial killers become addicted to the thrill but eventually will need to do things to heighten it. Exactly like a junkie. There's even some neurochemical support for the idea."

"Endorphins."

"Yep." Deevers nodded. "The other theory for escalation is that something happens in a killer's life, something that puts pressure on him that he responds to by his behavior."

"When that happens," Ellen asked, "is it some kind of general life pressure or is it something pretty specific, something that relates to whatever got him going in the first place?"

"Or an exciting combination of ingredients," Deevers said. "We don't know and probably won't until after we catch him."

Later, after they had finished their sausage and green pepper sandwiches, both women sipped their diet colas in silence while Deevers considered Ellen. She did not remember her from Ohio, though hearing her name had stirred old memories. The young woman, nonetheless, had given her the impression that she was... Deevers searched for the word.

Solid.

"Can I go on deep background?" Deevers asked, surprising herself. "Nothing appears in print until after we have him, nothing for attribution even then."

Karen looked at the FBI agent, her eyes slightly wide.

"Yes," she said. "Nothing in print until you catch him, and nothing for attribution." Ellen smiled slightly. "You don't want to see your name in print?"

"Publicity can ruin an agent's career," Deevers said, her voice very serious.

"Understood," Ellen said. "You've got my word."

Deevers nodded and took a breath. "This is a bad one," she said.

"My own theory is that this is the guy's last run. Before he killed two or three and could back off. He's up to eight in his current series. That's a pretty sharp break with the past. I'm guessing that he's at a point that he can't stop unless we catch him."

"He may have killed thirteen women," Ellen nodded.

"Maybe more we don't know of," Deevers said, "but that's not what I meant. There've been others who've killed many, many more. No, this is a bad one because he is very smart, very disciplined. Unless we get lucky, if he gets himself under control, he might get away with doing this forever. And that happens."

"How often?" Ellen suddenly realized most of the serial killers she had read about were the ones who were caught.

"We're not sure," Deevers said. "The problem is that some serial murderers are never detected. Maybe they are on the move so the pattern of their killings is never identified. There was a man who was killing tramps riding the rails – he worked over multiple states and the assumption by local law enforcement officers in each jurisdiction was that it was just another fight that got out of hand. And some may be just very, very good at what they do."

"That's pretty scary."

"Definitely," Deevers said. "That's my biggest concern."

"So how did you get into the business of tracking them down?"

"Just lucky, I guess," Deevers said. She glanced at her watch. "In part, I was interested in the work. I heard John Roberts give a talk one time and that sort of intrigued me. In the Bureau, it's easy to specialize. Depending on the area, you almost have to."

"What do you mean?"

"Banking fraud," Deevers said. "The technical and historical information you need to know is immense. I have a lot of respect for those people of ours who can really get into all that. CPAs with guns. Me, I always wanted to be a wind-up action toy." She smiled self wryly. "Right up to the point someone shot at me."

"Johnson," Ellen said, "says you worked in Hostage Rescue."

"I did," she said. "That was after Ohio. I got into the Behavioral Analysis Unit after that." She leaned back in her chair. "So, after Ohio, you finished school and went to college. Now you're a grad student."

"Much to my surprise," Ellen said. "Going in, I thought I was going to teach school. I took a journalism undergrad course, liked it, and took another. The rest is history."

"I've always enjoyed teaching," Deevers said. "But I'd rather be out in the field."

"Me, too," Ellen said and both women smiled.

Chapter 24

Klemmer, a mug of tea in his hand, stood beside Deputy Morgan as both men studied a carved chest that stood on brass casters. Across its dark top, inlaid mother of pearl traced loops and swirls in a symmetrical pattern around the edges.

"Korean?" Morgan said. "They know how to carve wood."

"They do," Klemmer said. "Now, the sides where there's no carving, that's a laminate. The maker wanted to have a contrast in tones. The dark front carved with those nature scenes and the sides lighter and perfectly smooth. But the eye is drawn, first, to the inlay."

"What's wrong with it?"

"A couple of places, the inlay is damaged. That's going to be the hard part. But there's another problem. Easier. It's the interior," Klemmer said. "The top lifts, so." He used one hand and the top rose, exposing brass hinges and fittings. Inside, the chest was divided by a shallow wall. "Someone stored old rags in it. You can see that the solvent on them attacked the divider and the bottom."

"That's pretty ugly."

"I think the bottom can be saved," Klemmer said. "But the divider, it pulls out, is going to have to be replaced. The problem there is…" He stopped as a small, bell-like tone sounded. "Someone's coming." Morgan raised his eyebrows.

"The previous owner," Klemmer said, as he led the way out of his shop, "had one of those infrared driveway detectors put in. It really is handy. I get so wrapped up in my work that a convoy could park and I wouldn't notice it. Not good for customer relations. I moved a bell repeater into the workshop so I can hear it if I'm here or in the barn."

Morgan nodded as he followed. He closed the door to the shop and they turned the corner. Someone in a large luxury SUV was just entering the parking area. Morgan saw the driver, an older man with white hair, open his eyes widely as he saw Morgan's uniform. Morgan hung back as Klemmer walked up to the stopping vehicle.

Morgan watched as Klemmer, leaning in the driver's window, spoke with the older man. He wondered what the visitor was thinking – the man's eyes kept coming back to Morgan. He knew the look; it was a mix of curiosity and anxiety. *Don't worry, buddy. You can't possibly be speeding sitting still.*

No one's reactions to a cop were ever neutral. Morgan had gotten used to it many years before. You had to or you stayed irritated. Besides, a lot of reactions were pretty positive. Many people like the reassurance of the uniform.

Morgan looked up; over the past few weeks it had gotten warmer and the skies, like now, were brighter. Pennsylvania had finally gotten the word that spring had arrived.

Morgan had gotten into stopping by Klemmer's after work to look in on his projects. Morgan classified himself as a clumsy carpenter who had done nothing more elaborate than some home repair projects, like replacing the roof of his house's porch. Klemmer, on the other hand, was a professional, what would be called a "cabinet maker." He shook his head. Score one for the prison job training program, though Klemmer had told him wood working had been a hobby prior to being sent away.

He watched the old man hand something to Klemmer. The SUV backed and turned around. Klemmer, an envelope in one hand, waved goodbye with the other as it left and then walked over to Morgan.

"The rich," Klemmer said, "are different."

"First off, they're rich."

"That's for sure," Klemmer smiled. He held up the envelope. "They also tend to be cavalier about paying. This is merely three months late."

"I hope it was worth the wait."

"Yes, it certainly was."

"Well," Morgan said, "I've got to get going. They're changing my shift to four to midnight temporarily. One of our guys was hurt."

"Nothing serious?" Klemmer looked disappointed.

"Tangled with a drunk driver," Morgan said. "Ended up with a broken arm." He tapped his own left shoulder. "He's in a sling and is looking at rehab. No patrol work for six weeks. He's stuck on a desk. I'm covering while we wait for another deputy to come back from vacation."

"Well," Klemmer said, "if you want to stop by on your way to work, I'm probably here."

"I'll do that," Morgan said. He nodded and walked over to his unmarked car. As he got into it, Klemmer waved and went back to his workshop.

Morgan drove east towards Kennett Square and then followed Lenape Road northeast to West Chester. His visits with Klemmer were something that he did not mention to Bobby Hamme. While Hamme apparently had backed off the idea that Klemmer might be involved in something, Morgan knew his partner simply didn't like the man.

He found it a little surprising that he, Morgan, did. He had never viewed a convicted felon in any way than with suspicion. There was something about Klemmer that attracted the eye beyond his arrest and conviction record. It wasn't just Morgan's interest in woodworking. That had opened the door, yes, but during his visits over the past two weeks Morgan had discovered that Klemmer had a quiet sense of humor. Obviously intelligent, he seemed to be basically a good man.

Morgan smiled. How bizarre was the world getting that he was calling a convicted killer "a good man?"

Still, there were boundaries. Klemmer liked to talk – Morgan thought the man was a little lonely living by himself and his visits to the Kennett coffee shop didn't totally meet his need to socialize. Once or twice Klemmer had referred to the task force's work but quickly pulled away from it. That was one of the boundaries. It was one Morgan shared.

On the whole, though, their conversations had gone well beyond wood and carpentry and Morgan knew that both of them were getting a need met. Morgan interacted with more people in a typical day than Klemmer did but, like Klemmer, he had few people that he felt close to.

Bobby Hamme was a friend, but not someone he hung out with after work. At work, there was a little distance between himself and the other deputies. Part of it was his seniority but part of it was the fall-out from *the incident*. Maybe it wasn't that anyone thought he'd done anything wrong. It was the kind of trap any police officer might have fallen into.

In killing, Morgan became something other than an ordinary deputy sheriff. He had taken a life. Whatever the reasons, there it was. He had done the ultimate act, the first crime mentioned in the Bible. Most people, most police officers, never killed anyone. It was a dark area on the map that few ever wanted to explore and chart.

He sighed. Morgan made no pretense to being a philosopher and he had found nothing among his brief examination of the scattered writings of such

149

people that had helped him. *People who wrote about it didn't do it and those who had didn't write about it.* That wasn't totally true, he knew. He had discovered some writers – former cops, former soldiers, mostly – who had killed and then talked about it. They had provided no answers for him but at least were able to reassure him that he was not alone in his struggle to find some peace with it.

Would time do it? It hadn't so far. Morgan smiled. He doubted the value of time and waiting. Things changed because of what you did.

The problem was, he didn't know what to do about being a killer.

"Sidebar's in," Johnson said to Ellen as she leaned into his office doorway to check in. "Framed up and will be in Sunday." He leaned back in his chair, his hands behind his head.

"Good," she said. "Anything else going on?" She had a list of background subjects Johnson wanted her to research and needed to get into it.

"Set up a time for a follow-up," Johnson said. "With Klemmer. He had some good answers in our 'Q&A' and I want to keep him as a source. I want you to run some of what you got from Callahan and Deevers last week past him. No attribution. Ideas *you've* been kicking around. Let's see if he's buying into some of their stuff."

"When do you need it?"

"Yesterday," Johnson said. "When else? What, did you think this was television? This is a newspaper, real news. Bang-bang, we gotta go."

"Right," Ellen said. "When do you need it?"

"No rush," Johnson said. "Clear the other projects. Today's, what day is it?, Thursday. If you can get the research done by the weekend, see if you can see him next week."

"All right," Ellen said. "You'll have the questions ready by then?"

"Questions?" He frowned. "What, you need questions? You still wearing water wings? Time to swim, woman."

"No questions?" Ellen stepped into the office. "You mean conduct an interview on my own?"

"No questions," Johnson said, still leaning back, though folding his arms. "We're not turning it into a story. This is background. But write it up as if it was going into print. Professional job. I'll critique. Two birds with one stone. You know him, you know the subject area. You get to practice writing. You don't need for me to write up the questions."

"Right, got it," Ellen said, barely suppressing a smile. "No questions."

"Questions?" Johnson said it a Hollywood accent to Ellen's retreating back. "We don' need no stinkin' questions."

Ellen quickly returned to her desk. Enfield and Stewart were conferring at the other intern desk. Stewart, sitting on the edge of the desk, watched Ellen sit down.

"The Fourth Horse*person* is smiling," he said. "What have you done, Ellen? Finally shot Johnson?"

"No," she said, pulling her keyboard to her. "He's letting me conduct an interview 'off the leash.'" Both Enfield and Stewart raised their eyebrows; "off the leash" was the current intern expression for being allowed to operate independently.

Like a real reporter.

"Damn," Stewart said. "How much did you pay him?"

"It was cheap," Ellen said. "Two-fifths of my soul and my first-born male child." Her fingers started typing.

"You're a graduate student," Enfield said dryly. "He must know you have no soul left."

"Congrats, Big E," Stewart said. He stood up and as he walked past Ellen held up her hand. He slapped it and grinned broadly. "All right, *girl*," he said.

"You've done well, young Skywalker," Enfield said. "You've snatched the pebbles from my hand. The force is strong within you. Who's the victim? I mean, who are you interviewing?"

"Klemmer," Ellen said. "This time without questions from Johnson. It won't be for publication but I get to run some ideas past him and see what he thinks. And I write it up as if it were going into column."

"Nice," Enfield said. "He must be impressed with your work."

Ellen thought for a moment while her fingers danced. Enfield was right. In her excitement, she hadn't thought about what the assignment meant. Immediately she felt the urge to downplay it. After all, all four interns had been given assignments to talk to people – that was part of the learning. But this was different. This was an *interview* with a *person of significance*. Unsupervised.

Things were looking *up*.

Chapter 25

Deputy Sheriff Craig Morgan was feeling pretty good, even if he was working the evening shift. He disliked getting home after midnight but, on the other hand, there wasn't much happening with the task force that he was immediately responsible for – the last briefing had gone over the autopsy reports, again, demonstrating similarities and then spent time on some work that had been done on the first five victims. Exhuming the bodies and turning them over to the "slicers and dicers," as several of the task force members called the medical examiners, had not given them much, other than some support for the idea they were the result of the same killer.

Morgan was feeling good primarily because, and he would not have said this and was hardly aware of it, he was developing a friendship with Klemmer. Men didn't talk much about friendships, they just noticed when they didn't have one. Even then, it tended to be something unnamed.

Morgan even had begun doing a few real woodworking projects again around his house. Nothing complex, nothing that Klemmer would do, just a pair of low bookshelf cabinets that would hold his stacks of police and American Rifleman magazines. It was the kind of project he had gradually stopped doing over the years. It was good to be back at it.

He had not stopped to see Klemmer before his Saturday night shift. Running a little late, he had checked in to the Sheriff's Department to pick up an assignment to set up a speed trap near Unionville on Doe Run Road. Backing his car into a clear area next to Hilltop View Road, he had, as the nearby road promised, a pretty good view of cars coming east or west. At the same time, local police were setting up down on 926 and up on 842. The concentrated effort, it was hoped, would serve as a blanket on speeders and have an effect on their behavior for perhaps 72 hours. And it would generate a little income for all the departments involved.

Morgan pointed his Stalker hand-held radar gun at an approaching car. The red LED numbers were just a few numbers above the posted limit; the rough rule of thumb he used, to avoid issues coming up over someone's speedometer and disputes about the gun's accuracy, was 15 MPH over the limit. Where he was parked, the limit was 45; few drove less than fifty without backing up cars and trucks behind them. Anything over 60 was fair game.

He listened closely for calls from the other cars working the area. Stopping someone at night, alone, was among the most dangerous things a police officer did. Whenever possible, once speeders stopped and while their license plates made their way through the law enforcement computers, police officers were to wait until another officer arrived. It wasn't always possible but it was the best way.

It was barely five but Morgan thought he had already been spotted and drivers were warning one another. He was not pulling down any speeders but it sounded like the boys, no, girl, down on 926 was hauling them in as fast as she could write tickets. She already had three. Morgan shook his head. It went like that sometimes.

He had a thermos cup with a closeable lid from which he sipped coffee between flashing approaching cars with the gun. It was promising to be a long four hours.

Morgan had just read the LED – *64, we have a winner* – when he heard the call from the county dispatcher.

County three-one and three-two, we have a 10-54 at Bartram and Sparrow. Officer on scene is off-duty and is in civilian clothes, green jacket and a white van. All available officers please respond.

Morgan threw the radar gun onto the passenger seat and started the car's engine. He levered the transmission into gear and slapped on his siren and lights. As the car vaulted onto the road, he grabbed the microphone.

"County Three One is responding," he said and dropped the microphone. He pressed the gas pedal and the Ford leapt down the road.

Sparrow Road was the road leading to the nursing home where Bobby Hamme's mother lived.

A County Sheriff marked unit, call sign County Three Two, beat Morgan to the scene. He recognized Hamme standing in front of his van, pointing into the field while talking with the other deputy. As he slowed, Deputy Collins ran over.

"Can you take the intersection?" Collins asked. "I'll go down to the entrance to the nursing home."

"Got it," Morgan said. He glanced at Hamme, still standing in front of his van. "Is he all right?"

"He's fine," Collins said. "He spotted it on his way back from visiting his mother. Tough." The deputy turned and ran back to his car.

Morgan turned the Ford around, quickly checked in with the dispatcher, and drove the short distance back to the intersection of Bartram and Sparrow. Bartram wasn't heavily traveled, Sparrow less so, but it was still the edge of rush hour and there would be an avalanche of emergency vehicles coming.

He parked on the shoulder of Sparrow and left his flashing lights on. From the trunk of the car he picked up several road flares which he ignited and placed as a barrier across Sparrow Road. It was getting cold and he took his jacket from the passenger side. He had just zipped it up when the others began arriving.

For a while, Morgan simply directed traffic; Collins did the same at the turn into the nursing home parking lot. The emergency vehicles, an ambulance and two marked police cars were first but others soon followed, parked in the field across from Hamme's van. A pair of county detectives arrived and waved to him as he pointed them through his barrier of flares.

He recognized an unmarked black Chevrolet SUV used by the FBI agents on the task force and waved it through. It stopped and the window slid down. Agent Karen Deevers was at the wheel and he could see Callahan in the passenger seat.

"Hamme found the victim?" Deevers asked.

"I think so," Morgan said, leaning so his elbow was on the door edge. "I saw him but haven't gotten any information."

"Any idea why he was here?"

"See those lights down the road?" Morgan pointed with his thumb. For some reason Deever's question irritated him. "That's where his mother is kept. It's a nursing home."

"Then we lucked out," Deevers said, nodding. "The first person on the scene is a police officer. Good."

Morgan stepped back and the SUV moved down to join the other vehicles. By now, it was dark enough that the flashing lights of all the cars and vans, silently contesting the darkness but only accenting it, gave the impression of a carnival where no one was having any fun.

He didn't see Hamme while he covered the intersection. After two hours, another officer relieved him at the road junction. Morgan left his car where it was – the field was getting crowded – and walked towards the white van.

He found Hamme sitting in the driver's seat, watching the police in the field.

"Hey," Morgan said. Hamme nodded.

"They are waiting for another set of lights to be set up," Hamme said, referring to the portable lights that were illuminated the field. Small groups of police, some in uniform, some in plain clothes, stood on the edge of the field. They all had something to drink and Morgan saw one of the local fire companies had gotten a critical incident support truck across the road from the van and was passing out coffee.

"What happened?" Morgan asked and immediately frowned; Hamme probably had been interrogated half a dozen times by now and talking about it yet again was likely to be the last thing he wanted to do. He was surprised when Hamme answered.

"I was heading north," Hamme said. "Coming from visiting my mother. I saw some color in the field. Turned out to be the victim's clothing, though I couldn't tell then. It didn't seem right so I stopped. Right here. I walked over and saw it was a victim." He shrugged. "Pretty clear she was dead but I checked for a pulse. She was gone. I got on my cell and called for help." He looked at Morgan. "I think it's another one. Clothes, hair, wound, it all matches."

"Damn," Morgan said. He glanced down the road toward the nursing home. It was less than two hundred yards away and there were people standing in the parking lot, staring at the flashing lights. "That's a hell of a thing to happen so close to your mother, Bobby."

"I don't think she knows," Hamme said. "She's losing responsiveness. I tried talking to her but I don't know that she heard much of it." He shook his head. "Not much longer now."

"Sorry to hear that, partner," Morgan said. "When are they going to release you so you can go home?"

"They already did," Hamme said. "I have to do a write-up tomorrow. I was just hanging around to see if there was anything else I could do." He nodded to one side. "There go the other lights they were waiting on."

The van blocked Morgan's view but he saw the surge of light as another bank of portable lights came to life. The generators powering all of the sets of lights filled the night with their smell and sound. Morgan stepped to the front and saw a small group of people crouched in the field. Standing back was a pair of dark jacketed EMTs with a collapsible stretcher standing on one end, calmly waiting to be called forward.

Hamme had good eyes and the elevated driver's seat of the van must have really helped. Judging from the position of the group, it looked like the body was two thirds of the way to the dark line of trees in the distance. Deevers was right; having a police officer spot the kill before anyone else might turn out to be a major break.

While there was some temptation to go out into the field, Morgan knew better. This was a time to stand back and let the forensics people do their thing. He patted the side of Hamme's door, got a nod, and walked across the road, heading for the support truck. He got a cup of coffee and then called the dispatcher with the microphone attached to his shirt. Carolyn had nothing for him, other than the traditional standby command.

Morgan walked towards the van and was surprised to see Deevers talking to Hamme. He stopped and sipped at his coffee. She nodded at something that was said and reached up and shook Hamme's hand. She looked over and saw Morgan. She said something to Hamme and then walked over to Morgan.

"You haven't been to the scene, have you?" Deevers asked after exchanging brief greetings.

"No," Morgan said.

"When did you get here?"

Morgan glanced at his watch.

"I'm not sure of the precise time," he admitted. "I was in too much of a hurry. But it could not have been more than twelve or fifteen minutes after the call."

"Dispatcher called at five oh seven," Deevers said, not consulting her notepad. "The other deputy called in at five oh seventeen upon arrival at Hamme's van. Hamme confirms the time. You arrived, then, both estimate about three minutes later. Sound about right?"

"Yes," Morgan said. Questions were routine but there was an edge to Deevers' voice. What was she tense about?

"What did you see when you got here?"

"I turned around almost immediately," Morgan said. "I set up at the intersection." He pointed north with his coffee. "Other than Deputy Collins and Deputy Hamme, he was at his van I think, I saw nothing."

"Nothing in the field?"

156

"No," Morgan said. "I didn't know where to look and, even if I did, I suspect I wouldn't have seen anything."

"Why not?"

"Too low," he said. "My cruiser sits the driver a lot lower than Hamme's van. What with the scattered brush and weeds, a low-lying body would be invisible." He looked towards the killing field. "Hell, even now I can't see anything. If it wasn't for those people out there, I wouldn't know where the body was."

Deevers didn't bother to glance at the field. She frowned slightly and pointed north.

"You came in there, right?"

"Yes," Morgan said.

"On you way in, did you see anyone turning off this road?"

"From Sparrow?" Morgan shook his head. "I didn't see anyone do that." He thought for a moment, understanding what Deevers was seeking. "There were a couple of oncoming cars once I turned onto Bartram. One Hyundai SUV, dark blue, and one old Ford Taurus – oval rear window. The Taurus was blue. I don't know if they got to Bartram from Sparrow Road. I observed no vehicles heading west."

"Deputy Hamme saw the Taurus," Deevers said. "He thought it was another visitor to the nursing home. We're checking on that." She looked at Morgan. "We lucked out in having an officer right on the scene. A civilian would not have been so observant."

"He's got good eyes," Morgan said. He grimaced. "It looks like his mother is dying."

"Hell of a thing," Deevers said. "He told me they changed your shift."

"Just temporarily," Morgan said. "One of our people got hurt."

"I heard." Deevers smiled slightly. "A head's up. Agent Callahan has talked with Sheriff Walsh about getting you off this evening shift. We need you full-time with us. Things are ratcheting up." She nodded towards the field. "This is part of that." She looked back at Morgan. "I hope Callahan's request doesn't put you in hot water with the Sheriff."

"I don't think it will," Morgan said but his uncertainty touched his voice. "Sheriff Walsh is pretty much about results and if the task force says they need me, I'm guessing she'll cooperate." He paused. "Does the request include Hamme?"

"It does," Deevers said. "Hell, now that he's in the witness category, so to speak, we've got a pretty good lever to get him full-time. Callahan, by the way, liked the project you deputies did in checking out the violent offenders."

"That was Sheriff Walsh's idea," Morgan said. "And the county detectives did part of the load."

"I'm surprised it wasn't Hamme's idea," Deevers said. "He's got some good insight." She grinned. "Even if he does think we couldn't find the end of our own noses."

"It's not that bad," Morgan said, coming to the defense of his partner. "Bobby just has been frustrated with the pace of operations."

"He doesn't think much of profilers."

"Well," Morgan said, "we haven't gotten much from them. I mean, most of what they've said so far is the kind of common-sense observation that anyone could make or get from some book." He paused. "I mean, hell, the profiles I've read so far are so general as to not be useful."

"I know what you mean," Deevers said. "The profiling business, though, helps to filter possible suspects. We don't have infinite resources. We can't investigate everyone. But if the profile limits the field, we can prioritize who we look at."

"Works fine in theory," Morgan said. "And I hope it pays off. But from the view of one of the troops, we don't see much happening with the profiles."

"I understand that," Deevers said. "And no offense is taken, including from Deputy Hamme. Just think of it as another tool that may pay off." She shrugged. "That's how it is a lot of the time. You never know what it is that is going to get the job done."

"True enough," Morgan agreed. "So where do we go from here?"

"Doctor Bennert is on his way back," Deevers said.

"I remember him."

"He's going to partner up with Doctor Maire," she said. "They're already chattering like crows on their cell phones. They're really eager to get to a body this fresh."

Morgan nodded; it sounded ghoulish but forensic pathologists approached death and the dead differently than other people.

"When do they go to work?"

"Tonight." She looked at Morgan's now empty paper cup. "I think I'm going to get one of those."

"It's not bad," Morgan said. As Deevers walked away his radio spoke to him.

County Three-One, 10-19.

"Three-One, roger," Morgan said. He walked back to the intersection and his car, the empty cup still in his hand. *Return to base?*

Morgan crushed the cup and, as he opened the door of the cruise, put it in a small plastic bag used for trash – Chester County Deputy Sheriffs were hell on litterers. He waved to the deputy covering the intersection, got a wave back, and pulled out onto Bartram Road.

Klemmer sat in his dining room, his eyes on the soft glowing screen of his small computer monitor. His folded hands were in front of his face, slightly pressing against his lips as if making an effort to keep from speaking. An untouched cup of tea was on the desktop near his elbow.

He read the email from Callahan again and slowly shook his head.

Do they really understand how close they are? And what that might mean?

Klemmer sat back in his chair and glanced out the window. There was nothing to see. The night had turned the windows into dim mirrors and all he could see was a faint reflection of his own face, though he stared at and through it as if seeking something outside his house, something crouched in the darkness.

He sighed and began typing a reply.

Regardless of whether or not we agree on my hypothesis, the most important element to keep in mind is what the killer will do when he perceives you closing in. The gauntlet is down. He will not go peacefully, Paul. His rage is so great and long-lasting that he will, if given the chance, become savagely violent.

Klemmer shook his head; police officers always thought they could handle anything that they encountered. They *had* to think it or they could not survive in their jobs. Most of the time they were right but there was always the unexpected, the unusual. Paul was a level-headed FBI agent and undoubtedly already was thinking about what would happen when they approached the killer and would take every precaution he could.

It won't be enough. Nothing will be enough.

Ellen Parker lay in her bed and stared up at the barely seen ceiling. The dream had jerked her awake, close enough to it that she remembered and felt it. She closed her eyes, as if to shut it out of her awareness but it still played out in her mind.

Eileen is just out of reach, caught in the Ohio River. Ellen knows it never happened but knows she has to save her cousin. The horror is that Ellen cannot get herself to move. She does not know what to do and seemingly cannot get herself to think of what needs to be done. Eileen is looking at her with disappointment and she thinks she hears her father's voice criticizing her inaction.

What stops her is the knowledge that she might do it wrong and Eileen will be lost. Again. She looks around for her grandfather. Thomas Luther Parker would know what to do, but he is not there. She is alone and she is not enough. The knowing of that judgment is crippling.

Finally, she picks up a branch; it folds as if made of limp spaghetti and she can't even throw it. She looks and looks but there are no other branches. Eileen starts to drift away. Finally, Ellen finds another branch. It is crooked but it is stiff. She runs down the riverbank, holding out the branch. It crookedly twists in her hand as if not satisfied with its shape. She feels it move in her grip but she holds on and runs into the water until she is knee deep. Then she cannot move forward any further; the Ohio is holding her feet. She reaches with the branch; it is long enough.

But a hand reaches from behind her and lifts the branch. Eileen cannot grab it. Ellen turns. It is a young man with brown hair, a face dimly remembered. Then she knows it is a bully, one she faced down on this same riverbank, and he smiles in pure enjoyment as he keeps her from saving Eileen. Her cousin is swept away. Ellen, her heart breaking, turns on the bully who just smiles and then says:

"Gotcha."

Chapter 26

The task force met in its offices across the street from the County Courthouse. Once again, they sat in the cramped conference room and talked quietly while waiting for things to begin.

Morgan stood against the wall with Hamme and watched as some of the other cops, already aware of Hamme's spotting of the latest victim, came up to his partner to ask brief questions.

Hamme seemed to be handling it well even though it sounded to Morgan like it was terribly repetitious. The questions were the same, mostly about what he saw, and about half of the conversations ended with a comment about hoping for the best for his mother. Hamme always thanked them for that. Morgan thought such continuous reminding of his mother's illness and terminal condition would be painful but Hamme did not seem bothered by it.

"Are you getting tired of that?" Morgan whispered, leaning over to his partner after a particularly gushing offering of hope.

"It's all right," Hamme said, his voice low. "That's just what people do. It doesn't hurt anything."

Morgan nodded; that was Hamme, always aware of what other people thought and felt. A good man, however you calculated it.

At that moment, Agent Callahan, accompanied by tired looking doctors Bennert and Maire, came into the room. He attached a laptop he carried to a small projector sitting on a table. Turning it on, he adjusted it until its white square of light centered on the portable screen behind the front table.

Karen Deevers followed a few seconds later and took up a position against the far wall. She nodded to both Morgan and Hamme and Morgan smiled back. Her prediction about his being pulled off the shift and being placed full-time in the task force had come true; news of it was responsible for his recall to department headquarters during the previous evening.

When the FBI wants something, they tend to get it.

Morgan didn't think there would be any negative repercussions; lots of police departments did not enjoy good relations with federal law enforcement but Sheriff Walsh was pretty diplomatic. Politics forced the development of that set of skills. More than that, she was a good cop and anything the task force needed she seemed ready to provide. When Morgan had passed her office before the task force meeting, she had called him in and talked about moving from part-time to full-time with them.

"They seem to think," Walsh had said, "you have your act together. I'm glad to see that."

Morgan had thanked her and then gone to the task force meeting. Deevers had met him and Hamme. They were assigned opposite sides of the same table – desks were hard to come by – and she spent several minutes with them. They already knew the task force and most of its procedures.

"We want you to be in your uniforms usually," Deevers said. "It's important to have a county presence each step of the way. But it would be a good idea to have a change of civilian clothes available in case we need you in plain clothes. There is a closet in the back of the conference room where you can hang your civvies. There's going to be a series of full field sweeps at the crime scene after this morning's meeting. Deputy Morgan, we'd like you to coordinate that. There will be other deputies there, the troopers are bringing in six, and our forensics team will be there. Callahan is going to try to be there but may get there late. I'll probably be there but we want you running the sweeps."

"Why?"

"Because these are all Pennsylvania people doing the work," Deevers said frankly. "It's usually a better idea to have one of the local officers out there with the black snake whip flogging people into formation than one of us feds."

"Probably true," Morgan said, grinning. "And Deputy Hamme...?"

"Same deal," Deevers said, looking at Hamme. "Get on the line and assist."

"Got it," Hamme said, nodding.

Morgan glanced at his watch as Callahan stood at the head table and lightly rapped his knuckles on it. The deputies and troopers were supposed to be at the scene, watched by a pair of deputies overnight, at 0830. He hoped the meeting wasn't going to run long.

Callahan made it clear it wouldn't.

"The technical reports are being written up," the FBI agent said. "But the piece we need to talk about is what we've gotten from the crime scene." Callahan nodded to someone and the lights dimmed. There was a pause and then the projector came to life by showing a slide with an FBI logo.

"This isn't going to be pretty," Callahan said in warning. "Our perpetrator got a little messy this time."

The picture changed to show the crime scene. Taken from some distance, the picture showed the entire scene lit by the camera's flash and the portable lights. The picture changed.

The body lay face down in the weeds. Her clothing lay to her left and her face was turned away from the camera as if in embarrassment. Her light blond hair had been severely hacked and Morgan saw it was scattered in several directions. Blood had streamed down her back and discolored her scalp.

The next picture established the orientation of the body. Taken from a position from beyond the woman's head, Sparrow Road appeared in the background, discernable primarily by the lights of the vehicles parked on the other side of the road. Morgan thought he could just make out Hamme's van.

Then followed a series of close-up shots of the corpse. The killer had stabbed her multiple times and not just because he cut her clothes off of her. The wound to her throat looked like it was broad and deep enough to nearly have beheaded her.

"Single edge weapon," Doctor Bennert said, his voice heavy with fatigue and perhaps something else. "Not previously used. Certainly right-handed. Very strong. He pierced a thoracic vertebra, splintered it, and cut the medulla spinalis. The spinal cord. The wound to the throat was, at the time it was delivered, utterly unnecessary. She was already dead." He paused and nodded to Maire.

"Time of death," Maire said, "was about midnight. No apparent evidence of sexual assault, though some additional tests are being run along with the blood work."

"God," Morgan said as the images flashed and then disappeared. He looked at Hamme who just silently shook his head.

The pictures came and went. There weren't many. Callahan was limiting them to those that reflected the violence of the scene.

The projector switched off and the lights came back on.

"We've been concerned," Callahan said, "about an escalation in violence. Perhaps as a function of a gradual deterioration in control, perhaps as a need for greater thrills. We're seeing it now. This killing was closer in time to number eight than any of the others were to one another. We think he's losing it and is making mistakes. He probably has not taken the time to dispose of the weapon and perhaps not even the clothes he wore at the time. He's in a hurry and not thinking clearly. We think he's missing things."

"The victim is Janet Gracen," Callahan said. "That's 'c-e-n.' She was a semi-pro working in Downingtown at the Red Dog Tavern on Lincoln. Biker bar. Her brother will do the official identification but we have a match on prints. She did some shoplifting a couple of years ago. Earrings and rings missing." He paused. "Deputies Morgan and Hamme are with us full-time now. Good news. They'll be coordinating the scene sweeps this morning. I think we have a good chance of finding something if our boy is not being as careful as he usually was. Karen?" He looked to one side at Deevers. She shook her head negatively and Callahan looked across the group.

"All right, let's get to work."

Morgan and Hamme left the conference room quickly. As they waited for the elevator, Morgan looked at Hamme.

"What do you think of the idea that our killer is getting sloppy?"

"It's a possibility," Hamme said. He thought for a moment. "That's happened before."

"Those pictures looked like he's losing control."

"Hey," a woman said and Hamme turned. It was Karen Deevers.

"We got your transport set up," she said, quickly walking up to them. She held out a set of car keys to Morgan. "Black Chevy SUV in our lot, license is on the key ring." She turned to Hamme. "Sheriff Walsh has okayed you using one of the Sheriff vehicles. Go ahead and pick it up as it will give us a little more flexibility if you both have your own sets of wheels."

"All right," Hamme said.

"Sounds good," Morgan agreed. He led the way onto the elevator with Hamme and Deevers close behind.

The Chevy was minimally equipped. While Pro-Gard push bumpers and a vertical shotgun rack – a Remington 870 12-gauge shotgun with a pistol grip and small flashlight attachment occupied it – suggested it was not your ordinary gas-guzzler, there was no computer over the central console. Morgan had gotten used to using one while on patrol but the FBI did not do traffic stops. The radio was programmable, with one frequency reserved for the task force, another for the state troopers, and one linked to the Sheriff's department, each carefully labeled with plastic tape. The front grill hid flashers but for the overhead there was only a flasher the driver had to reach around and put on the roof. Plugged into a power outlet, it currently resided in the center console.

In the back, raising the back hatch accessed a large first aid kit, held to the side with hook and loop straps. A small evidence kit was stored opposite it.

Morgan checked the shotgun rack. The rack had a lock that any handcuff key would open, a common police practice. The Remington was loaded though no shell was chambered. He emptied the weapon of its shells and checked the trigger pull. As was usual with police shotguns, the pull was harder than what one might expect in a civilian version of the same weapon. He carefully slid the shells of "double-ought" buckshot into the weapon and locked it in its rack.

He worked all the lights, stepping out of the vehicle to check the rear turn signals. A quick blip of the siren and he was done. Ten minutes later, Morgan was driving to the crime scene on Sparrow Road. The big Chevy handled like what it was, a truck disguised as a car. He preferred his nimbler and more responsive Ford cruiser but the Chevy had a certain solidness that suggested it was a no-nonsense vehicle. Morgan smiled; he always had felt that there ought to be a license qualification for trucks and SUVs like there was for motorcycle operation. The skills were different from driving a car and he had seen enough rolled over SUVs to know that most people didn't have those skills.

Getting the search sweeps set was pretty simple; this was something all cops had done, usually several times. Because of the low brush and weeds, the line spacing was tight. Everyone was within arm's reach of one another. The procedure was straightforward. The line moved forward together with its center aimed at where the body had been. If someone found anything, they called out, the line stopped, and the forensics people trotted over to pick it up. If they were busy, a marker – a red triangle pennant on the end of a steel wire – was plunged into the ground to guide the forensics team.

While Bobby Hamme walked at one end of the line, checking its speed, Deevers stayed with the forensics team.

The plan was for the line to sweep first east to west, from fifty feet from the body to fifty feet beyond it. Then they would do a sweep from north to south. The third and last sweep would be on a diagonal. It was slow work, with the dead weeds and just emerging new growth hampering their views of the ground. They were thorough and soon the little marker pennants littered the field as the forensics people fell behind. Deevers, Morgan saw, helped the team collecting and bagging items found in the field.

Before starting the second sweep, Morgan gave everyone a twenty-minute break to allow the forensics people a chance to catch up. He looked toward the nursing home. The parking lot held only cars; there was no crowd watching in the morning cold. He squinted at the building for a moment.

"Hey, Bobby," he said. "If you want to take a moment and check on your mom, I've got it covered here."

Hamme looked up and then nodded.

"Thanks," he said. "I'll be back before the break's over." He turned and walked quickly towards the nursing home.

Hell, it wasn't procedure but sometimes you had to show your people some support. Morgan watched Deevers talking with a forensics technician who was on his hands and knees, working on something. After several minutes she looked at him and then towards the nursing home. Hamme was just going into the main entrance.

"Where's he going?" Deevers asked as she walked over.

"Check in on his mother," Morgan said. "What have we got so far?"

"It doesn't look like much," Deevers said. "A fair amount of probable trash. Items from the body, mostly hair, missed last night when they moved it." She looked towards the nursing home. "Is that place any good?"

"Supposed to be," Morgan said. "It looked all right when I was there with Bobby. He thinks they do a good job."

"Is his mom on a common ward or...?"

"She has a room," Morgan said. "That wing to the left, that's the one she's in."

"Probably not a great idea," Deevers said, "to put him to work here, where his mother is."

"He can handle it," Morgan said. He hesitated, not eager to talk about his partner on a personal level but wanting to reassure the FBI agent. "Bobby's pretty solid, the kind of man you can depend on. Sure, he's going through some stress but it would be hard to tell it."

"One of those cops who doesn't show much," Deevers said.

"Well," Morgan said, "more like one of those cops who can stay focused on the job. When he's off work, I don't know. Maybe he beats the hell out of punching bag over at the 'Y'."

"That's what I do," Deevers said. "I run my legs off. He really joined the YMCA?"

"I think he's been a life-long member," Morgan said, happy to talk about something that wasn't so personal as how his partner was dealing with his mother's approaching death. "Works out several nights a week. All kinds of cardio. Me, I do my push-ups, sit-ups, and pull-ups and get in the occasional jog, that's enough."

"Does he have a girl friend?"

"You interested?"

"No," Deevers said with a grin. "But he looks like the kind of guy who ought to be married."

"I've tried to talk him out of that idea," Morgan said, returning the grin. "Personally, I haven't been too successful at it."

"Me, neither."

"He dates," Morgan said, "but there's not been anyone special, not yet at least." He saw Hamme emerging from the nursing home. "That was short."

"We should have brought more techs," Deevers said. "I'll be with them."

Morgan nodded absently, watching Hamme walk back.

"She was sleeping," Hamme said as he approached Morgan. "They said she'd been tossing and turning all night but was peaceful now. I didn't want to wake her."

"Well," Morgan said, "let's set them up for the next sweep."

"All right," Hamme said. "Did they find anything?"

"Deevers doesn't think so," Morgan said. He clapped his hands to get everyone's attention and the line formed again.

By lunch time, the field had been thoroughly swept. The forensics technicians had a couple of boxes full of plastic bags of various kinds but Deevers had not been optimistic about what they might have turned up.

"No," she said as everyone got into their vehicles, "we didn't find the perp's driver's license."

"I was counting on that," Morgan said in reply and Hamme smiled slightly.

Morgan made a point of thanking each member of the search team for their help. It didn't take that much time and the verbal recognition would be all any of them got for the several hours of slowly examining the cold ground. Besides, the possibility existed that he would be working with one or the other of them at some time in the future and building good relations among law enforcement officers was always a good idea.

Morgan followed Hamme who followed the technician van back to the task force headquarters. Once there, he watched them for a few minutes record the arrival of each bag. The techs would be distributing the material found in the sweeps to several labs; Morgan did not envy them the record keeping needed to avoid breaking the chain of evidence.

The task force had been expanded by more than making Morgan and Hamme full-time. The state was providing several more detectives from the troopers and the FBI supplied another handful of agents – Morgan thought that odd, given that Agent Bargan had been sent south and wondered if there wasn't more to the story – and a senior forensics technician. Along with them, police officers from throughout the county came to the task force's second floor headquarters. Callahan decided to conduct a briefing to bring all the new arrivals and the local cops up to speed.

Callahan asked Morgan and Hamme to be present though he reassured them did not have to say anything. Deevers apparently managed to escape and was away doing something far more useful, Morgan suspected.

Actually, in spite of his expectation, the briefing was a good one. Callahan had a way with presenting material that linked it all together. He even managed to use PowerPoint in a fashion that didn't put anyone to sleep nor did it distract from the points he made.

On the other hand, the briefing seemed to go on forever. Part of it was, of course, Morgan had heard all of the information before, but Callahan seemed to be drawing it out. Morgan smiled; perhaps the agent liked being in front.

Morgan guessed that he and Hamme were there to provide some window dressing, so the local cops would see that the FBI and the commonwealth investigators, the people actually running things, were taking the local law enforcement community seriously. Morgan thought that was true for the most part and didn't resent being used in that fashion. Besides, technically the investigation was led by Sheriff Walsh. As a practical matter, once the FBI and other federal agencies moved in, the real power shifted. Still, if there were any major announcements for the news, they would come from the Sheriff's office.

The local cops had most of the questions and Morgan guessed the others figured to get more, in-depth information during later discussions. He was surprised when Callahan responded to a question about the latest killing by nodding at Hamme.

"Actually," Callahan said, "that officer you referred to is here. Deputy Hamme, can you walk the group through what you saw and what you did yesterday?"

Hamme also was surprised but he recovered quickly and stood up. Callahan did something with his laptop and the projector suddenly flashed an aerial map of the intersection of Bartram and Sparrow Roads. He adjusted it and soon the entire area from the nursing home up to Bartram filled the screen.

Hamme did pretty well, Morgan thought, especially for someone who was not expecting to be called on. Maybe especially for someone whose mother was dying in the white, U-shaped building that sat in the bottom of the picture. As Hamme finished, there were a couple of follow-up questions and Hamme handled them well, using his hand as a guide as he indicated a position in the field. He nodded to Callahan and returned to his seat.

"Preliminary evidence gathering beyond the body," Callahan said, "took place last night. This included the victim's clothing, hair and a few items that might or might not relate to the crime. This morning, Deputy Craig Morgan oversaw a thorough sweep of the area utilizing deputies from the Chester County Sheriff's Department, several local police, and troopers of the Pennsylvania State Police." Morgan noticed that Callahan got the troopers' agency right – they weren't the "Highway Patrol."

Callahan turned to Morgan and asked him to discuss the sweeps and Morgan stood up. He could see the reaction of the group – all of them probably had done dozens of such sweeps in their careers and this was going to be very boring unless he had something dramatic to give them. He didn't, so he made it brief.

"We used thirty officers," he said, not bothering to move from his chair, "and did three sweeps from different angles. Special Agent Deevers supervised the techs who bagged what we found. We found a ton of stuff and most of it will be crap, of course." He paused when a few people chuckled and the rest smiled. "All the material found is being processed in three different forensics labs to speed things up." That got a few approving nods. "Questions?" There were none and Morgan happily sat down. Talking to groups of people, in spite of the Sheriff's Department's many community outreach functions, still was not easy for him.

Callahan seemed reluctant to quit and launched himself into a discussion of the chains of command among the various law enforcement agencies.

Morgan could see he was losing the audience's attention but the agent kept on. He paused as Karen Deevers entered the room.

Morgan glanced at his watch. The whole briefing had taken a lot longer than he had anticipated and, though there were times when it seemed to drag, things seemed to have moved along. It was probably a measure of Callahan's speaking ability that the time had gone by so quickly.

Deevers stood in the back and made eye contact with Callahan. She gently shook her head negatively and he raised his eyebrows but continued for a moment before closing the meeting. With everything done, the local police formed small groups and talked among themselves for a few minutes, doing a little networking before they left. The new people to the task force followed Callahan out of the conference room, probably to get individual briefings.

Deevers walked over to Morgan and Hamme.

"That was a good sweep this morning," she said. She looked at Hamme. "You remember when we stopped the line for that red-headed tech?"

"I think so," Hamme said. "Second sweep?"

"Right," she said. She turned back to Morgan. "A trooper found a scrap of paper. It was away from the shortest direct line from Sparrow Road to the site but it was dry and on top of the weeds."

"Windblown?" Morgan asked.

"Might have been," Deevers said. "It's very fresh. The techs say it can't have been in the field for more than one night. It still had some of its crispness."

"What was it?" Hamme asked.

"A receipt of some kind," Deevers said. "Maybe for gas."

"You think the killer may have dropped it?" Morgan asked. It seemed improbable. The killer was very thorough and some of the investigators thought he policed the area after himself and probably made a point of not taking anything into the site.

"It hasn't been there very long," Deevers said. "Maybe it belongs to the victim. But it's the kind of thing that may turn into a break."

Morgan nodded; they were due for some luck but he didn't want to get his hopes up. It was far more likely that it blew into the field from some passing car, maybe even one of the responders that parked across the road last night.

Later, Morgan and Hamme went to their table. Though they had to share the same table, they each had their own laptop computer tied into the local area network though not into the internet. With a few clicks, Morgan saw the preliminary autopsy report of the latest victim – he did not use her name, a common self-defense practice of police officers – and it confirmed everything the doctors had said. He shook his head but read every word. When he was done, he leaned back in his chair and stretched.

"That receipt," he started to say to Hamme but the other deputy interrupted him.

"That *possible* receipt," Hamme said.

"Right," Morgan agreed. "Possible. I was thinking, I don't think it likely that the killer dropped it."

"Why not?" Hamme leaned forward, putting his elbows on the table.

"I think he goes clean into the site," Morgan said. "Right, he probably wears rain gear of some kind to keep the blood off. Maybe one of those disposable rain suits and burns it afterwards and they think he checks the area before leaving. But I don't think he brings anything into the site other than the victim and his knife. You know, he might empty his pockets before he goes on the prowl and keeps his wallet in his vehicle so he has I.D. in case he's stopped. But nothing goes with him."

"Could be," Hamme said. "So, the receipt has nothing to do with him?"

"I didn't say that," Morgan said. "It might have come from his vehicle. You know, he got gas some place, maybe weeks ago, and stuffed the receipt down beside the seat or something, or he used a trash bag and it's torn. In any case, it was flopping around inside his car and when he got out with her, it fell outside. The breeze put it in the field."

"I suppose that's possible," Hamme said, nodding. "If it's a gas receipt, then he's toast. The date-time stamp, the station number, and the last four of his credit card will be on it. We have him even if there isn't a fingerprint on it."

"It's not a gas receipt," Morgan said. "She could see what it was and a gas station receipt is pretty clear."

"I think I agree," Hamme said, pausing as he thought back to what the FBI agent had said. "But maybe Deevers was just being typical conservative Fee-Bee. She won't say positively it is a gas receipt until the some friggin' Saudi prince flies in and lays his hands on it and a ray of light descends from heaven and the angels sing."

"No," Morgan said, smiling. "She could see it through the plastic evidence bag. And if it's that fresh, then they can read what it says. If it was a gas receipt, or any kind of a receipt with credit card info on it, they would have run it before we left the field. Right about now we'd all be converging on the perp's house, guns drawn."

"What you're saying is, it's not a credit card receipt." Hamme shook his head and smiled slightly. "You just made a good case how it might have gotten into the field. That could happen, despite the perpetrator's care. Part of the risk of the game. Question is, what do you think they have?"

"Probably a receipt, sure," Morgan said. "Obviously not one that has credit card info on it. That would be too sweet. No, it's probably a cash receipt, maybe from a pizza place or some other outfit." He shrugged. "It will be a lead to check out but…"

Morgan didn't have to add anything and Hamme nodded. *If* it was a receipt and *if* it belonged to the killer, then it would be useful *if* some clerk somewhere could remember who it was made a purchase just like a hundred other people at about the same time on the same day. Unlike television, people's memories of who they sold something to even the day before tended to be unreliable. They wouldn't know if it belonged to the killer or some passing motorist littering from the day before the body was found.

"Pretty thin," Hamme said.

"Better than nothing," Morgan said and smiled ironically. He was grasping at straws and knew it. "Hey, catch the time."

"I've got to finish the autopsy report," Hamme said, gesturing at his LCD screen. "They never use one word where five will fit."

"Doctors," Morgan said. He got up and walked down the hall to the task force dispatcher.

"Don't forget to log out," the dispatcher, a young man who was reading a copy of a computer magazine. He pointed at a display screen that was swiveled so people walking by could see it. "That will show you gone for the day."

Morgan looked and saw that a number of the federal people already were gone and had left a half hour before. *Slipping out a little early?* He shook his head as he walked back to his table. It made no sense that the day after the discovery of the body people would leave work early. Hell, just reviewing the generated paperwork from the autopsy had taken him more than an hour and Hamme was still at it.

Then he remembered that they all had left at the same time and nodded to himself, grimacing. He wouldn't mention to Hamme his suspicion that the feds were having a private meeting away from the other task force members. *Just like those people.*

"Forgot to log out," Morgan said to Hamme as he walked past. With a few keystrokes, he completed the task. "You have a good evening," he said to Hamme.

"You, too," Hamme said, his eyes still on his screen.

"Hey," Morgan said, turning. "I hope your mom is better."

"Thanks," Hamme said. He held up his hand and waved but kept reading.

Morgan went downstairs and then walked to the parking garage used by the deputies for their private cars. He got into his older model Subaru Forester and slowly made his way out to the street.

He glanced at the time and decided to swing by Klemmer's and see what the former psychologist was working on. He smiled slightly to himself. After the work of the day, this would be something a little different for his mind to get around.

Chapter 27

Ellen Parker put down the telephone receiver and looked around the crowded floor; the usual afternoon scurry was well underway as people hurried to get their pieces done. Johnson, though, was gone; the board outside his office was not helpful: the magnetic marker lay on "Gone Fishin'," which probably meant something in Johnson-code. She wanted to talk with him about Klemmer.

Since a county deputy found the ninth victim, Johnson had been gone a lot, mostly trying to look over the shoulders of Special Agent Callahan. Apparently, Callahan had sealed his lips tight and Johnson, to his disappointment, was not getting anything from the task force that the other reporters weren't getting.

Still, that didn't keep him from trying. Besides, all reporters simultaneously worked more than one story at a time and Johnson had more irons in the fire than the serial killer story. He wasn't like some who would save time by simply rewriting the press releases handed to him. Her supervisor had a desperate need to *know*, something that Ellen identified with, so he was probably somewhere interviewing someone.

And, as usual, Johnson did not answer his cell phone, content to let callers be diverted to his voice messaging. She had left messages but there had been no response.

Now Klemmer was willing to talk to her again and Ellen wanted to go but she couldn't find Johnson. She was "off the leash" but technically she still had to check out with her supervisor.

Finally, Ellen picked up her coat – she wouldn't need it; Philadelphia was pretending it was summer today but might snow tomorrow – and put a sticky note on Johnson's desk.

Gone to see Klemmer.

Better to ask forgiveness than permission.

An hour later, she eased her car onto Klemmer's long driveway and heard the gravel ping lightly against the bottom as she made her way to the parking area. She got out of her car without her coat and heard the high whine of a powered saw coming from the workshop.

Ellen paused and looked into the barn. The barn was very dark and, though the floor seemed solid and in good repair, Ellen had not, in her previous visit, learned where the light switch was and she did not want to trip over some piece of rare and expensive wood trying to get to the connecting door to the path to the workshop. As if accentuating the darkness, the back door of the barn was slightly open but the light did not help much. She turned away and walked around the corner of the workshop.

Klemmer had the workshop door open, probably to let in the fresh spring air. Ellen paused at the opening and watched Klemmer work for a moment. He was cutting long, thin lengths of wood from a heavy board and was wearing a set of ear protectors; Ellen kept her fingers in her ears. She waited until he reached up and turned off the saw.

"Good afternoon," she said. Klemmer gave a small start and then he turned. He smiled as he saw her.

"Ah," he replied, "Ms. Parker." He put down the length wood he held and took off the headset then walked forward, extending his hand. "Good afternoon."

They shook hands and Ellen looked around.

"New project?"

"Ongoing," he said. "Home repair. My home. Never buy an old house. Especially one made of wood. Will you take coffee or tea?" He led the way from the workshop, turning off the lights as he stepped through the door.

"Tea would be great," she said. "I didn't mention it before but this is a nice place you have here."

"Thanks," Klemmer said. "It's a little isolated for some people's taste but I like it. My saws might disturb close neighbors." He stopped as he was about to turn the corner of the workshop. "Out back there," he said pointing, "beyond the corn field, do you see the tree line?" Ellen nodded.

"There's a horse ranch over there," he said. "One of their ponies got out and I found her. She had made her way through the corn leavings and got caught in the rain. She actually stuck her head into the barn. Poor thing had gotten loose, got wet and was looking for shelter." He smiled. "I got a rope around her, she didn't mind, and called around and they came and got her. I'm a hero to the horsey-set now." He winked at Ellen. "I never cared for horses;

anything that big with teeth should be avoided, not ridden, but they've offered to teach me to ride."

"I already know," Ellen said. "It's fun."

"Country girl," Klemmer said and continued on, Ellen close behind.

They were soon at the kitchen table. Klemmer stirred his tea and then looked up.

"No pre-arranged questions?"

"No," Ellen said. "Regular interview. I write it up but it won't be published."

"Ah," Klemmer said, "an exercise."

"More than that," she said quickly. 'We really want to get your perspective. It helped a lot with the sidebar."

"I read it," Klemmer said. "Interesting but obvious." Before Ellen could reply, he continued. "Tell me, how are you handling all of this, if you don't mind my asking?"

"Handling...?"

"Graduate school, for one," Klemmer said. "I hated it. Half was busy work, a portion was detrimental to good mental health, and the last minority piece actually made a contribution to my development as a psychologist." He sipped from his tea, his eyes on Ellen.

"It's all right," Ellen said. "The program is well designed. The part I liked was the use of journalists – we had all kinds coming in talking about their work and issues."

"I can see how that would help," Klemmer said. "Sort of a reality check. My program was strictly academics. On the personal side, what's it been like?"

"There's no time for a 'personal side,'" Ellen grinned.

"No," Klemmer said. "I meant for you, being exposed to all this, having to delve into the area of human violence. What is that like?" He held up a hand. "If you don't mind discussing it."

"That's all right," Ellen said slowly. She paused and then looked at Klemmer, her eyes sharp, the falcon-brown looking more like the bird. "You've learned about my history."

"No offense intended," Klemmer said. His voice was calm, matter of fact. "I wanted to know who I was talking to. I got onto the internet and found your student listing. It mentioned you were from Ohio. I followed that and read some things online from the local papers. I hope you are not offended."

"I'm not," Ellen said after a second. "It's a reasonable thing to do." She smiled slightly. "I do it with just about everyone whose name crosses my desk." The smile faded. "It is not easy."

"From what I read," Klemmer said slowly, "you lost a cousin to violence. I would guess the reminders of that are not pleasant."

"That's not the problem," Ellen said. She stopped but Klemmer remained silent. Finally, she continued. "It used to be. Any time I would see something violent, even make-believe violence on television, I would be disturbed. Bad dreams, all that."

"That changed." Klemmer was not asking.

"Yes," Ellen said. She looked at her teacup. "I don't want to go into the details. But one of the things I learned from the death of Eileen and the aftermath was how easy it is to kill." She looked up at Klemmer. "Is it my turn to say 'no offense intended'?"

Klemmer simply smiled and shook his head.

"Anyway, I'm afraid much of the time when I think about this stuff," Ellen said. "I guess I'm afraid of what it might do to me."

"Reasonable fears," Klemmer said. "Reality based." He paused. "It is very easy to kill, easier than a lot of people can comprehend, including, unfortunately, many people who kill." He sipped at his tea and then looked at Ellen. "But, nonetheless, here you are, sitting at the table of a convicted murderer. How did that happen?"

"Just lucky, I guess," Ellen said, smiling wryly.

Klemmer laughed.

"Well, perhaps," he said. "Look, being afraid, that happens. Having fear, though, doesn't say much about you. It's what you do when you are afraid that matters."

"That's what my Grandpa Tom said," Ellen said. "He said that courage is doing the right thing when you were so afraid you thought you were going to pee yourself." She smiled. "He phrased it differently when I was very young and I took it as a sign of his recognition of my maturity when he let himself say 'pee' and 'damn' in front of me."

"I'm glad to see my position is endorsed by your grandfather," Klemmer said and made a half bow. "Nice to get support from someone who isn't a killer."

Ellen smiled and said nothing.

"Now, what did you want to interview me about?"

"The latest killing," Ellen said as she pulled her small bag up. She took out a micro-recorder and raised her eyebrows and Klemmer nodded. She turned it on and a tiny red light appeared. "The information we've gotten suggests the killer was particularly savage this time. Even the official news release from the police indicated a higher level of violence. And doing it between two traveled roads, a couple of hundred yards from a nursing home staffed 24-7, that seemed to me to be a pretty good sign he's escalating the violence."

"You're right," Klemmer said. "If you look at the dates of the killings, you'll see that, after number three of the latest nine, each killing took place in time a little closer to the previous one. His drive is increasing."

"Why?"

"Well," Klemmer said, "that's the key question. The obvious answer, and I think it is definitely playing a role, essentially is internal. The addiction to the violence, over time, requires a greater degree of risk-taking to get the same thrill."

"Sort of like sky divers who become BASE jumpers."

"Exactly like them," Klemmer said. "Probably the same reinforcing brain chemistry. So that's one of the internal drives. The other is the deterioration of his control mechanisms. Some serial killers are very well disciplined and can shut down their activities for years at a time, either from choice or because of circumstances, such as incarceration. But that discipline is under assault all the time – what they do is addicting and satisfies needs that are exceptionally powerful."

"His controls may be falling apart?"

"Yes," Klemmer said. "I would expect he will eventually reassert his control, possibly after a close-call with the law. He seems to have done that in the past. But all that is obvious, those internal sources of pressure. I think there's an external source."

"What do you mean?"

"Remember," Klemmer said, "a lot of investigators think serial killers are made, not born. Whatever the genetics or biochemistry, something special has to happen to affect the normally developed social links that define us human beings. That's an external source of stress that the killer responds to. Killers like this are not oblivious to stress, they are not 'Terminators.' They're not robots."

"Cyborgs."

"They're not them, either," Klemmer said, smiling at Ellen's correction. "There can be events in the killer's life that he responds to by going out and killing."

"Like what kinds of stress?"

"Bad relationships are big on the trigger list. A rotten, over-bearing boss, a nasty spouse, and it really hinges on the killer's *perception* of the source of the stress. In other words, the wife might not be nasty. Maybe she is passive, bland, non-provocative, but she wears a color that reminds him of someone who was, like his mother or an abusive uncle." He sipped at his tea.

"Can we tell what's going on in this man's life?"

"I don't know the specifics," Klemmer said. "I think the rate of escalation is so sharp there has to be something else going on than simply needing a greater thrill. Maybe someone is kicking his ass at work in a way that hasn't happened before. Maybe he's feeling pressured to make his point by a particular time."

"What point?"

"'I am powerful,' 'I have control,' 'I can get revenge,' all of the above, probably more." Klemmer shrugged. "'I can show *you*,' is a favorite, with the *you* being the person the killer views as the source of their pain."

"Why don't they just kill *that* person? Why hurt anyone else?"

"Fear," Klemmer said. "They often can't get themselves to go after that all-powerful person who so damaged them. Sometimes they do. They start with their father, for example, but it's not enough so they keep on. It will never be enough. Those scales can never be balanced."

Ellen nodded. She thought for a moment.

"You're a psychologist…"

"*Was*," Klemmer emphasized.

"All right," she said. "Whatever. My question is, how do you treat someone like this?"

"You don't," Klemmer said. "Psychotherapy has nothing to offer serial murderers. First off, they don't see themselves as having a problem. 'Catch me before I kill again' is a taunt, not a plea for help. The things you read about 'cooperative' serial killers in prison are people who are still trying to control the world around them. They read the same books as you do and know what to say to sound sincere." He shook his head. "They are not like other killers." He pursed his lips for a moment.

179

"They are not like me," he said quietly. "Typically, they are incapable of regret. The wiring of their brains is different, I believe." He sighed. "As individuals, humans can barely survive."

"You mean in the wild or in prehistoric times."

"Not just physical survival," Klemmer said. "We need people; it's one of our defining characteristics." He licked his lips and folded his arms, thinking. "Look, take a bunch of newborns, take care of every physical need they might have. Food, water, shelter. Medicine. But don't touch them, maybe because you're concerned about spreading germs. Lots of hospitals operated in that fashion in the past." He reached for his cup and found it empty. He held it up and looked at Ellen, raising an eyebrow as he stood.

"I'm fine," she said.

Klemmer put his cup in the sink and then opened the refrigerator. He took out a bottle of root beer and popped the cap. He sat down across from Ellen.

"Where was I?"

"Untouched babies," Ellen said.

"Right. A certain number of them will die. Now, and there's been research on this, have your nurses hold and talk to each baby every day. The death rate goes down. The same kind of data came out of the Korean War prisoner of war experience. We cannot tolerate prolonged isolation. Worst thing you can do is send someone to prison. Worst thing you can do *there* is send someone to solitary confinement. It can drive people crazy and makes the crazy crazier. But that doesn't do much to a serial killer. They lack the ability to form the social links that define us as human. Without that ability, we're not human."

"Whoa," Ellen said. "Are you saying a serial killer is not a human being?"

"Only legally," Klemmer said. "A human is more than a body. You can have someone lose their body parts and still be a human. The brain defines us as human. Serial killers' brains are different. Similar shape and form and chemistry but, no, not human. We are closer to wolves than to serial killers." He smiled slightly. "I like wolves, so that's my bias."

"If we accept your definition of the need for social linkage to define someone as human…"

"Even babies have it," Klemmer said, interrupting. "It's innate, not learned." He took a sip of soda. "Almost every species on earth has that need for social linkage, by the way. That lack makes for aliens, something not of this earth."

"But if we accept that idea," Ellen said, "then what do we do with them?"

"Good question," Klemmer said. "I had a conversation with Agent Callahan about that question. All we could agree on was they would have to be locked away forever." He shrugged. "And I am not the person to be saying that the alternative is to take them out in the forest some place and put a bullet through their head. That, by the way, is what our ever-pragmatic Russian friends do."

"Has there been research into treating serial murderers?"

"Yes," Klemmer said, nodding. "No one's found the magic cure. I think it's because there are too many ways to arrive at that kind of behavior *and* we simply don't know enough about the working of the brain. Drugs might suppress behavior but the individual has not changed and remains dangerous indefinitely."

"This one," Ellen said, "he's been pretty good at covering his tracks. If he's losing control, won't he start to leave clues?"

"True," Klemmer replied. "Probably. He may have been leaving them behind all along and we just haven't recognized them." He smiled. "Or the investigators have and they haven't told me. They play their cards close to the vest." He took another drink. "But you're right. We may see more." He paused. "This one has been meticulous."

"He's been very careful."

"Indeed," Klemmer said. "He may be familiar with forensic procedures." He shook his head. "Like a police officer."

"A police officer who's a serial killer," Ellen said, "seems to be a tough thing to believe. And wouldn't such a person be spotted by the people around him?"

"It's very rare," Klemmer admitted. "There was Gerard Schaefer. And you are right about being spotted. Schaefer was when he concocted a story about two girls he had had under his control briefly but had left and they escaped." He shook his head. "He was becoming disorganized but it is generally thought he had other victims never identified. There may be other police officers who were serial killers, but it would be very hard for someone so lacking in empathy to remain a police officer for a prolonged period of time." He smiled. "It's the empathy that makes being a cop so hard. A lot of them crash and burn, traumatized by all that they see. A serial killer would not have that empathy. But it can happen. On the other hand, lots of people are *CSI:* fanatics and a bright killer would read and refine his technique even without knowing the details of the science."

"So, you *don't* think it is a police officer."

"I *hope* it isn't," Klemmer said. He smiled almost shyly. "Such a killer would be very well camouflaged. If self-disciplined, unlike Schaefer he might never be suspected. The task force profilers don't think it is, or so they say. I can't be sure *what* they think. Agent Callahan is very careful about that kind of thing. He doesn't want me to be a leak."

"We're still on deep background," Ellen reminded him. "Informational purposes only, no attribution."

"Good," Klemmer said. He eyed the recorder and then stretched. "All the guesses aside, I think the only thing I'm sure of is, whoever the killer is, he's on the edge of losing it."

Chapter 28

It is like walking with thunder. With every beat of his heart, he feels the pressure. There is so little time left and the need to strike intensifies with each passing minute. He stares at his cell phone lying in his hand and expects it to ring.

He knows what they will say; they've said such things before. They will do it automatically, needing to distance themselves from the flood of grief they anticipate he will feel.

They are, of course, wrong. He does not feel grief, has not felt it in decades. He feels...

The Excitement. Of course, he feels that, feels it now as it reaches from deep inside him and touches his heart. It is the source of the thunder and it is strong.

Anger. And hate. Yes, he feels them. Perhaps they are the fire that super-heats The Excitement. He mentally shrugs. He doesn't care about explanations. Fear? He has not felt fear since his childhood and those memories are not, he admits, terribly reliable. What he is has changed, he knows, how he sees the past.

There is little else he feels. There is no love, no guilt. He is immune to those weaknesses.

He is careful, precise, and being that way makes him feel... What? Satisfaction?

The people around him do not suspect what he does, he is certain of that, and that is another reason he holds them all in contempt. What does he have to do, hang a woman spread-eagle from his porch roof for the school kids to see while they wait for their bus? The idea has a certain attractiveness but he pushes it away. Just because they are all blind idiots does not mean he needs to be a fool.

He looks at the cell phone; it does not ring. He wants it to ring. He wants it to ring more than he's wanted anything in his life. And he doesn't want it to ring. He wants more time, more time to send his message, his proof, to the one he hates.

He has told her. She cannot respond, trapped inside her destroyed body and brain. But he has told her. He has told her what he has done and what she has created. He has offered the proof of her vileness in the form of those dead women, dead women whose hair is like hers. Dead whores more important in her life than he was.

He smiles. Not that more proof is needed. Perhaps he has made his point. Perhaps that was all it was when he began. But now what he does, taking down those worthless women, it has a life – he sees no irony in the word – of its own, a power of its own. And in considering the idea he discovers he has one emotion he has not thought was his.

Joy.

Bobby Hamme smiles.

Paul Callahan and Karen Deevers sat in silence, each reading a handful of papers. Deevers finished first and put the papers back on Callahan's desk.

"Damn," she said.

Callahan nodded and kept reading. As he did, he reached and pulled Deever's papers face-down to him; he did not want anyone else seeing them. Finally, he looked up.

"He holds his mother responsible for the death of his father. But the evidence of childhood abuse is a little thin."

"You're a profiler, Paul," Deevers said. "You know it often is." She nodded at the report. "But that background information is pretty solid. She was at least neglectful at a time when he needed support and even before. The police report said her BAL was positive on the scene. She had a prior DUI offense." She shrugged. "The woman was an alcoholic. By definition, that's abuse. After his father's death, Hamme was alone. She was away from home a lot, heavily involved in social and charity functions."

"It's an impressive list," Callahan said. "The dates of involvement certainly spike upward after her husband's death."

"Wind sprint," Deevers said. "Trying to race to the finish line of acceptance from the Main Line. I guess she never really made it."

"And where did all that disappointment go?" He leaned back in his chair. "It might have become resentment towards her son. A single mother would have a tough time breaking into that social arena."

"Kerosene to a fire already burning." She leaned back in her chair. "I do not think Bobby Hamme had any happy times as a child."

"These reports," he gestured at the papers, "give us historical and evidentiary data. He had a lousy upbringing. He might not have been able to see the body's clothes the way he says he did."

"I don't think it takes us to trial," Deevers said.

"What seals it for me," Callahan said, "is he did the latest one in the field, near where his mother is kept."

"It's worse than that," she said. "Did you know you can see the field from her room? I checked."

"He wanted to send her a message," Callahan said. "He doesn't have much time left to send that kind of message. She could go at any time. There's one source of pressure."

"His judgment is falling apart," Deevers said. "The risk he took was extraordinary. He had to know that someone might have driven up that road while he was in the field…"

"And someone did," Callahan said, tapping lightly the small stack of papers.

"No license number, unfortunately."

"What, you want it easy?" Callahan grinned.

"Yes, please," Deevers replied. "A 'light-colored' van from a glasses-wearing witness who admits to being exhausted and who drove by in the dark. She's not even sure where along Sparrow Road she saw it. And Hamme, probably so wrapped up in what he was doing, never looked over his shoulder."

"Such vans were seen in possible connection with several other killings." Callahan's voice was cautious.

"Such vans may be the most common vehicle in America," Deevers said. "Remember DC?"

Callahan nodded. A serial sniper and his young protégé had killed ten people in 2002 around DC. Though they used a blue Chevrolet Caprice, reports of a "white van" near several killings had led to target fixation; after the two killers were caught it turned out that police had several times seen the blue car and even stopped it but did not realize what it was. Even after the blue Chevrolet was suspected, police officers who ran across the car did not get the word about it and let it go. It took an alert civilian finally to catch the two while they slept in the car.

"His van is white," Callahan said.

"We don't have enough for a warrant. We can't search it."

"He could not have seen the body. You checked."

"We don't *think* he could have seen the body," Deevers said. "The height of his head while in the van doesn't look like it would permit seeing any of the victim's clothing." She shook her head. "I took that rental van up and down the road, running the video camera. The forensic techs are pretty emphatic that too many of the dead weeds had been crushed during the sweeps to be sure if they shielded the clothing." She shrugged. "The site photos suggest they *probably* were high enough to block the view but it's not clear."

"Hamme volunteered to watch sites."

"Just so he could get his jollies on company time," Deevers said. "That means something to profilers but isn't proof of anything other than a desire to score some overtime."

"We've ratcheted up the pressure on him," Callahan said. "The business of the receipt…"

"I still think that was a good move. The problem is keeping eyes on him." She shook her head. "I think that kind of thing may push him into reacting but the problem is continuous covert surveillance on a police officer is hard. He's been out of sight several times. Maybe he took the opportunity to destroy his souvenirs or other evidence. Maybe we'll get lucky."

"He doesn't know the new people," Callahan said. "He doesn't know we brought them in to watch him. He doesn't know of the others we have who have not been introduced to the team."

"Maybe the Air Force can loan us a Predator," Deevers said. "Now that the war's over, they might have one to spare."

"I'll look into it," Callahan said. "Look, we have to be patient. Robert Hamme is our man. We have people watching him, though not yet 24/7. We're gathering information on his whereabouts for all of the killings, including the past ones. We have to walk on tip-toes but we are walking." He smiled slightly. "Sooner or later we will have him."

Morgan looked across the highly polished wood on Klemmer's work table, his eye almost even with the tabletop, and nodded.

"About two feet down," he said and Klemmer nodded. "I'll be damned."

"The light has to be right," Klemmer said. He swept the tabletop with his hand. "You can't feel it."

"A tiny trapdoor in a dining table?" Morgan said, standing up. "What did they use it for?"

186

"The story is that the owner, who was some kind of nobleman, hid poison there to sprinkle on his guests' food." He pointed at one of the detached legs. "A thin wire came down in a narrow groove in that leg. He could pull it, the small trapdoor drops open, he reaches in and takes out the vial."

"And if he has a big bird for carving in front of him," Morgan said, nodding, "no one might notice. Puts the poison on the slice he gives the guest." He smiled. "That's pretty slick."

"Well," Klemmer said, "that's the story, anyway. I tend to think this was just a large writing table, a desk for some official, and the trapdoor opened a small space for storing ink or maybe even secret messages."

"The French, man," Morgan said, shaking his head.

Morgan followed Klemmer from the workshop and across the parking area to the kitchen. They took their usual seats at the table as Klemmer opened the refrigerator.

"Do you like root beer?"

"Sure," Morgan said. "Haven't had any since I was a kid."

Klemmer walked to the table and put a brown bottle in front of him.

"Try this," he said. "It's local." He smiled. "I'm an evangelist for local goods and services."

Morgan took a large swallow.

"That is good," he said.

"Dutch make it," Klemmer said. "I think this is better than their birch beer but I like that, too."

"Where'd you get it?"

"Farmer's market," Klemmer said. "Up at 23 and 10."

"The one at Morgantown?" Morgan asked. Klemmer nodded. "I know it. I'll have to stop by."

"I don't go that far north usually," Klemmer said. "There's another place in Lancaster and, of course, I do a lot of shopping over in Kennett."

"I get over to Kennett for Mexican food," Morgan said. "Couple of good places there."

"If all the posters are in Spanish," Klemmer said, "you know it's a good place."

Their conversations were often like this and Morgan enjoyed the process of talking about things that weren't serious, that had nothing to do with police work or hunting a serial killer. Cabinet working, food, that kind of thing. It was comfortable, relaxed. It was… Normal. He smiled.

Sometimes the subject of the killer came up and Morgan was not surprised when it did.

"Had that reporter intern out again yesterday," Klemmer said. He was slouched in his chair, obviously a little tired after a long day of restoration work.

"Ellen Parker?" Morgan was surprised he remembered her name.

"That's the one. She's getting background stuff from me."

"She know what she's talking about?" Morgan frowned slightly. "A lot of these reporters seem pretty ignorant."

"She's pretty bright," Klemmer said. He waved his bottle as he spoke. "I know what you mean about reporters in general, though. She did her homework and has good questions." He landed the bottle on the table and leaned forward. "Nice person. Callahan referred her to me. He knows her supervisor."

"Ah," Morgan said, not thinking of anything else to say. He took a sip.

"We're mostly talking theory," Klemmer said. "Nothing in terms of actual evidence. I don't get exposed to that."

"Not much to get exposed to," Morgan said, "as far as I can tell." He raised an eyebrow; Callahan talked to Klemmer about the killings? He had not guessed.

"Well," Klemmer said, "do you think they withhold information from members of the task force?"

"Sure," Morgan said. "You know, officially the investigation is being conducted by the county prosecutor's detectives and Sheriff Walsh, but the task force is led by Callahan. He's careful to refer to it as a *coordinating* body only that works for the county but, hell, the task force has all the resources."

"Have to be careful of turf issues," Klemmer said, nodding. "If you catch him, the county prosecutor will do the announcement."

"Or the Sheriff," Morgan said. He smiled. "If she beats him to the microphones."

"The FBI people will fade into the background," Klemmer said, "but they'll make sure every reporter knows their role."

"And then some," Morgan added. "They're not shy about getting the stage lights on." He took a sip and then looked at Klemmer. "You said, *if* we catch him. You don't think we will."

"He's been on and off over the years," Klemmer said. "He may be taking things so intense he's going to have to shut it all down again. He's also very sharp."

"He hasn't left much behind," Morgan agreed. "He knows forensics or he's been pretty lucky."

"Luck has nothing to do with it," Klemmer said. He shrugged and then said, "He might be a cop."

Morgan chuckled.

"No way," he said. "Someone like that, we'd notice."

Klemmer realized immediately he had said too much and silently cursed himself; it had happened before. Was his need for companionship so great that he would babble uncontrollably?

"You're right about that," Klemmer said quickly. "What I meant was, he might be someone who is well educated in police procedures. Someone who's done a lot of reading on evidence gathering, the work of other serial killers, that kind of thing."

"Right," Morgan said. "If he's not some kind of schizophrenic, I figure he's spent a lot of time educating himself. Hell, you can get on the internet and learn just about everything you need to know to be a killer." He took another sip. "Did you get that set of bookshelves finished?"

Grateful for the change in topic, Klemmer nodded.

"Last night," Klemmer said. "Take a look."

He led the way to the front of the house, into the living room. A set of bookshelves with glass-fronted shelves occupied a space against a wall.

"Looks good," Morgan said. He lifted one of the wood-framed covers and slid it into the bookshelf. It moved firmly but smoothly. "I like the different heights. Ordinary sized books on the top shelves and the big kind on the bottom. Nice." He pulled the cover out and gently closed it. There was a soft click as the latch engaged.

"Thanks," Klemmer said. "Now I've got a place to unpack all my books. Nick of time. I joined the History Book Club last month and I can't say no."

"It can be an addiction," Morgan said. "I'm a western and detective novels nut. Only paperbacks but every year I have to clear my shelves of books I won't read again."

The two men continued to talk and made their way back to the kitchen. After a while, Morgan left and Klemmer watched him turn around in the parking area, the black SUV slowly crunching the gravel. Then the car was gone and Klemmer was alone.

It was several minutes before he went back into his house. Klemmer thought about what he had said and, tight-lipped, shook his head. How stupid, how really, really stupid.

He thought about calling Callahan about his slip but did not. He did not want to embarrass himself and, besides, the damage was done, if there was going to be damage. And if he made Callahan angry, then…

Then Klemmer would lose one of the few people he had to talk to and that seemed like the worst thing that could happen.

He was wrong.

Chapter 29

"How did you manage it?" Morgan asked Hamme as the two met in the Sheriff's Department. Hamme was in plain clothes but Morgan was in uniform. Around them, deputies came and went, checking on messages in their mailboxes and exchanging greetings with the two and the dispatcher. Everyone seemed to carry a cup of coffee.

Hamme, a tall Starbucks coffee cup beside him, glanced down at himself and his civilian clothes. He smiled slightly.

"I think they want you to do a briefing this morning," Hamme said. "Put on a dog and pony show for some of the new people. I was over there before coming back to check on my mail and Deevers mentioned it. They said I would be in civvies all day."

"Well, we all have to make sacrifices," Morgan said. Like all the deputies, he griped about wearing his uniform with its bright patches and insignia but, like most, secretly he liked it. "So why the plain clothes?"

"I'm driving one of the new people to some the sites," Hamme said. "The techs have a new man, a real top-notch guy to hear Callahan talk about him. He wants him to see the sites."

"Sounds boring," Morgan said.

"Probably will be," Hamme agreed. "We're taking along the tech that used to be the lead to explain some things. That might be colorful."

"Feds fighting? Sure, we can use it on cable."

"Better than wrestling," Hamme said. "How's Klemmer?"

"All right," Morgan said. He had told Hamme about visiting Klemmer and the look on the deputy's face made it clear he did not approve of talking to the convicted murderer. "I've learned a few things."

"About woodworking?"

"That, for sure," Morgan said. He reached into his mailbox and pulled out a police equipment catalog. He shook his head and dropped it into the trashcan. "He's had a few things to say about our case. They're not giving him any special information but you know he has talked to Callahan."

"Is he still doing that?" Hamme idly leafed through several envelopes and, one by one, dropped them into the trash. "I thought he might be, since Callahan kind of intervened on his behalf."

"Apparently."

"What's he thinking?" Hamme's tone verged on boredom. "Anything useful?"

"Blind guessing," Morgan said, shaking his head. He reached for his own cup of coffee; it was cold but he took a sip anyway. "Thinks the perp knows something about forensics, that's why we don't find much."

"There's a surprise," Hamme said. "The profilers have been saying that for a while."

"He thinks it might be a cop," Morgan said. He frowned at his cup, finished the last of the coffee and dropped it into the trash.

"A cop?" Hamme seemed more interested in some notices on a bulletin board.

"Maybe," Morgan said. "I'm going on over. You coming?"

"No," Hamme said. "I'm picking up the techs at the motel they're using. Catch you later."

Morgan nodded, tugged unconsciously at his shiny leather equipment belt, and left the dispatcher's office.

Hamme, his eyes unseeing, stared at the bulletin board and no one noticed the small bead of sweat that formed on his temple.

The floor was, oddly, calm, as if the newspaper building had slipped into the eye of its usual hurricane. Ellen Parker waved at Jay Enfield, who nodded in return as he typed steadily on his keyboard. She draped her coat – it hadn't been needed this morning – over the back of her chair and walked to Johnson's office.

Jefferson Johnson was in and reading a copy of the newspaper as Ellen appeared in his office doorway.

"I was just thinking of you," Johnson said. "Good morning."

"'Morning," Ellen said. "What's up?"

"Mayor is having a news conference at nine," Johnson said. "I'm going. Come along. I want you to meet a couple of people who are going to be there."

Ellen nodded; Johnson had a network of people he cultivated in the city government. Most were in middle management. *High enough to know what's going on, low enough they're willing to crap on the boss*, was how he referred to them. He regarded learning how to talk to them, to draw them out, as an important skill for Ellen.

"Sounds good," she said.

"And did you get my email about your Klemmer interview?"

"No," Ellen said. "I haven't logged on yet."

"Good idea to do that first," Johnson said. "Take a look at it. I enclosed my critique. I have a few follow-up questions I'd like you to pursue."

"When?"

"How about today?"

"My car's in the shop," Ellen said.

"Not a problem," Johnson said. "Enfield is off the leash to Kennett Square to do some mushrooms. Check with him about times and then give Klemmer a call."

"All right."

Ellen went back to her desk; the placid nature of the floor was gone and everything was settling into its usual morning bustle.

"Are you going to Kennett today?" she asked Enfield as she sat down. "Doing mushrooms?"

"Mushrooms," Enfield repeated, his eyes on the screen. He looked over at Ellen. "I am not doing mushrooms, young woman. Too much driving involved." He smiled slightly. "Yes, this afternoon. What's up?"

"Johnson wants me to see Klemmer for follow-up..."

"Again?"

"Again," she said. Her computer screen came to life and she rapidly called up her inter-office email. Ellen read while talking. "He has a couple of questions based on my interview. I'll try to do it by phone but Klemmer probably will want it to be face to face."

"I remember you saying that was one of his conditions," Enfield said. "No sweat. Don't bother him with it. Just set up a time. The people I'm talking to I meet at five. I can either drop you off and pick you up after my interview or you can take the car and drop me off, depending on the time Klemmer can see you."

"Thanks," Ellen said. "Dinner's on me on the way back."

"Great," Enfield said. "Mexican."

Ellen nodded. Mexican food was something that was still relatively rare to her and it had been a while before she learned that what she had called "Mexican" was, at best, what people called "Tex-Mex."

She glanced at the time and over at Johnson's office. They wouldn't be leaving for the news conference right away. Ellen opened his critique of her interview and began reading.

Hamme was finding it difficult to think. The new forensic technician, someone called Carl Denton, was very talkative but his questions went to the other technician.

I could provide you some answers…

Their chatter seemed to fill the FBI SUV, almost echoing, and breaking almost every thought he had.

Hamme gritted his teeth. He had to think. He forced his thoughts into small sentences, focusing on them.

Klemmer thinks the killer is a cop. Klemmer talks to Callahan. So maybe Callahan thinks it might be a cop. How do I get them to think about something else?

That was the problem. He could not think of an answer.

It was while they were stopped at the Hibernia Park site that Hamme finally had a chance to think it through. While the two techs walked around the area, it came to him.

Klemmer is a known killer. Morgan talks to him. What if Klemmer was up to something, what if Morgan suspected him of something? Hamme felt *The Excitement* building, anticipating where his thoughts were taking him. *What if…?*

Chapter 30

Klemmer was willing, almost eager, to see Ellen again. She explained Enfield's appointment in Kennett Square and her own lack of transportation.

"Any time," he said.

"Great," Enfield said when told. "I'll drop you off and then scoot into Kennett. I'll probably be an hour and then come on out and we'll go get something to eat."

"Sounds like a plan," Ellen agreed.

"Are you going to see Klemmer today?" Hamme asked. He and Morgan were having late lunch at a sandwich shop close to the courthouse.

"Probably," Morgan said. "Why?" Morgan was guarded in his tone. Bobby had made it clear in the past he didn't think much of the convicted murderer.

"Do me a favor when you get out there," Hamme said. He pulled his clamshell cell phone from his pocket. "Give me a call from there. I've been having some reception problems when someone is more than one tower away. They say they've fixed it but…"

"Phone companies," Morgan said. He licked some mustard off his fingertips. "Sure, I can do that. Any particular time?"

"When are you going out there? Right after work?"

"Yes," Morgan said.

"Great," Hamme said. "Sure, as soon as you get there, that would be fine. Thanks a lot."

"Not a problem," Morgan said. He took a bite of his sandwich and felt a little pleased. Hamme had referred to his seeing Klemmer and there hadn't been anything negative in his tone. It seemed his partner finally was settled about Klemmer and him.

The ride from Philadelphia was uneventful, which is to say Enfield drove conservatively. It helped they were going ahead of the worst of the flow of the beginning rush hour traffic. Enfield slipped off 202 and used a series of back roads to get around the traffic lights of small towns. He remembered the directions to Klemmer's drive and was soon easing into the parking area.

"Hey," Enfield said, "he's got company." He nodded towards a large black SUV. It was parked so its front bumper was in line with the side of the barn. The barn had one of its doors slid back but there was nothing to be seen in the darkness. Enfield stopped and Ellen got out.

"I should be back in an hour," Enfield said, leaning across the passenger seat. "You got my number and I have yours if anything comes up to cause a change."

"Got it," Ellen said. "Thanks."

She closed the door and turned towards the barn. Emerging from the darkness was Klemmer closely followed by Deputy Sheriff Morgan. Morgan nodded while Klemmer smiled as he walked forward.

"We heard you coming," Klemmer said. He nodded towards Enfield, who was turning around. "He's not staying?"

"He has an interview in Kennett," Ellen said. "Hello, Deputy Morgan."

"Good to see you, Ms. Parker," Morgan said. "Hell, I almost forgot." He took out his cell phone. "Excuse me," he said and walked a few feet away.

"Cup of tea?" Klemmer asked Ellen who nodded and the two went into the house.

Bobby Hamme stood in the Sheriff's dispatcher office, waiting. It was taking longer than he thought it would but he forced himself to be patient. *The Excitement* told him it would happen and happen exactly as he planned.

Other deputies came and went and Hamme tried to be casual. Someone commented on his being in civilian clothes and Hamme tried to make a joke about it. It was clumsy but he knew he was not known for his wit and a clumsy joke was about his speed normally.

"Did Craig say where he was going after work?" Hamme asked Carolyn, who looked up slightly surprised. Hamme did not engage in ordinary conversation very much.

"No," she said. Curious, she asked, "Did he say anything to you?"

"Something odd," Hamme replied. "He said he wanted to check out something with that Klemmer fellow."

"Task force business? He would have let their dispatcher know."

"I think it was something else," Hamme said. "Just something about that guy…"

At that moment, as if it had been rehearsed, Hamme's cell phone rang. He turned away as he opened it but did not step out of the dispatcher's hearing. He wanted her as a witness.

"Bobby Hamme," he said. "Hey, Morg. How goes it?"

Just fine, Bobby. Are you hearing me all right?

"Fine," Hamme said. "Everything there all right?"

You're coming through loud and clear. No static at all.

Hamme paused for a moment as if listening to something Morgan was saying. He nodded, feeling Carolyn's eyes on his back.

Bobby? You still getting me?

"I got you," Hamme said. "Watch yourself."

Always. See you later.

"Bye." Hamme closed his phone and turned back towards Carolyn, a worried look on his face.

"Everything all right?"

"I don't know," Hamme said. He looked at his cell phone for a moment and then slipped it into his pocket. "That was kind of odd. He said there was something going on with Klemmer and he was checking out a few things at his place."

"Like what?" Carolyn now looked worried.

"He didn't say," Hamme lied. He looked up at the clock on the wall. "You know, just for my own peace of mind I think I'll swing by there on my way home."

"It couldn't hurt," Carolyn said.

"I'll call in when I get there," Hamme said. He tapped the top of the counter and left her office.

Morgan joined the other two in Klemmer's kitchen. He waved off a cup of tea.

"I'm beginning to slosh," he said, smiling. He looked at Ellen. "He just got in some mahogany. It's got a really nice grain and looks as solid as iron."

"I'm using it for a restoration," Klemmer said.

"It's an armoire," Morgan said. "You ought to see it."

"I'd like to," Ellen said. "Where is it?"

"In the workshop," Klemmer said. "The mahogany is in the barn. Finish your tea and we'll take a look. We've got plenty of time."

197

Bobby Hamme resisted the urge to run to his car. It was, he realized, important to keep thinking. He even walked across the street and went up to the task force headquarters. The night shift was on but the area was almost totally deserted. He stood in front of the dispatcher.

"Did Deputy Morgan take a task force vehicle?"

"Yes," the dispatcher said. "Why?"

"Just checking," Hamme said. "I got a call from him a few minutes ago. I wasn't sure if he was in a Sheriff's vehicle or a task force one."

"One of ours," the dispatcher said.

"All right, thanks," Hamme said and turned back to the elevator.

Perfect.

Klemmer obviously loved his work. That much was clear to Ellen. And Deputy Morgan wasn't far behind in his appreciation of the magic that could be done with wood. As Klemmer went into far more detail than was needed, Ellen found she was studying the two men's reactions more than the tall armoire. She smiled. *Now who is the shrink and who is the reporter?*

They went into the barn and Klemmer flipped on the overhead lights. The mahogany consisted of several six-inch wide boards. It was very dark but the grain was darker. To Ellen's eyes, wood was wood but she picked up a little of the enthusiasm of Klemmer and Morgan. After all, the wood *was* beautiful.

The late afternoon light was fading when Klemmer shut off the lights, plunging the barn into darkness.

"Watch your footing," Morgan said. He was at the opening of the barn. "A lot of stuff on the floor."

"It's not that bad," Klemmer protested. He looked over his shoulder at Ellen. "He's always saying I need to get all this reorganized."

Ellen was not having a problem; the light from the slid back barn door formed a path to follow. And it helped a little that both the door to the workshop path and the one out the back of the barn were open.

She had taken a few steps when they heard the low bong of the driveway sensor.

"Ah," Klemmer said. "Someone's coming."

Chapter 31

For Bobby Hamme, it went exactly as he anticipated. He drove his white van into the parking area and stopped beside the black Chevy SUV. Quickly he got out and half-ran the few feet to the SUV's driver's door. He opened it and, using his handcuff key, opened the shotgun rack and pulled free the Remington 870 tactical shotgun.

He walked around the back of the SUV, racking the pump-action slide. Just emerging from the barn was Morgan, looking back over his shoulder, smiling. *Another one of the idiots, talking to his murderer friend.*

Hamme walked forward and Morgan turned to him. For a moment, Morgan looked puzzled, not understanding the significance of the shotgun. Then Hamme whipped the shotgun up to his shoulder, aimed, and fired.

For Craig Morgan, it began as he walked into the light. He looked back at Klemmer and Parker; the young woman was hard to see in the barn's dense shadows. He heard Klemmer say something.

"What?" he asked. Klemmer did not reply and Morgan turned his head and saw Bobby Hamme walking along the side of the SUV. Then Hamme raised the shotgun he carried – Morgan had an instant to wonder what was he doing with a shotgun? – and fired.

There was no time to react, no more time to think. There was only the blast of the shotgun, so loud as to almost be silent, and then darkness.

For Michael Klemmer, it began as he looked toward the stopping van. He saw someone get out and run around its front. It was a second before he recognized Bobby Hamme. By the time he did, Hamme had been in and out of the black SUV.

Klemmer stepped forward to see, his view of the back of the SUV blocked by the barn. He saw the gun in Hamme's hands and his eyes widened. He looked over his shoulder at Ellen. She still had a chance.

"Run," he said, trying to keep his voice low. "Out the back. He has a gun. I'm right behind you."

"What?" Morgan asked, peering back into the darkness of the barn.

For a second, the young woman did not move but then the shotgun fired. Her eyes wide, she turned and ran.

Klemmer turned back toward Morgan; his body lay limply on the ground. When he looked at Hamme, he saw the younger man had laid the shotgun against the side of the black SUV and had drawn his pistol.

Walking forward smoothly, he pointed his pistol at Klemmer and motioned with it for him to move out of the barn. Klemmer did not dare look to see if Ellen was gone. Instead, he stepped forward.

It was time finally to pay off an old debt. He would buy Ellen the time she needed. Klemmer raised his hands and walked slowly out of the barn. He smiled.

For Ellen Parker it began with seeing Deputy Morgan walk ahead as the vehicle – she could not see it from her position within the barn – came to a halt. She heard car doors open and close as she watched her footing. Klemmer was several feet in front of her when he turned.

"Run," the man said, his voice a hurried whisper. "Out the back. He has a gun. I'm right behind you."

Morgan said something but Ellen did not make it out. Klemmer's words sank into her and she froze as if they pinned her to the old planks of the barn floor. What was Klemmer talking about? She could not see Hamme but she was looking directly at Morgan when the shotgun fired. The deputy jerked as part of his uniform shirt flew into the air and then he fell backwards, almost into the barn opening.

She turned for the back door and ran. Her soft shoes were almost silent but she did not appreciate her good fortune in the selection of her footwear. Fear carried her like a wave, though each step seemed to be mired in a nightmare-like substance that held her back.

Ellen skidded to a stop just outside the door. Ahead lay an open field, the previous year's stunted corn rows pointing towards a dark tree line in the distance as if indicating where safety lay. She looked over her shoulder; Klemmer was not with her. She turned further and saw him leaving the barn through the front opening, walking slowly past Morgan, his hands in the air. Just coming into view was a man holding a pistol aimed at Klemmer.

Ellen was terrified and felt the warmth of her urine between her legs. She looked across the field and then towards the corner of the barn. She had to get out of the doorway. She ran to the corner and glanced around it.

She could not see anyone, just the back portion of the SUV Morgan had driven. Beyond it was a white van.

And lying against the black vehicle was a shotgun.

It was happening exactly as it should. Hamme was elated, fully enthralled with *The Excitement*. He had not killed men before; Morgan, who lay still on the ground, was his first and Klemmer would be the second. With his Glock on Klemmer, Hamme looked down at Morgan.

The other deputy was motionless. The 12-guage had hit him in the upper chest and slightly to one side, above his badge. It was hard to tell from the torn uniform shirt and blood, but it looked like the primary point of impact had been at the clavicle. Hamme nodded; he had aimed for the center of Morgan's chest but it wasn't a bad shot. He looked up at Klemmer.

"You've won," Klemmer said, still walking away from the barn.

"Of course," Hamme said. "That's far enough."

The plan was simple. He had witnesses, cell phone records. Morgan had called him. He, Bobby Hamme, loyal partner, had been concerned about his partner talking to the convicted murderer Klemmer. Out of that concern, carefully voiced in front of the dispatcher, he had driven out to Klemmer's, just to check. It was probably nothing. He was shocked to find that Klemmer had gotten his hands on Morgan's shotgun and killed him. Hamme had shot and killed the cop-killer.

That would get everyone's attention and discredit anything Klemmer had said to anyone.

Getting Klemmer's prints on the shotgun would be easy once he was dead. He would even fire a round so the forensic techs could find some powder residue – give those morons something to do.

"So," Klemmer said, "this was all about your mother?"

Hamme's finger, slowly tightening on the trigger, stopped. He could not help himself.

"What the hell do you know about anything?" His voice was a rasp.

"Oh, come on," Klemmer said. His tone was almost conversational. "You're almost a stereotype, a caricature. Do you think it was hard figuring out that you were the one?" He shook his head.

"You don't know," Hamme said. His voice was tense. "No one knows."
"Everyone knows," Klemmer said calmly.

Ellen stared at the shotgun and then looked back across the field. Her mouth was dry as if she had never had a drink of any liquid in her life. She thought she heard voices from the front of the barn.

Get out of here!

The thought was almost a scream within her mind. It repeated and seemed to dominate her thinking so thoroughly she could not hear the voices.

A picture of the Ohio River, stones underfoot, Grandpa Tom gone.

I'm alone.

Eileen…

Then came a thought, a realization that seemed to slip past the screaming thought.

Klemmer is buying me time to get away. He's going to die. For me.

For a second, her heart was on a knife's edge as her fear pulled at her like some kind of viscous undertow. Her lips tightened. One word formed.

No.

She walked quickly forward, towards the SUV, her first steps taken before she fully realized what she was doing. Her lips remained tight and she bit her tongue to keep from crying. Every part of her wanted to go in the other direction. But still she stepped forward.

Ellen looked around the barn's corner. She saw a man, his back to her, his arm stretched forward and holding a pistol. Klemmer stood beyond him, his eye tightly focused on the man, an odd small smile on his face.

"You don't know," Hamme said. "No one knows."
"Everyone knows," Klemmer replied.

Ellen took a breath and stepped to the SUV.

She picked up the Remington. As a girl, her grandfather had taken her to a skeet range exactly once before her father vetoed any more such trips, but her hands handled the weapon with a surprising grace, as if they had never forgotten that morning in the Ohio summer.

The pistol grip was unfamiliar but it helped balance the heavy weapon. She pressed the butt to her shoulder and laid her cheek on the stock. The front sight wavered and Ellen realized she was shaking. Still biting her tongue, she pulled the pump slide all the way to the rear and shoved it forward; the sound was almost a cliché, used in every cheap gun movie she had seen. But now it was real and it sounded like nothing else; a sound of mechanical competency that was more than moving parts made of steel.

It was a warning.

"Everyone knows," Klemmer repeated. "They know what she did to you. They know what you've done since. Your behavior was kind of an obvious response, don't you think?"

He had Hamme's attention and that was all he wanted. Each second meant Ellen was that much further away. Klemmer smiled. He had noticed the Adidas shoes she wore and she looked like one of those young women who ran every day. Perhaps by now she was in the cover of the trees, well on her way to the neighbors' and...

Klemmer saw Ellen come around the corner of the barn, walking steadily forward though he could see the tight tension in her face. He was horrified but he fought to keep his expression steady, his eyes holding Hamme's.

Hamme's eyes narrowed at Klemmer's quick glance past him but it was the sound of the Remington jacking a shotgun shell into its chamber that made him turn his head; it was a sound impossible to mistake for anything else, as distinctive and as dangerous as the buzz of a diamondback.

For a moment, for an eternity, nothing happened. Klemmer understood immediately that Ellen would not fire, could not kill. It was over.

"Put your gun down," Ellen said, her voice wavering. She could not get the heavy shotgun to hold still.

Looking over his shoulder, Hamme saw a young woman. *Who the hell...?* Then he had it – one of the reporters from the park, the one who talked to Callahan. Despite the shotgun in her hands, she was obviously terrified. He moved his eyes. Klemmer was frozen, his face showing nothing but shock, no longer trying to maintain his amused expression. Hamme understood what had happened. *You tried to be a hero, maybe do some penance, and it was for nothing. Too fucking bad.*

The muzzle of the shotgun was all over the place and Hamme knew it wasn't a lack of strength. The girl was shaking. He smiled.

"No," he said. "You put *yours* down." The response struck him as amusing and it was all Hamme could do to keep from laughing. He knew how this was going to go. *The Excitement* grew. "Or I'll shoot him."

Ellen had no reply. She tried to slow her breathing down – from the distant past she remembered that was important when shooting. She could see the side of Hamme's face, could see his smile. He turned a little more and she saw the smile was part of an expression of contempt.

Klemmer saw what was happening and knew he and Ellen were dead. He could think of nothing else to do except what he did. He started to run, his feet slipping in the gravel and doing little more than attracting Hamme's attention. The deputy fired, snapping off a quick shot.

The bullet hit Klemmer's leg like a burning ball peen hammer and he sprawled into the gravel, almost knocking the wind out of him. Hamme looked back at Ellen as the hollow, flat echo of his Glock faded.

The pistol in his hand smoothly moved along an arc, taking it from Klemmer towards Ellen. Ellen knew death was near and then the part of her that had chosen to walk to the shotgun rather than save her own life, the part of her that ran so deep that she had never known it was there until a killer with a gun came into her life, that part surfaced. She felt something, something like anger, like determination, come from within and fill her.

"You don't want to do this," Hamme said, turning. "You'll never be able to live with it."

For a second, a year, everything seemed to freeze.

"I can learn," Ellen said and the red dot on the shotgun's front sight steadied on Hamme.

Hamme spun and crouched at the same time, bringing his gun around to face Ellen. He moved with the speed of madness. Ellen saw him turn and she tracked him, the Remington following her eyes just like she'd been taught that morning in Ohio.

Hamme's eyes were on Ellen's face as he brought the gun around. He felt the thrill. *I have you!* The thought was a joy. Then he saw her eyes and everything changed.

Ellen fired; the Remington tore the air in its fury and punched her shoulder. Eight double-ought buckshot pellets, each a third of an inch wide, slammed into Hamme, ripping open the right side of his chest, exploding a spray of blood, tissue, and cloth. He pitched forward onto his face, curled into a tight ball, his pistol sliding to one side.

Ellen stood still for a second and then jacked another round into the shotgun. The empty shell bounced with a hollow click on the gravel, its sound magnified by the absolute silence left by the shotgun's blast. She walked forward, the red dot of the front sight on Hamme's head.

She stood over him and eased the shotgun from her shoulder but she kept it pointed at the side of his skull. Hamme's body looked like a mad dog from hell had ripped a gaping wound out of his side. His legs slowly moved as the last nerves fired but his half-closed eyes showed no recognition of her and lost their focus as Ellen stared down at him.

Her waver was gone; the muzzle was inches from Hamme's skull. Ellen tightened her grip and felt the trigger move slightly under her finger. Her eyes were those of a raptor as she breathed slowly and deeply as if she had finished a long, difficult race.

"Ellen," Klemmer said. His voice was just loud enough for her to hear. "Ellen." He spoke as if cautioning someone who had stepped near the edge of a cliff.

She looked up at Klemmer. Her eyes were hard, brown and gold. Finally, she nodded. She pushed up the safety of the Remington and stepped away from Hamme's body. She moved his pistol to one side with her foot and watched him for several seconds. The slow movements stopped.

"How are you?" she asked as she approached Klemmer. Her eyes softened as she looked at Klemmer and then the motionless deputy.

"Check Craig," Klemmer said. He had taken off his shirt and was tying its sleeves to bind his wound.

Ellen knelt beside Morgan. The wound was bloody and she could see *in* his body; a broken bit of bone lay in the torn flesh. She bit her lips, touched his wrist and then looked at Klemmer.

"He's alive," she said.

Klemmer had out his cell phone. He punched in numbers that he had trouble seeing because of the tears that ran down his face.

Chester County Nine One One. How may I help you?

He couldn't speak; for perhaps the second time in his life Klemmer could not find any words. Ellen took the cell phone from his hands.

"This is Ellen Parker," she said, her voice calm, the shotgun still in her other hand. "We've had several shootings. There is an officer down. We need emergency medical and police at..."

Klemmer leaned back onto his elbows and looked across at Morgan's still body. He still could think of nothing to say.

Chapter 32

Ellen remembered that the black SUV was a police vehicle of some kind. Laying the shotgun down next to Klemmer, she ran to it and found strapped in the back a first aid kit.

Opening it beside Morgan, the kit contained things that Ellen didn't understand, but the bags of Celox said "Haemostatic Granules," which meant nothing to her, and "For Life Threatening Emergency Bleeding," which meant everything. She ripped open a pair of them and dumped them into Morgan's wound. Then she put almost every bandage in the kit onto the wound and held them in place with her hand. Klemmer watched her hands move smoothly, though her expression was tense.

She was using the last bag of Celox on Klemmer when they heard the first sirens in the distance.

The first vehicle was a Chester County Deputy Sheriff marked car driven by Deputy Collins. He deliberately drove across the parking area and slid his car to a stop just inches from the workshop. He shut off his siren but didn't bother to close his door as he ran to Morgan and dropped to his knees, another first aid kit in his fist.

"I told him," he said, "I told him. And he did." He shook his head as he added to Ellen's bandages and fingered the ballistic vest Morgan wore.

Ellen had no idea what the man was talking about and finished securing the bandage around Klemmer's leg.

Soon there were ambulances and police cars from more jurisdictions than Ellen thought existed in Chester County. The expression *Officer Down* had triggered a tsunami of vehicles with flashing lights and bright decals. The vehicles spilled over into the fields and only some quick movement and direction by the county deputies cleared the driveway to get the ambulance with Klemmer and Morgan out and away.

She stood to one side as police filled the area. For several minutes, she found herself trying to explain what had happened, starting over again and again, to five or six different officers. Finally, a slightly short but muscular state trooper – he looked to Ellen like a football player from her childhood, a man named Emmitt Smith, and she did not know why she remembered him – moved her to one side and waved the other officers off.

"We'll wait on the detectives," he said with a voice that sounded like that of a friend. "The perp is down. Let's secure the place. Get everyone out of the parking area."

He the kind of authority that was more than his uniform and the other police moved out. Gradually, the area was cleared. He looked at Ellen.

"How are you doing, miss?" he asked, his clear voice soft, and that was the trigger.

Ellen began crying and the state trooper, slightly more than five and a half feet of muscle but fifteen years of seeing the worst, held her as gently as he would have a baby. After a moment, he motioned with his fingers and a woman officer came over.

"Hang onto her," he said and the police officer nodded.

It was a quarter of an hour later that Special Agent Karen Deevers drove up in another black Chevy SUV. Deputy Collins guided her off the drive and into the field. Getting out of the vehicle, she had a small yellow backpack with her. She paused to talk with the young deputy and Sheriff Walsh. She nodded, talking quietly with the pair. Then she went looking for Ellen.

She found her sitting on the steps to the kitchen, a female Chester County Deputy standing beside her. Ellen looked exhausted. There was a smear of blood on her face. Deevers exchanged looks with the deputy and the woman nodded and moved a few steps away.

It was becoming dark outside the lit parking area. Technicians had placed little yellow plastic markers on the ground, plastic monuments in the gravel, and still took pictures. Deevers sat on the steps beside Ellen and, for a moment, remained silent.

"I want to apologize," Deevers finally said, her voice low. "This should never have happened." She took a pair of small packets from the yellow pack and opened them. The faint medicinal smell of alcohol filled the air. Deevers took out disposable towels and wiped Ellen's face and then put one in her hands.

Ellen just nodded, her hands operating mechanically as they cleansed themselves. Her eyes were on the portion of Hamme's body visible beyond the vehicles.

"We thought it might be him," Deevers said. "We were trying to follow him. We brought in people he didn't know to do it, but they were still getting set. There was no one on him today. I'm sorry."

"It's all right," Ellen said almost absently. She wanted to say something else but there were no words. She looked down at the stained towel and Deevers took it from her and put it into a small paper bag.

Deevers saw Callahan talking with someone wearing a coat and tie she didn't recognize but who was hovering over Hamme's body as if it was a road kill and he was a vulture. *Probably a medical examiner.* She smiled at the mental image and glanced at Ellen out of the corner of her eye. The young woman was still staring across the parking area but Deevers didn't know how much she was taking in.

Deevers opened the backpack and handed Ellen a plastic bottle of water. The young woman opened it automatically and took a drink, then another, a large one. After the third swallow, her hand went to her mouth and she stood up. Deevers held her elbow and, as the deputy stepped aside, guided her to the edge of the house.

Ellen threw up all the water she had drunk. Her head down, she felt her stomach push whatever was left and then it stopped. It was a moment before she let herself straighten up.

Deevers handed her some tissues and Ellen used them to wipe her mouth. Then she rinsed her mouth with water and spat it out. She took a tentative sip and swallowed it. It stayed down.

"Have they interviewed you?"

"Yes," Ellen said. "A couple of times. Sheriff Walsh said I can go home." Her eyes widened. "Oh, hell, I forgot about Jay."

Deevers frowned, not understanding, but Ellen took a cell phone from her pocket and punched in some numbers. She waited and then she spoke.

"Hi," she said. "It's Ellen. No, no, I'm all right. You're where? They won't let you in?" She looked at Deevers. "It's my ride, Jay Enfield. They won't let him in. He's parked out on the road."

"Let me see what I can do," Deevers said and walked away.

"Hold on," Ellen said into the phone. "They may be able to let you through." She paused and nodded. "No, I'm all right," she repeated and then paused, looking at Hamme's body as it was put into a black body bag. "I'm fine."

Chapter 33

"That'll do it," Jefferson Johnson said. "Thank you," he added.

Ellen Parker nodded.

"Big Sam had a hernia when he heard," Johnson said. He smiled. "He'll heal quickly. This is the thing editors live for, a first-person exclusive."

"Of course," she said. She sat in his office with her hands resting on her small handbag.

"When I talked with Callahan," Johnson said, "he told me they found residue of bleach in Hamme's van. He apparently cleaned it out after every use; a neighbor said he used the do-it-yourself carwash down the street."

"I see."

"He never cleaned the roof, though. One of the women must have slapped it with her hand when he pulled her in. They have a perfect palm print."

"Good."

"They still haven't found the jewelry," Johnson said, eyeing Ellen. "But they've got a court order for a storage locker up near Downingtown. They're probably there now, popping it open. We have someone with them. I wanted to do your interview."

Ellen nodded.

"So how are you doing?"

"I'm a little tired," she said. "With all the statements and police interviews, I didn't get home until late. Jay was pretty patient."

"A real taxi driver is Mr. Enfield," Johnson said. *She has no idea the poor bastard is in love with her. Oh, well, she can work that out on her own time.*

"If we're done," Ellen said, "I'd like to get out and see Mr. Klemmer and Deputy Morgan. They're both at Brandywine Trauma Center."

"I know," Johnson said. "Of course. Take the day off. You deserve…"

"No," Ellen said as she stood. "I'll be back after lunch." Slipping her handbag strap over her head, she left Johnson's office.

Jefferson Johnson watched her go. *Thomas Luther Parker's granddaughter…* Then he went to writing up his exclusive interview.

They found nothing in Bobby Hamme's house. There was nothing in the attic or basement, there were no hidden rooms. It was just a house that looked like every other house, though perhaps a bit cleaner than some. The same was true of the storage locker. There were several cardboard boxes of old clothes, another box of travel magazines, and a last one holding old year-end reports of several charitable organizations from the southeast Pennsylvania area.

It was one of the forensic technicians who found the thing that mattered. Inventorying the things found on Hamme, she made her way through the key ring attached to his belt. In her first pass, she found four that could not be immediately identified. A deputy sent by Sheriff Walsh to assist identified one for a locker in the Sheriff's Department; people immediately went across the street to check it out. One was for the Downingtown storage locker. The third was for a padlock that was never found.

The fourth was a house key but did not match the front and back keys for Hamme's home. It was a duplicate key with no number, nothing that made identification easier. After speaking to the deputy, she called Agent Paul Callahan. Callahan looked at the key and then remembered that Hamme's mother had lived in Paoli, less than thirty minutes away. In a few moments, the house address was found. They quickly obtained a search warrant.

Callahan and Deevers led the small convoy of four vehicles through the morning rush hour traffic. They moved quickly, their flashing lights breaking into the awareness of the other drivers.

Hamme's mother lived in a medium-sized house with an attached garage just off Paoli Pike, less than a half mile from the center of town. Waiting for the task force were two cruisers of the Malvern Borough Police Department.

The key was a perfect fit for the front door. With neighbors on their way to school or work pausing to watch, the task force members entered the house.

Dust covered the furniture, all of which looked expensive. The agents and technicians fanned out. Callahan went upstairs to the attic while Deevers worked in the bedrooms but it was a technician in the basement, another of Hamme's despised morons, who found it.

Deevers arrived first with Callahan a close second. Already the dark basement alternated between light and darkness, revealed then hidden, by a tech with a camera and flash.

"It was behind this plywood panel," the technician explained, pointing at a broad sheet of plywood lying to one side. "False wall. I guess at some point he got sloppy about making sure it fit properly or the wood was warping a little or something. I saw the seam and it came right off."

Flash. A map of southern Pennsylvania suddenly existed and just as suddenly faded into darkness. *Flash.* Little glints scattered across the map, some forming clusters. *Flash.* The glints resolved themselves into pieces of jewelry. *Flash.* They were rings and earrings, pinned to the map. *Flash.* Spare sets of earrings bordered the map, tacked in place. *Flash.*

The photographer paused and someone set up a large portable spotlight on the furnace so it illuminated the map.

"Your Quantico map was right," Callahan said. He shook his head. "Holy Mother Mary."

"But not complete," Deevers nodded. She pointed at earrings just west and north of Philadelphia. "We didn't get these."

"We have now."

Dave Maddux whistled to get Cracker's attention and the Border Collie paused and looked towards him. He pointed to one side and the dog moved to Maddux's left, checking the wind.

Maddux liked these morning exercises. Getting out into the trees with the dog was just plain enjoyable. He smiled; it wasn't terribly sophisticated, it wasn't some resort, just a patch of woods in southern Pennsylvania, but it felt good.

Cracker, his orange vest glowing in the morning sun, slipped behind a tree and then reappeared. The black and white dog paused, looking downhill. Then he looked at Maddux.

Do you smell what I smell?

Maddux looked where Cracker had looked but saw nothing. The dog, though, was in full alert.

"Show me," Maddux said, and Cracker trotted forward and stopped at a jumble of logs. He walked to them and peered over.

"Hi, Dave," Jack said.

"Hi, Jack," Maddux replied. "Good boy," Maddux added, reaching down to Cracker and scratching his ears. He grinned as he looked up. "That was for Cracker, Jack, not you."

"I hoped that was the case," Jack said as he stood up. "Nice run."

The two men walked down the hill with Cracker moving alongside Maddux and investigating things on the way only he noticed.

Some of the rest of the team – not everyone could take Friday mornings off, though half the team was retired –gathered in the parking area, quietly talking over cups of coffee and tea poured from large thermoses.

"Hey, Dave," one of them said. "Did you catch the news?"

"What happened?"

"That guy," the man said, "the one who killed that woman you found. They got him. Shot him dead yesterday, found all kinds of evidence today, the radio was saying."

Maddux nodded and tossed Cracker a small dog biscuit.

"They said they would."

A Chester County Deputy stood outside Morgan's room and summoned a nurse when Ellen appeared. The nurse was helpful and escorted Ellen into the room where she stood watching the unconscious man breathing.

"He'll make it," the nurse said again and Ellen nodded. "The vest took most of it. That's what saved him." Ellen nodded again as if agreeing but her thoughts were not spoken.

No. What saved him was a Remington 870 twelve gauge held in my hands.

Klemmer was not in the intensive care unit. He was in a room that he shared with another person, an older man who was asleep when Ellen walked in.

Klemmer was reading a magazine and looked up as she arrived and smiled. He looked a little tired. His leg was propped up and well bandaged.

On an impulse, Ellen leaned forward and kissed Klemmer on the cheek.

"Well," he said, "thank you. That's better than the breakfast they tried to feed me."

"How are you?" Ellen sat in a chair next to the bed.

"I'm fine," Klemmer replied. He waved at his leg. "They call it 't-n-t;' through and through. The bullet made a very small hole all the way through my leg. Didn't touch the bone or anything important." He looked at Ellen. "And, how are you?"

"All right," she said. She smiled and then pressed her lips together. Tears filled her eyes and she blinked them back. "Better than yesterday. At least now I'm not throwing up."

"Progress," Klemmer said. "You saved us all." He paused. "I want you to keep repeating that to yourself, no matter what images or feelings come into your head." He smiled. "I wouldn't be here, enjoying all this good food if it wasn't for you." The smile vanished. "Thank you."

"You're welcome," Ellen said. She took a breath. "And thank you. I know what you were willing to do to save me."

"I think," the killer said, "I was trying to save myself."

"I still am," the other killer said. "Now, can I do an interview?" Ellen took a small recorder from her purse and raised her eyebrows, a grin spreading across her face, and then both killers laughed.

It is The Dream. It comes every few weeks, perhaps less often as the months mount up since the fight at Klemmer's home.

Ellen stands near a barn and she recognizes that it's not Klemmer's but Grandpa Tom's. It has been years since she's seen it and she knows it no longer looks like this, that her Uncle John had it worked on and repainted a few years ago. In her dream, it looks like it did when she was a girl of thirteen and the farm was her sanctuary.

Eileen is there and the two of them walk out into the sunshine. Eileen looks like she did and, oddly, like she would have had she lived. The two girls/women walk up a hillside and there is a blanket and a lunch spread out.

They talk though Ellen can't quite make out what the subject is but that was how they often talked, bouncing from one subject to another, not bothering to go deeply into anything, just enjoying each other's company.

Sometimes in the dream, there is something distant, something threatening. Ellen sees the concern in Eileen's young girl's/young woman's face as she searches the horizon and then she turns in the same direction and she feels what she felt in Klemmer's parking area and the thing on the horizon flees.

Ellen turns back to Eileen and smiles and that is all there is.

Killers cover by Eric Strehl
Blackheart Studios, http://www.ejstrehl.com

Also by Steven M. Silver

With Susan Rogers, Ph.D. *Light in the heart of darkness: EMDR and the treatment of war and terrorism survivors.*

Poetry

American Travelers
Hot Chrome, Smooth Leather, and a Red Bandanna
Victor Echo Zero Five

Fiction

The Wild Geese Saga
Mercenary's Heart
Mercenary's Honor
Mercenary's Code
Mercenary's Logic
Mercenary's Destiny
Mercenary's Soldiers
Mercenary's Redemption
Mercenary's Courage
Mercenary's Peace
Mercenary's Justice
Mercenary's Humanity
Mercenary's Promise

The Ellen Parker Series
A Dangerous Man
Killers
Woman on the Wire
Hidden Things
Child in the Dark

Excerpt from "Woman on the Wire," the third Ellen Parker novel.

Chapter 1

"She's been dead not much more than twelve hours," the medical examiner said. He had a blue windbreaker on over his brown suit; the tall, yellow "ME" on his back was as crisp and sharp as the early morning air. Still squatting beside the corpse, he turned to the two police officers standing behind him and pushed his glasses up on his nose with a latex-gloved pinky.

"She wasn't killed here," he said. "Lividity, what I can see so far, lack of blood around her, and her wrists," he nodded to one side, "all say she was dead before she was tied to the fence."

The woman leaned into the ancient barbed wire. Her arms were outstretched, her wrists bound to the upper strand with stiff wire folded over on itself. Her head slumped forward, her long blond hair straggling down. Several obvious stab wounds marked her breasts and dried blood from them covered her torso down to her reddish-blond pubic hair.

"Cause of death?" The tall cop, a black man with gray at his temples, was in civilian clothes. The white man next to him was in the uniform of a Pennsylvania State Trooper and wore his broad brimmed hat pulled low, shadowing his pink face from the morning light.

"Need to look," the M.E. said. He stood, brushing his gloved hands together. "The stabbing might have done it but it looks like she took some hits to the skull that were pretty severe." He shook his head.

"Yeah," the cop said to the M.E.'s unspoken words. "Nasty."

"She didn't go peaceably," the M.E. said. He stepped to one of her hands and pointed. "It looks like she hit something with her knuckles." He looked at the cop. "I think there's material under the fingernails of the other hand. Bruise on the top of her right foot. Maybe from the perpetrator, maybe from kicking someone."

"The top of the foot?" the trooper asked. He frowned as he considered the comment.

"A lot of kicks impact in that fashion," the M.E. said. He took plastic bags from his jacket's pockets and put one around her hand. "Some martial arts teach kicking like that."

"The marks on the inner thighs, those are post mortem," he said. "Some kind of design. Drawn, not slashed. He wasn't in a rage when he did those."

The black cop squatted to see better.

"Yeah," he said, examining the cuts. His gloved hands touched nothing but he held a finger close to the cuts, measuring their dimensions. They were small, no more than a couple of inches in length. They had not bled. They looked a little like stylized lightning marks, a pair close together on each thigh.

"Advertising," he said. The M.E. raised an eyebrow but the black cop added nothing. He stood, his eyes still on the cuts.

"The forensic services unit people are on their way," the black cop said to the white one. "Remind them not to cut the wire around her wrists." As the trooper nodded, he added. "I don't suppose they will but it won't hurt to say it." He looked up at several people at the side of the road standing next to a green tractor. "Is that the man who found her?"

"Yes, sir," the trooper said. A small notepad appeared almost magically in his hands. "Carl Tailor. Trooper Johnson is with him. Owns this patch of woods and the land on both sides of the road all the way down into that hollow." He motioned with his chin. "He said he was cutting the weeds along the shoulder and saw her hair."

"Good eyes. Has to be twenty yards from here to where his tractor is stopped."

"The fence parallels the road before it turns in here but remains about fifteen feet from the shoulder the whole side of the woods." The trooper looked up. "He says this is one of the few places where it is up and intact, that it's twenty or thirty years old. The wood lot grew up around it."

"Someone pulled off the road, carried her into the woods, and wired her up to the barbed wire. Twelve or so hours ago it was dark." He looked down the road. "I can't see his house."

"Down in the hollow. The road climbs back up and goes behind the far hill. Next house is a quarter of a mile beyond at the end of a lane."

"He see anything before spotting her?"

"Says not. Watched the Phillies lose. Wife went to bed at ten, game was over a little after eleven. He didn't notice any traffic."

"They get any?"

"Usually not," the trooper said. "That farm I mentioned, he says they would go in the other direction to pick up U.S. 30 to get anywhere. Occasionally kids drive by, looking for a deserted place to make out." He pointed. "At the edge of the lot, there's a dirt track between the wood lot and the corn field. Once or twice a year a kid will park there. He said he found a bunch of empty beer cans there last fall but nothing since."

"All right. I'll talk to him." He looked around; the scene was too ugly for the morning light. "Tell everyone to keep things sharp." He nodded to the medical examiner. "Doc, we're going to have visitors."

"The federal variety?"

"Yes."

"This has happened before." The ME wasn't asking a question.

"'Fraid so. About six weeks ago here in Pennsylvania, and Maryland, last year. Maybe other ones. There's a task force with the Fee-Bees, they'll be taking over, so let's keep it sharp."

"I always do."

"Of course." Doctors were always a little sensitive. He turned back to the uniformed trooper. "We'll walk the track and a broad front sweep from here to the road and to the track." He looked at the dead woman. She had once been pretty but murder and wounds had taken it all away. "Maybe we can find some trace of the son of a bitch who did this."

Chapter 2

On the other side of county, as emergency lights flashed silently near the body of a woman on an old wire fence, four men rode inside a black Chevrolet SUV and thought about their morning's chore. Robert Jacks – only a rare handful called him Bobby – closely studied the land around him with the intensity of a man looking for hope.

Given his occupation, some might have found this odd but everyone hopes and Bobby Jacks was living proof that people hope for the damnedest things.

Spring had come reluctantly to eastern Pennsylvania; the gray, cold misery of winter had held on like a dead hand in full rigor. But even the dead let go eventually, Jacks thought as he stared out the window of the big SUV. Green seemed to show in reluctant spots among the dead brown of the wooded lots they passed, but it showed.

He nodded. He liked spring. More exactly, he hated winter. Bobby Jacks glanced behind him at the men in the back seats. The one on the left, the young one, had his pistol in his lap. Jacks shook his head.

"You want to point that thing at the floor?"

"Sorry, Bobby."

"Mister Jacks – Tallman calls me Bobby. You don't."

"Got it, Mister Jacks."

"There it is, up ahead." The driver nodded as he spoke and Jacks turned to the front.

The trailer park was nothing much to look at. Someone had given up on grounds keeping a couple of years back and the blackberry bushes, their thin, reddish-brown arcs marking their territory, looked to make a fight of it if anything else tried to grow around them. The white fence bordering the road was missing pickets, drawing the eye to what wasn't there. Beyond them, the house trailers seemed few and some looked like they had been abandoned.

Maybe business would pick up when summer showed up, maybe not. Jacks thought not, though the large lake beyond the trailers might be an invitation to people looking for fishing or whatever the hell people did around lakes.

"All this place needs are tumbleweeds and crickets," the older man in the back seat said. Jacks agreed but he didn't show it; Jonesy, as the man was known, was an asshole. It was not Jack's idea to bring him along with the younger one. But Mr. Tallman wanted to give both a tryout and so here they were.

The black SUV turned into the entrance slowly. The place seemed deserted. Few of the trailers had a car near them. There were more empty slots than Jacks had thought there were. He shook his head again; Jonesy was right about tumbleweed rolling through it.

Sure, these "mom and pop" meth operations were everywhere and it made sense to keep them organized and under control so they didn't interfere with Mr. Tallman's operation. Yes, they were handy to take up the slack if there was a problem in the supply chain and there was money to be made moving their product. On the other hand, Mr. Tallman used industrial-sized supplies of ephedrine from India and Mexico and didn't mess with any over-the-counter bullshit, leaving that to the small producers he controlled.

But Jacks thought the small operators were more trouble than they were worth. They were disorganized, unreliable, and had a tendency to try to cheat. Case in point. He glanced at the driver as he scanned the area, looking for anything that might be trouble.

"Which one?"

"The white one," the driver said. He was the only one who had ever been here before, delivering and picking up. "The one with the, what you call it, garden shed behind it. Got the gray car parked beside it."

"OK, pull over here for a minute."

"Yes sir."

"Anyone see anything going on with any of the other trailers?"

"No."

"I got nothin'."

"Me, neither."

"Here's how we're going to do it, just like I told you before we left. We're going to pull in behind their car, it's on the far side. Leave the keys."

"Yes sir." That was the young one again. He was called Books but Jacks didn't know if that was his real name or some kind of nickname. Jacks figured he was trying to make an impression.

"Don't interrupt. They make the crystal in the shed." He looked at the driver, who nodded in confirmation. "Driver stays with our car in case they try to come out a window. You two follow me. I go to the shed. You keep going to the door and go in. Get them down, put two in their heads, two each. Everyone, keep your guns out of sight except in the trailer or if they come out.

Don't cowboy it. Get them down, then the head. Don't spray. Fucking rounds will go through that thing. It's just aluminum. We know the cash and product are in the shed – I'll get it. They keep the money in a blue backpack but the product may be bagged or loose, so be ready to lend a hand in gathering it up. We all go into the trailer to help look for the money if I don't find it immediately. Any questions?"

"No."

"Got it, Mister Jacks." Young guy again. At least he seemed to learn his manners.

"They have a kid." The driver rubbed his upper lip.

"So? If the kid is there, do it. Kid I.D.s you, you go down. Besides, part of this is to send people a message that Tallman is serious." Jacks paused. Of the three, the driver, in his opinion, had the most reliable credentials – everything he had said about the place had been true so far and he had never worked with the other two before, though Tallman seemed to think they were all right. He threw the driver a bone. "Thing is, we're coming at ten in the morning; kid's in school, right? Probably won't be there."

"Not a problem, just askin'."

"Any other questions? No? Ok, go ahead and pull around to the other side. Yeah, that's it, nice and easy. Middle of the day, just someone visiting. Guns out of sight. This is good. Stop here. Keep your eyes open. You two, out. Let's go."

"I see a car, babe." His voice was thin, tired, but she was used to hearing it that way and no longer noticed.

"We're in a fuckin' trailer park. Everyone's got a…"

"They're coming here."

"Let me see. Shit. Sharon! Sharon! Take out the ear things. Come on, just like we practiced." She half-dragged the little girl forward as if getting to the television that no longer worked was important.

"Not again. Davy, do I have to?"

"Do what she says, Sherrie. Hurry!"

"This is stupid." Her mother did not hear her. She grabbed a blue backpack and shoved it into the girl's hands, though it was a little large for a child.

"Hurry up. Here's your stuff. Good. Remember, whatever, you stay still until…"

"Until you open the trap door. This is stupid."

221

"Down. Down you go." Then the woman's desperation spoke. "I love you."

"All right, all right."

"Put it down, get the rug back."

"Got it, babe, got it. Where's my .45?"

"Here's one."

"Fuck. I don't like the Glock. Where's the shotgun?"

"By the bed, hurry!"

Books, the one who called Mister Jacks "Bobby," felt like he needed to get everything right so Mister Jacks would see that he was cool and not some cowboy. A professional, someone reliable. And maybe get a better nickname than "Books," which wasn't really a nickname, just his last name.

You look for your chances in life, your opportunities to get ahead. That's what this was for Books, an opportunity. He regarded himself only occupying a step above that of "entry level" – he had read an article about employment and the phrase had stuck with him. To get into "middle management" – same article – he was going to have to show something to the real decision makers in his organization, and Tallman and Jacks were not easily impressed.

Sure, dealing with a low-level manufacturer was a small assignment but it meant working with Mister Jacks, and Jacks had a very serious reputation. Books figured that this was one of those opportunities the article had talked about.

All it would take was two in the head.

He walked to the small stairs at the base of the trailer's entrance. He noticed that Jonesy walked well behind him, as if reluctant. Well, that was his problem. If he wanted to look reluctant, that was fine; it would make Books look better.

"Stay close," Books said over his shoulder. Jonesy said nothing but looked irritated; Books didn't know him very well but his reputation was he did not like taking orders. On the other hand, he was supposed to have killed someone a few months back, and that made him a potential rival for advancement.

Books stood with one foot on the top step, his hand on the butt of an automatic pistol resting in the small of his back. Mister Jacks already was at the large garden shed, a small pry bar in his hand. Jacks looked at the shed's padlock and then turned around and made eye contact.

He nodded to go ahead. Books nodded back, glanced at Jonesy standing behind him, and reached for the door handle.

Trying to turn the handle triggered four quick shots from inside the trailer, all of which were just over Books' head, tearing through the thin aluminum and leaving neat, uniform holes. Terrified, he dropped to the ground, his reflexes working even as the first bullet came. Jonesy crouched and pulled his pistol out of his jacket. He fired into the door, emptying the gun's fifteen rounds in a few seconds and squeezing even after the gun was emptied.

"Shit!" Books now was terrified of Jonesy, thinking the man had closed his eyes while he fired. He rolled to one side and then got to one knee. He pointed his own gun at the door just as Jacks arrived. Jacks impatiently held up his hand at him and then, standing to one side, tried the door.

The door swung open, revealing an interior too dark to see anything well. Books strained to see without standing but, other than the edge of a chair, he saw nothing worth shooting at. Jacks glanced at him and Jonesy and then snapped his head around the corner of the doorframe and then jerked it back. Drawing his pistol, he paused for a second, thinking.

Jacks, holding his gun with both hands, jumped into the trailer, just hitting the top step. Books scrambled to follow.

A woman, thin, stringy hair, lay on the carpet, her legs moving idly while her hands – they seemed almost like chicken feet they were so thin – pulled weakly at her bloody t-shirt; some of Jonesy's wild rounds had done some good. The t-shirt was something about Hawk Mountain, which Books had heard of, and looked like it was dirty before she got shot.

Books saw Jacks ignored her except to kick her pistol further away. Still holding his pistol out in front of him with both hands, he looked towards the front of the trailer but there was little to see except an old television and a filthy couch that Books didn't think he would sit on even if offered money. He turned with Jacks and faced the back.

Beyond a simple kitchen where dirty dishes seemed to be breeding with each other, a hallway formed by what was probably the bathroom ended in a cheap door marking the bedroom. He guessed the man was back there and copied Jacks' stance, moving to one side.

As he raised his pistol, the man appeared in the bedroom doorway. He had a shotgun leveled and Books thought for the third time he was about to be killed. Instinctively he fired and knew immediately he missed.

Jacks, though, did not miss. His shot, incredibly loud in the trailer, caused the man to flinch, folding into himself as if he had been punched. Jacks fired once more and the man convulsed, dropping the shotgun, and fell backwards, bouncing off the bed before landing on the floor.

Jacks walked forward, still holding his gun with both hands. He stood over the man and fired twice more. Then he looked back at Books.

"Finish her," he said, his voice seeming to come from very far away. Books looked down.

The woman still moved, though only slightly. Blood soaked into the ratty carpet. Books lowered his gun and pointed at her face. The woman did not see him. She mouthed words he could not hear. Then she seemed to gather herself.

"Run, Sherrie," she said. Her voice came from very far away. "Run."

Even as Books wondered if he could really do it, his finger squeezed. The nine-millimeter pistol barely bucked in his hand and a black dot about the size of the tip of his little finger appeared below her right eye. Her hands dropped away. The second shot, this one went into her temple, was so easy he smiled and considered a third until he remembered Jacks' instructions back in the car. *Two in the head.*

Jacks moved quickly but controlled, like a dancer who knew exactly where a foot was going to be before it started to move. Books followed him back to the garden shed and Jacks had the pry bar in his hand before they reached the door.

The shed was big enough that it could have held a couple of riding mowers but that's not what was in it. A table on which glass jars, plastic jugs, and other paraphernalia used in the making of methamphetamine took up most of the space. Jacks ignored nearly all of it, his hands reaching for a pile of thick, plastic kitchen self-sealing bags, crammed with white powder.

"Pick up all of these," he said to Books and turned to meet the driver who came running around the corner. "What's the problem?"

"I think I saw the kid," the man said, gasping a little. "She's headed to the lake."

"Show me," Jacks said. He looked at Books. "All of the bags."

It took Books only a moment to scoop up all the bags – they were a little unwieldy but he made it to the SUV without the disaster of dropping one. He looked up as Jacks and the driver jogged back to them.

"All right," Jacks said and everyone leaned towards him; Books admired his ability to hold everyone's attention like that. That's how he wanted to be.

"The money's gone," Jacks said. "The backpack is missing. The kid may have it. And she may have seen us, so we've got to get her. She's got to be going around the lake in that direction," he waved his hand to one side. "You two," he nodded at Books and Jonesy, "are going to chase her. We know she went that way because there's brush and shit that she could hide in; the other way is wide open and we can't see her. While you go after her, we're going to take the car and circle around the other way. We'll get to the other side of the lake and then we'll have her between us." He paused.

"Here's the thing. She may have the money in a blue backpack. Driver says they kept the cash in one and thinks he saw it on her. Even if she doesn't, she has to go down. Most of the houses around the lake are empty this time of year he says," nodding at the driver, "just like the few trailers here. But don't be stupid. Stay close to the lake. People be less likely to see you. Keep moving, don't give her a chance to stop and think. Got it?"

Everyone nodded. Books looked at Jonesy.

"Let's go," he said, not waiting for Jacks to tell him to move. He jogged towards the lake, crossing over an empty trailer pad, and then turned in the direction they thought the girl had gone. The way ahead looked like heavy forest. It didn't matter. Jacks would circle around and they would find her.

And then it would be time for two in the head. He smiled.

www.ingramcontent.com/pod-product-compliance
Lightning Source LLC
Chambersburg PA
CBHW060636260626
47161CB00008B/2905